Obedience

From his peers

"Taut, twisty, and highly original: the pages turned themselves."
—Peter Abrahams, author of *Into the Dark*

"*Obedience* draws you in and never lets go—and what a ride!"
—David Baldacci, author of *The Whole Truth*

"A devilishly inventive debut that reads like a house of mirrors. Nothing is what it seems, right up to the devastating finale."
—Brian Freeman, author of *Immoral* and *Stalked*

"A taut, clever puzzle so artfully crafted and tightly wound that it springs open its trap when you least expect it to."
—Carol Goodman, author of *The Lake of Dead Languages* and
The Sonnet Lover

"A taut and timely thriller that explores the dark side of academia, where classrooms are dangerous and paranoia abounds."
—Karin Slaughter, author of *Fractured*

"In his dream-like and labyrinthine debut, Will Lavender delivers a clever, intricate page-turner that kept me guessing late into the night. . . . *Obedience* is not to be missed."
—Lisa Unger, author of *Beautiful Lies* and *Black Out*

From the reviews

"A thriller that will strike some as a mix of John Fowles's *The Magus* and Stephen King's *The Shining*. . . . The conspiracy becomes so all-encompassing, so elaborate." —*Publishers Weekly*

"It's a genuine, if slightly perverse, kick to follow every Byzantine clue in this bizarre game. If you solve this one without peeking at the last chapter, it's an automatic A." —*New York Times*

"Terrific debut . . . A wonderful book with an emotional punch at the end." —*St. Petersburg Times*

"Quite a twisty tale . . . Haunting . . . Irresistible." —*New York Daily News*

"*Obedience* is a full course load of sinister fun." —Salon.com

"Tautly strung debut . . . Lavender tears a page out of Milgram's notebooks and sets into motion a chain of events that escalates far beyond its intended intellectual exercise. . . . Mystery fans will be satisfied to hang on around the story's hairpin turns as the list of suspects swells and narrows with the unearthing of each clue, but Lavender . . . is aiming at a broader target and posing deeper questions." —*Bookpage*

"Evidence that crime fiction is hardly a played-out genre . . . a mystery as ambitious as one could imagine." —*The Wall Street Journal*

"Chilling, unpredictable . . . a delicious mystery."
   —*Sacramento News and Review*

"With superb confidence, Lavender constructs a brilliant fictional web of lies, inventively warping the psychological thriller to fit the confines of a scholarly investigation. An inspired thriller." —*Kirkus Reviews*

"Lavender's first novel suggests he has a bright future. *Obedience* builds to a swirling conclusion." —*Tampa Bay Tribune*

"Will Lavender stuns with this compelling thriller . . . a new master of the genre." —*Louisville Courier-Journal*

"Infuriating, brilliant puzzle . . . [An] intriguing and addicting psychological thriller from a talented new writer worthy of our undivided attention." —Bookreporter.com

"As a fan, reading—and reviewing—many, many crime novels, it is a pleasure to discover a book that goes out of its way to try something different and really makes the reader think. Will Lavender has done this." —Crimesquad.com

"Lavender has a knack for creepy characters and red herrings."
   —*Library Journal*

"Lavender has sprinkled his text with enough red herrings to feed the biblical 5,000 but uses them to build page-turning suspense." —*Booklist*

"The most gripping book of this or any other year."
   —*Edmonton Journal* (Canada)

Obedience

A Novel

Will Lavender

THREE RIVERS PRESS

New York

Copyright © 2008 by Will Lavender

All rights reserved.
Published in the United States by Three Rivers Press, an imprint of the Crown Publishing Group, a division of Random House, Inc., New York.
www.crownpublishing.com

THREE RIVERS PRESS and the Tugboat design are registered trademarks of Random House, Inc.

Originally published in hardcover in the United States by Shaye Areheart Books, an imprint of the Crown Publishing Group, a division of Random House, Inc., New York, in 2008.

Library of Congress Cataloging-in-Publication Data

Lavender, Will, 1977–
Obedience : a novel / Will Lavender.—1st ed.
1. Missing persons—Fiction. 2. College teachers—Fiction. 3. Indiana—Fiction. 4. College stories. I. Title.
PS3612.A94424O24 2008
813'.6—dc22   2007015005

ISBN 978-0-307-39638-9

Printed in the United States of America

Design by Chris Welch

10 9 8 7 6 5 4 3 2 1

First Paperback Edition

When bewilderment on a subject seemed to have peaked, often with the class baffled into silence, Zechman would move on to another topic. But he never made a positive statement, never gave anything which resembled an answer, not even a hint. He just stood up there in his black suit with an expression of muted concern and kept asking questions; and as confusion grew, so did dissatisfaction. No one was quite sure what Zechman wanted from us. Were we stupid? Were the questions bad? What were we supposed to be learning? It was almost as if Zechman had set out to intensify that plague of uncertainty which afflicted us all.

By Friday, the level of anxiety in the class had mounted to a kind of fury.

—Scott Turow, *One L*

Run an Internet search using the name Deanna Ward.

You will get over 275 hits. Click on the first one. This is an article by a man named Nicholas Bourdoix.

Read this article. You will learn that eighteen-year-old Deanna Ward went missing from Cale, Indiana, on August 1, 1986. Police thought they had found Deanna four days later, on August 5, but they had not; this was a girl who simply *looked like* Deanna. The Deanna Ward case remains unsolved.

Run another search: "Nicholas Bourdoix."

You will get over 6,500 hits. Mr. Bourdoix graduated from Winchester University in DeLane, Indiana. He worked for fourteen years at the *Cale* (Indiana) *Star* before moving to the *New York Times* in 1995.

Run an Amazon search for Mr. Bourdoix. His latest book is a memoir about his career as a crime journalist. It is called *The Beaten Trail: My Life Covering Horrors and Hoaxes*. There are exactly twelve pages given to his years in Indiana.

There is a customer review of this book toward the bottom of the page. You will know it because it is the only review given. The reviewer awards the book one star and suggests, in rather harsh language, that readers not buy Mr. Bourdoix's "lying crap."

The reviewer's name is Deanna Ward.

Winchester

Present Day

SIX WEEKS LEFT

1

The strange thing about Williams was that nobody had ever seen him. The faculty guidebook showed a gray box labeled NOT PICTURED; group photos in the Winchester yearbooks only showed Williams's hand or arm, even though the captions advertised his presence. The college's website gave a brief curriculum vitae but no photographic evidence. By that Monday afternoon, the first day of classes for the fall term at Winchester University, the search for Williams had, for some of his students, become almost compulsive.

It was as if Williams were hiding himself from them, as if he were teasing them somehow. It had become a tradition at Winchester for students to find a picture of their professors before classes began; in this way, it was commonly believed, they could allay some of the anxiety when the man or woman strode into the room. It was a method of one-upping the faculty, of stealing some of their precious authority.

And so this thing with Williams had become *a big deal.* Some of the students of Logic and Reasoning 204 were so incensed over Williams's invisibility that they were convinced they were being tricked. One student, a Young Republican who carried a briefcase to each class, brought out his battered and veined Code of Conduct, and much of the class hovered over him while he searched the index for words like *Deception* and *Faculty Misconduct*.

It was as they were doing this that Williams himself walked into the room. He was wearing faded blue jeans, which was highly unusual for a professor at Winchester. He was also carrying *nothing*, which was even more curious than his dress. No papers, no manila envelopes, no coffee mug. He was wearing a flannel shirt that he had tucked in. No belt. Nikes. The professor was clean-shaven, another anomaly on campus, and his face was youthful (for a man clearly in his early sixties) and pitted with acne scars on the left side that brought to mind, both in their color and shape, pennies flattened on a railroad track. Yet he was handsome in a certain light, and he moved so softly and quietly that he gave the impression of extreme gentleness, his hands sometimes out before him as if he were feeling his way into the dark or perhaps gesturing, *Don't be scared; I'm right behind you.*

Professor Williams took his place at the podium at the front of the room. There were fifteen students in the class. Eight female, seven male. They were all white, which was the rule rather than the exception in a Winchester classroom. They were all sharply dressed in clothes their parents had bought them over the summer. Many of them were upperclassmen, as this course was a prerequisite for third-year seminars in philosophy and English. Because the students were mostly philosophy and lit majors, the room had an air of uncertainty. These were students who did not know where they were going in life but were generally accomplished. "Smart kids," a Winchester professor once wryly said of his philosophy students, "who were all seduced by Descartes' brain-in-a-vat theory in Philo 101."

Williams opened his mouth to speak, but before he could say a word, someone's cell phone chirped. He waited while the student shamefully dug in her bag to find the offending object. In fact, the professor seemed more anxious than the girl: he looked down, red-faced, at his podium while the girl furiously mashed buttons. Some professors would embarrass the girl further, make her hum the ring tone or have the conversation while standing in front of the class or something just as discomforting.

But Williams simply waited. And when the phone had been silenced he said, in a voice that was soft and commanding at the same time, "There's been a murder."

No one knew how to take this announcement. A young man in the back row laughed aloud.

Williams smiled. He stared down at his podium again and brushed something off the surface. "Not a real murder," he said. "No. This is a murder that may happen in the future. A . . ." The man paused, looked up at the class, waved his hand in the air as if he were trying to come up with the word by catching it in his palm.

"A hypothetical," said a girl in the front row.

"Yes!" said Williams. He was pleased with the word, as it suited the conditions of his story quite well. "A *hypothetical*. A potential murder. Murder in the future tense. Because, you see, many things have to happen before this murder is to occur. Many things that you, if you are clever enough, can keep from happening."

He fell silent. They met in the Seminary Building, the oldest of Winchester's classroom buildings. Sunlight poured in through the high, bare windows and a few students were shielding their eyes from it. This was a bane of this particular classroom, Seminary East. *The sun thing*, as it was referred to, had become such a problem that afternoon classes, as Logic and Reasoning 204 was, were often canceled because the fierce light would give the lecturer or the students migraine headaches.

"What kinds of things?" someone finally said.

Williams turned toward the dry erase board and searched the tray for something to write with, but because it was the first day of classes and professors were hoarding their supplies, no one had left a marker there. Sighing, he turned back to the class.

"Time, for instance," he said. "There is the variable of time. If the victim and her killer or killers—"

"*Potential* killer," said the girl who had offered *hypothetical*. She was into it now. She was tapping notes on her laptop and nodding feverishly as Williams spoke.

"Yes. If the victim and her potential killer or killers are not found in a certain amount of time, then she will die."

"How long?" someone asked.

"Six weeks from Wednesday," the professor said, and everyone noted that the fall term was exactly six weeks long. The fall term was followed by what students referred to as Winchester term, an eight-week session when many students studied abroad. Logic and Reasoning 204—and all the classes during the fall term—promised to be highly competitive, because so many students would be trying to impress the Europe and South America Committees to win a coveted spot on a foreign campus.

"The other variables," Williams went on, "are these: place, motive, and circumstance."

It was obvious that Williams would have written these four words on the board if he'd had the means. The girl in front put each word on the screen of her laptop: TIME, PLACE, MOTIVE, CIRCUM- STANCE. Bolded them all.

"So," he said then. "I'll see you Wednesday."

The professor turned to walk out the door of Seminary East, which was still standing open. Class had lasted just ten minutes. Almost imperceptibly, a moment of panic passed over the students. They were trapped between wanting to get out and enjoy the rest of the day (Williams's class, so late in the afternoon, would be their last) and finding out what Williams and his missing girl were really about.

"Wait," the girl with the laptop finally said.

Williams was almost out the door, but he spun in the threshold and said, "Yes?"

"How are we supposed to stop it?" she asked.

Williams came back into the room. He had a cautious expression on his face, as if he were wary about his students, so young and innocent, getting involved in such a mess.

"What kinds of questions are pertinent?" he asked.

The girl seemed confused. She looked at Williams over the top of her computer. She knew that she needed to tread lightly here. She was caught, as she often was, between the impulse to dominate the action in the classroom and remaining so silent that the teacher forgot her presence. Thus the laptop; she had found that the sound of her fingers on the keys made her noticeable. She didn't need to talk, didn't need to fear getting on the other students' nerves with her theories and ideas. She could peck at the keyboard during lectures and the professor would know she was engaged. And it had worked. She passed all her classes with high marks and remained well liked on campus, not a bookish nerd at all but rather as popular as a firmly middle-class girl with frizzy, stubborn hair and square-lens glasses (the kind she saw Joan Didion wearing on C-Span) who read Willa Cather in her free time could possibly be. She was most definitely *in*, as the Delta sisters she hung around with might say. She and her friend Summer McCoy referred to themselves as Betweeners—those girls who were comfortable enough to refuse to rush a sorority but connected enough to party at sorority and fraternity houses. Between worlds: it was, the girl felt, the best place to be at Winchester.

Yet here was Williams asking, *What kinds of questions are pertinent?*—a question that begged other, deeper questions, and she was stumped. If she answered, whole *philosophies* might open up and the class might run down an irrelevant current that would take up the full hour. If she remained silent, Williams might take her for a passive-aggressive brownnoser who hollowly pecked on computer keys.

"Who is she?" asked a boy in the back row, saving the girl from having to make her decision. He was the student who had laughed earlier, his normal classroom gesture. So many things seemed, for some reason, ridiculously absurd to him. Meaningless. Logic, for instance. He had signed up for Williams's class and had immediately wondered why he would waste his time. There was no logic, he knew. There were only vague choices to be made, problems to be contemplated but not solved, areas of the strictest gray to subjectively drone on about (because if you solved those questions, what would future classes have to talk about?). Yet after those choices were made and the problems considered, the world stayed pretty much how it was: maddeningly off-kilter.

His name was Brian House. Like a lot of people, Brian had learned to act at Winchester, to be someone he wasn't. No one knew, for instance, of the secret pain he had been suffering for the past ten months. No one knew that he didn't listen to those bands—Built to Spill, Spoon, the Shins—that he wore on his T-shirts. He went about his business—the fraternities, the intramurals, the study sessions—as if he cared, but really he loathed the whole process. He had thought about not returning to Winchester after the summer, but how could he tell his parents that? After the void that his older brother's death had left in their lives, there was no way they could understand why he, the one who had been spared, would squander his opportunities. His mother had even begun wearing Winchester U sweatshirts; she had slapped a MY CHILD IS A WINCHESTER COLONEL bumper sticker on her Volvo. Brian knew that he couldn't disappoint her by letting her in on his dirty secret: that it had all become, after Marcus, pitifully insignificant to him.

Brian was tall, nearly lanky, and he had been shaving his head because that's what his brother had done. The girls at Winchester took Brian's apathy for a sort of sexy rebellion, and they were often eager to share ideas with him in his dorm room late at night. And that was another thing. He had a girlfriend back home in New York, and shouldn't he feel bad about deceiving her? He did and he didn't. On one hand, what he was doing was clearly a kind of betrayal. He knew what that felt like. Yet a part of him, that uncaring and atrophied part of his soul, could not bring himself to feel sorry for his actions. In the end it wouldn't amount to anything but a girl being hurt. It was, like all things, illogical. It wasn't life and death.

"That is the first question," said Williams now. He was becoming more engaged. It appeared that he wanted to give answers to certain questions, but the *right* questions had to be asked first. "Who is she? Her name is Polly."

Some of the students laughed. "Funny name," said someone.

"Yes, it is funny," agreed Williams.

" 'Polly wants a cracker,' " said Brian, " 'but I think I should get off her first.' It's a Kurt Cobain song." The boy frowned. He did not like artifice, especially artifice that had been stolen from popular culture, perhaps because his own artificialness—his own insistence to put on a face and conform—was what he most disliked about himself. He decided that he was not going to like this class, no matter what happened from this point forward.

"That's right," Williams said. "But there are other questions."

"How old is she?" called a student from the back.

"She is eighteen years old." The average age of the class when they first came to Winchester.

"What does she look like?" asked another student.

"She's petite. She wears a lot of jewelry. She has various piercings: high on her ears, in her earlobes, in her navel. She has a tattoo of a Chinese symbol on her lower back. She has auburn streaks in her hair and is self-conscious about her height. She wishes she were taller." In short, she looked just like many of them.

"Where is she?" asked Brian.

"Place," said Williams.

"How did she get there?" wondered the boy.

"Circumstance." The last of the underscored ideas. Translation: we aren't that far along yet.

"Bullshit," Brian muttered.

"Maybe," said Williams. "Maybe it is all bullshit. But Polly is in danger, and if you do not find her before your six weeks are up, then she will be murdered."

The class was silent once again. Seminary East's internal clock ticked further forward, the light touching the face of Williams's podium.

"What does all this have to do with logic?" asked the boy with the briefcase. He was the most practical of the bunch. He was the only student in the class taking Logic and Reasoning 204 as an elective— that is, as a chosen punishment. He was a liberal arts major, a throw-back at Winchester. In the education reform–obsessed 1980s, Winchester had become a university. This small college in the central Indiana town of DeLane would always be overshadowed by the famous Catholic school 150 miles to the northwest, which was unfortunate, considering, as the brochures gladly pointed out, Winchester graduated more Rhodes and Fulbright scholars than Notre Dame and IU Bloomington combined.

When Winchester became a university, the curriculum predictably became more technical. More specific. Almost twenty years later there was still a rift among the faculty, and on some of the old guard's letterhead the seal still read *Winchester College*. The father of the boy with the briefcase had gone to the old Winchester and was now a professor at Temple in mathematics. His son was not nearly as brilliant with numbers, but he was always the one to take the straightest and least difficult line to the end of the maze.

His real name was Dennis Flaherty, but on campus he was jokingly called Dennis the Menace, which was irony in the highest degree: Dennis would not menace anyone even if he deserved it. His pragmatism was used mostly to keep him out of confrontation, and because of his ability to play the devil's advocate so adroitly he was an esteemed member of his father's fraternity, Phi Kappa Tau. Dennis lived on the top floor of the Tau house in a single room that could have housed ten. He had dark, curly hair that he liked to shake down over his eyes. It was mystifying to the other Taus how he could attract women so effortlessly. These girls would come to Dennis's room, prompting the brothers to sweep by and cast glances inside to see four feet on the floor, which was an old (and oft-broken) rule of the fraternity houses. But an hour later and the door would be shut and some soft music (Mingus or Coltrane or Monk) would be playing. The Taus wondered, for example, how he had attracted Savannah Kleppers, who was a 9 on the infamous Tau Scale. Yet there she was, disappearing into Dennis's room almost every evening.

The answer was *charm*. Dennis had it in spades. He could talk himself out of any lie, any malfeasance, and yet the same skill allowed him to talk himself *into* situations as well. When the fraternity was fined, as they often were, it was Dennis they sent to the Greek Authority as a liaison. If the head of the committee was a female, the fine would inevitably be lessened or struck from the record altogether. Dennis dressed differently (he favored Brooks Brothers suits and Mephisto shoes and his omnipresent briefcase), he spoke differently (he often used words like *corollary* and *incentive* in regular conversation), and he carried himself differently. Indeed,

Dennis Flaherty *was* different from most of the young men on the Winchester campus, and he was well aware of that fact.

"Logic is the destruction of fallacy," said Williams, answering Dennis's question bluntly. "It's an inherently inductive or deductive process that builds meaning out of a set of abstract notions." Everyone in the class braced for a lecture. Some students took out their notebooks from their backpacks and clicked up the tips of their pens. But Williams veered back to Polly. "Logic will help you find out where she is," he said. And then, as if it were just an afterthought: *"In time."*

"What are our clues?" asked the girl with the computer.

"The first set will be e-mailed to you this evening," the professor answered.

When there were no more questions, Williams walked out of the room. He did not say good-bye. He did not say anything as he left. Afterward, many of the students of Logic and Reasoning 204 convened in the hallway, which was empty by this time of day, and talked about the strangeness of the class. Some of them were happy that they would ostensibly not have to put in any work. The students at Winchester called these classes "float credits"—classes where you just had to be there to pass. When they speculated on what the e-mailed "clues" might contain, Brian said that he didn't know and didn't care because he wasn't going to access them anyway.

The girl with the computer was intrigued, however. She stood outside the circle of students, her warm laptop clutched to her chest. She was thinking about Dr. Williams and wondering how she was going to crack the code of the class. This is the way it was, at Winchester and at her Catholic high school back in Kentucky. There was always a code, always a design that had to be divined. Once it was cracked, passing the class was easy. But in Williams's class, there seemed to be no apparent code. Or at least not yet. This appealed to the girl because finally, for the first time in her two years at

Winchester, she was going to face a real challenge: how to solve
Williams and his strange class. No syllabus, no text, no notes. No
code! There was a certain novelty to it all, and this intrigued her—
but of course she couldn't tell anyone that. When Dennis asked her
how she had liked the lecture, she muttered a neutral "Okay." (He,
she saw in his face, had liked it very much. But he would, wouldn't
he?) *Okay* was not how she felt about Williams, however. She felt,
as she walked out the doors of Seminary that afternoon, strangely
electric.

2

The girl's name was Mary Butler. She was a junior, an English
major like her mother had been. She lived in the largest female dorm on campus, Brown Hall, in one of the dorm's most ex-
pansive single rooms. It wasn't that she couldn't get along with
roommates. To the contrary: she and Summer McCoy had roomed
together for two years and had become very good friends. (When
Summer had mono during their sophomore year, it was Mary who
took care of her and nursed her back to health. When Mary and
Dennis Flaherty broke up, Summer was there every night with
Grasshopper cookies and Agatha Christie mysteries on VHS—they
both agreed that there was something hot about Poirot.) No, Mary
lived alone because for the last year she had found herself wanting
some *space*. Some of her own space: to think, to decide on where
she was going with her life, to be silent and careful with her emotions. So her decision to single was a matter of "trust"—a word she
used often and without hyperbole.

It hadn't always been that way. In the time Before Dennis, as she referred to it, she was much more trusting. After Dennis, after he had dumped her and started going with Savannah Kleppers, she drew herself in a little and began to suspect that the world wasn't as clean-edged as it had once seemed.

She had truly loved Dennis. They had dated their freshman year for about six months. Theirs was a relationship of politeness, of soft awkwardness. He brought her candy, cards inscribed with poetry, flowers. She had dated in high school but was still relatively new at it; he sensed this and treated her like an acolyte, as if she were some precious thing that he was initiating into the adult world. Mary at once hated that and desperately wanted it, and afterward, in the After Dennis phase, she wondered if he had been setting her up for betrayal all that time. It had been, after all, so easy to do.

Mary told Dennis she loved him. She said it aloud, something she had never done before. And she thought—she *thought*, but she could not be sure—that he had told her that he loved her, too. In those days After Dennis she caught herself thinking, *Never again*. Never again would she be taken for granted. She was still well liked, still popular, still "so sweet," as the Delta girls usually said of her, but inside she was always looking out for those who would do her harm. "It's a different world up there," her mother said on the phone. "They'll take you for all you're worth." It was easy to dismiss her mom, a woman who had been out of Kentucky only twice, both times on vacation. But there was something truthful about it. Winchester *was* a different place. There was so much drama here, so many tenuous alliances that it was difficult to decide what you could talk about and what you must keep to yourself.

And that wasn't a bad thing. In fact, it was quite nice in her single room at Brown, peaceful and quiet and serene. It overlooked the quad, so she could look out the window and see the campus from behind glass, like a diorama, but not be forced to live it 24/7. She loved the parties, the people, the act you put on when you were *out there*. But After Dennis she found that she couldn't do it all the time. Up here, Mary didn't have to act in that soap opera if she didn't want to. She could stand well outside of it and pity the girls who flung themselves into the game so readily.

Sometimes she looked out that window and wondered what Dennis was doing right then. Sometimes she thought she saw him, his curly hair bouncing along, down below her. Every time this happened her heart squeezed, her breath caught in her throat. For a long time she had gone out of her way to avoid him, but inevitably they had begun to run into each other on campus. And now, of course, he was in one of her classes. She nearly died when he walked in to Seminary East. He saw her and winked—only Dennis Flaherty could wink in the twenty-first century and get away with it—and sat four chairs to her right. It was the closest he'd been to her in two years.

She was thinking about how she was going to drop the class and pick up something else on such short notice when Williams walked in.

Immediately, Mary noticed something different about him. The way he walked, the way he spoke to his class: so *not* like a professor. And when he launched into his story about the girl named Polly, Mary forgot all about Dennis and was lost in this bizarre class.

"Who's the prof?" Summer asked her when they met up in the dining commons that evening.

"Williams," Mary said.

"Hmm. Never heard of him," the other girl said.

And neither had Mary. Which was strange, because she had gofered for at least ten professors around campus. Surely *someone* would have mentioned him to her. Surely she would have seen him at a Christmas party or something. Not only did Williams fail to appear in any of her three face books, he was also missing from her annuals. There were no publications listed in the campus magazine, no news of him on the faculty page, no references in the recent edition of the school paper. It didn't make any sense. It was, as Summer liked to say, *freaky.*

That night, Mary browsed Winchester's website, trying to find information about him. He was a member of the philosophy faculty, and he was listed as an associate professor. There was a CV: BA from Indiana University, 1964; MA from same, 1970; PhD from Tulane, 1976. That was all. *Google him*, she thought, but then she remembered that she didn't know his first name. All she knew was the initial that was on her schedule of classes: L.

Earlier, she had repeatedly refreshed her screen, attempting to be the first to read the e-mailed clues. But now it was 8:00 p.m., and still no message from Williams had arrived in her in-box.

She took a shower (along with the biggest single room in the dorm, she also had her own bathroom and kitchenette; some girls on the third floor had taken to calling Mary's room the Hyatt) and tried to take her mind off the class, but she couldn't. She had been intrigued by Professor L. Williams, and had even found him to be kind of sexy. This was not unusual for Mary. She had formed a nagging and perhaps unhealthy crush on Dr. Cunningham last year. This would not have been odd had Dr. Cunningham not been strange in most every way, from his lisp to the pink ten-speed with a basket that he rode about campus, and it did not escape Mary that maybe she found some professors attractive only because the other students did not. Many of the students in Logic and Reasoning 204 had found Williams creepy—they had said as much in the hallway after class.

Out of the shower now, her hair wet and a towel around her— another perk of the single room was Mary's ability to walk around naked—she logged on to her Winchester account and checked her e-mail again.

There was a message from Professor Williams. The subject line read, "First Clue."

Mary opened the e-mail and read.

Time

Polly was last seen on Friday, August the first at a party. This was a going-away party in Polly's honor, because she would be leaving for college soon. All her friends were there, including an ex-boyfriend named Mike. Mike and Polly had problems. Mike would sometimes hit Polly.

One night toward the end of their relationship Polly had to call the police, but she refused to press charges once they showed up. Polly returned from the going-away party that night to her father's home on During Street, where she was staying for the summer. Her father was awake when she came home, watching David Letterman. He told the police that he had sat with Polly and watched television, and when she fell asleep he carried her to bed, "like I used to do when she was a girl." He hasn't seen her since.

Police speculate that early in the morning of August the second, Polly left the house. Her red Honda Civic was found beside Stribbling Road, about twenty miles out of town. When Mike Reynolds, Polly's ex-boyfriend, was questioned, he of course denied seeing Polly after the going-away party. The problem with Mike's culpability in Polly's disappearance is this: Mike was at the party until the next morning, and many witnesses told investigators that they had seen Mike sleeping on the couch. In Polly's car, investigators found no traces that Polly had been planning to leave for an extended time: there were no bags in the trunk, no changes of clothes in the backseat. The only fingerprints in the car were Polly's. There was no sign of struggle.

Polly's father received a telephone call on Monday, August 4.

The caller sounded distant, as if she were "at the bottom of the well." Polly's father thought he had heard the caller say, "I'm here," but by the time he was questioned by police he couldn't be sure. Investigators traced all calls made to the During Street residence on the fourth of August, and there was one unusual call made at 7:13 that evening. Unfortunately, the number was unknown.

When Mary returned to her in-box, she saw that Professor Williams had sent another message. It was called "The Syllabus." Mary clicked on it and waited while an image materialized on her monitor. The image was of a man being executed at the gallows. Mary could see the smudged expressions of some onlookers who stood below, watching. There was a blurring around the edges of the photograph, as if it had been taken just as the man dropped through the trapdoor. The man was hooded, and someone had cropped an image onto the velvet hood. Mary squinted to see it, and finally she made it out.

It was a question mark.

The mark was like a shadow, vaguely discernible. It was, Mary thought, as if it had been knitted into the fabric.

3

On Wednesday Mary noticed that two or three of the female students were not in class. She wondered if they had been scared away by the picture of the execution. She wondered if any of them would report Williams and if he could get in trouble for sending a picture like that through campus e-mail. But mostly she wondered about Polly, and she was eager to run her theories by Professor Williams. She had spent most of the previous night fleshing out those theories, and even though she had been exhausted for Dr. Kiseley's lit class that morning, she was feeling that hum again, that electric charge she'd felt Monday after class.

When he came in—today he wore blue jeans again and a Winchester U T-shirt—he was carrying a dry erase marker and a few loose pieces of transparency paper. He took his position at the podium. "Any questions?" he asked without any greeting.

Mary got her first theory organized in her mind, but just when she was about to speak Brian House said from behind her, "We all want to know what this is."

"What what is?" asked Williams softly.

"This," said the boy. "All of this. This class. Polly. That . . ." He couldn't bring himself to say "picture."

"This is Logic and Reasoning 204," Williams said dismissively. A few students laughed.

"That's not what I mean and you know it," Brian said. He was sitting up straight now. He was pointing at the professor, accusing him.

"Do you mean to say, Mr. House"—and this was the first time, they all noted, that he had called any of them by name—"that this is all a dupe?"

"Well, yeah. Exactly. That's exactly what I'm saying."

"Isn't all knowledge a dupe? Isn't the rational world itself full of inconsistencies and tricks? Trapdoors? False challenges? How do you know that every day when you walk across campus, you're actually swimming through a sea of *monads*? Because we tell you that it is. How do you know that *Pride and Prejudice* is a masterpiece? Because we say it is. How do you know that a certain proof explains the meaning of light or the speed of sound? Because it is written in the book. But what if the equation is not square? What if the proof is a little off? What if the measurements were proved to be false? What if that which you had always believed to be logical thought turned out to be—God forbid—*wrong*. The world is dictated by a set of principles, and most of those principles are granted to you here, in these decorated halls." Williams raised his arms, encompassing the walls and the light and the dancing dust of Seminary East.

"Are you saying that what we learn at Winchester is a lie?" asked someone else.

"Not all of it, no," said Williams. "Not all. But certainly some. The trick is finding out what is the real and what is the fake."

"What's that have to do with this class?" asked Brian.

"Only this," Williams said sharply. "I am telling you that the best way to learn logic is to decode a puzzle. And this is what Polly's disappearance is: an intricate puzzle. Now some of you may take offense to this. Some of you may be bewildered by my choice of pedagogy. But you will learn to think, and induce, and carve out the blight of lazy thought—those fallacies and indiscretions and wrong turns. Only the best thinkers among you will find Polly, and those are the students to whom I will grant As."

Brian rested. He seemed to be satisfied with that answer. He began to inspect his quick-bitten fingernails.

Mary had her theory formed now. "Polly's father abducted her," she said, more quickly than she would have liked. By the time she was finished, she was nearly breathless. She didn't want to appear desperate, not this early in the game.

"How?" the professor replied.

"Why?" Dennis Flaherty put in, leaning forward in the front row to look quizzically at Mary.

"Motive," said Professor Williams. "What I want to know now is how? How could the father possibly be responsible?"

"Because . . . ," Mary began, but she could not go on. The professor was questioning her again, and she failed that test for a second time.

"Because of Mike," said Brian.

"Ah," said Williams. "Mike. The father and Mike—they don't like each other?"

"Probably not," Brian offered, perhaps because he had experienced a similar situation: a bitter father, a beautiful girl, threatening phone calls from the despondent old man.

"You're right," said the professor. "They don't like each other. In fact, they hate each other. Polly's father once told Mike that he would kill him if he ever caught him out alone. But this doesn't answer the question that Miss Butler is implicitly posing: *Why the father?* Why abduct your own daughter?"

"To protect her!" Mary almost shouted. She was feeling that cold, familiar rush when she put the pieces into place. That old energy in the blood. She had to be close.

"That's interesting," said Williams gently. Mary looked at Williams and saw that he was staring at her in a way that betrayed his interest in her. She knew that he was keeping her on a line, tethering her to all the intricate possibilities. Blushing, she finally looked away. "To protect her," he went on. "So you're saying that Mike is such a danger to Polly that her own father must abduct her, lie to the police, grieve publicly about his daughter's false disappearance, and manage to keep the ruse intact for almost a month? That's impressive for a little old schoolteacher with not much money in the bank."

Mary realized how ridiculous it sounded now, coming from him. She could only look at the flickering cursor on her laptop monitor.

"But if this Mike is really dangerous," said Dennis, taking up for Mary, "if he's psychopathic in some way, maybe Polly's father feels that her life is threatened enough to hide her."

"Hide her where?" Williams asked.

"An aunt's house," he said. Mary wasn't sure if Dennis really believed in her theory or was just grabbing the loose strand of the idea and running with it to save her the shame.

"How many of you believe this?" Professor Williams asked the class. The light from the window was approaching him. Their time was running out. No one in the class raised a hand.

"But in a murder—" said Brian now.

"A kidnapping," the professor corrected him.

"—in a kidnapping, isn't the father the immediate suspect? Isn't that the rule? A girl is taken and her father did it. Maybe he's a sexual deviant."

"Polly's father was a suspect," Professor Williams said then, and Mary's heart started up again. "But he was never a suspect for the convoluted reason that Ms. Butler suggests he should be. Class: what is the real problem with the theory Ms. Butler is presenting?"

Again she crashed down shamefully, her gaze on the hot light of the screen.

Limply, a girl in Mary's row raised her hand. "She is going to be murdered," the girl said, casting a look at Mary that said, *Sorry.*

"Think about it," the professor said, his impatience with them showing for the first time. "I've told you that she is to be murdered in six weeks. That is a given. So why would the father 'rescue' Polly from Mike if he—Daddy—were going to kill her in six short weeks?"

Williams shuffled the papers he had brought in. He turned off Seminary East's lights, and the room fell as dark as it could given the natural light that poured in through the windows. Then there was the whir of an overhead projector, and a square of yellow, sickly light blanched the northern wall. The professor slipped the topmost sheet off the stack and put it on the machine. It was a photograph of a girl in a summer dress. She was standing barefoot on the grass and holding out her arm, palm forward, as if she didn't want her picture taken. Williams didn't have to tell them: this was Polly. He put on the next page. This was a shot of a tattooed young man sitting on a couch. He had drunk too much and his eyes were rimmed red. He was shirtless and sunburned, his bare shoulders pink and peeling. An invisible girl, who was off to the right of the shot, had her arm around him. Mike. The third page: an overweight man standing to the right of a class of young children. Polly's father. The children all had their eyes censored out by thin black bars. And then a fourth page: a house, a simple Cape Cod with a dead vegetable garden off to one side and an American flag blowing against the eaves. Polly's house, the last place she had been seen.

"So now," said Professor Williams, turning to write on the board, "you know these things." He wrote *August 1*. "This is the last day Polly was seen. You also know the date when her car was found." He wrote, *August 2*. "You know that Mike was in the house of the party all night on August first. You know Polly's father was the last to see her late on the evening of August first, and that he watched television with his daughter before she went to bed. And you know that whoever kidnapped Polly is her potential murderer. Is that it?"

No one in the class spoke. Upstairs, in Seminary High, students were getting out of class, their desks scooting almost musically across the floor.

Mary thought, *Something else*. But she couldn't organize the thought, much less verbalize it. It was there, right in front of her, floating nebulously.

"All right then," said Williams. He gathered up the papers and put the marker in the tray, a gift to whomever used the classroom next, and turned off his machine. "It's important to remember that this class is an NF." He was referring to a "No Friday"; Williams's class was coveted mostly because it would be held on Mondays and Wednesdays only. The students would have Friday afternoons off, and so Mary knew she would not be able to talk to him again before next week. Any theories she had would have to be laid out now, or else she risked other students beating her to the punch.

"The phone call," Mary said then. Her heart was beating fast again, and her face was growing hot.

"What's that?" asked Williams.

" 'I'm here,' " she said. "The strange phone call to her father. The one with the girl in the well. Polly was calling him. She got to a phone somehow. She . . ."

"Circumstance," said Brian mockingly, and the back row cracked up.

Williams took up the marker and wrote on the board, *August 4*.

Then he said softly, " 'I'm here,' she said. 'I'm here.' Was it Polly? Was it a prank? And where is 'here'?" He didn't turn on the fluorescents, and the room was yellow, almost golden with the streaking light. He was outside of the light, behind it, frontlit, nearly invisible behind a curtain of Seminary dust. "Now, ladies and gentlemen," Williams said, capping his marker with a sharp click, "you know that you have just over five weeks to find Polly, or else she will be murdered."

4

Winchester University is split into two hemispheres: Down Campus, home to all of the classroom buildings and underclassmen dorms, and Up Campus, where the Greek houses are located and where much of the faculty lives. The great creation myth of Winchester comes from the 1950s, when Down Campus was the women's college and Up Campus was a sparsely attended divinity school. Down Campus was the first to accept a minority, a black woman named Grace Murphy. The students at Up were so incensed over this that they rioted on Down Campus. A now-infamous town cop named Henry Rodram was involved in these riots, and the narrative goes like this:

Rodram and some divinity students carried twenty gallons of gasoline the half mile between Up and Down and poured it around the base of Trigby Hall, where Grace Murphy lived. Trigby and all the buildings around it—Norris, Filmont, the Gray Brick Building—went up in flames. In fact most of Down Campus burned that night: May 27, 1955. The next day Grace Murphy withdrew from Winchester, and it was not until the mid-1960s, a year after Winchester became a coed liberal arts institution, that a minority was allowed to enroll.

A small stream called Miller's Creek cuts through the geographic middle of campus, a viaduct connecting the two hemispheres to take students from Down Campus to Up. This is where Brian House was walking on Saturday evening. The viaduct had myths of its own: attempted suicides, accidental deaths, an infamous and botched demolition attempt by a mentally ill student in the 1980s. During the Vietnam War, students had formed a makeshift boundary at one end of the bridge so that professors could not get from Up to Down without driving Route 17 all the way into downtown DeLane. The faculty was too proud to do this, so for a week classes were canceled altogether or held on the banks of the creek, the professors on one bank and the students sitting on the muddy grass of the other. After a six-day standoff, the students grudgingly returned to class.

Brian had already had a little to drink, and he planned on drinking much more as the night went on. It was a cool, breezy twilight in early September. High up in Norris Hall, some freshmen had their window open, and the sound of a basketball game wafted down and echoed off the buildings on each side of Miller's Creek.

Brian stopped midway across the bridge and looked down, as he often did, and listened intently to the metallic burble of the creek. Standing here always reminded him of being a kid, of the tinny sound of a faraway stream in the woods when he and his father and brother would take long hikes through the Catskills. On one of these excursions they got lost, and his father had told Brian and Marcus, "We'll stay right here. You aren't supposed to panic when you get lost. People walk these trails all the time." But three hours later they were still in the same spot and no one had come for them. It was getting dark. Brian could see that his father was scared, or maybe he was cold, because he was trembling, legs and arms and shoulders all vibrating as if he had been strummed. Finally, when it was almost too dark to see, they began to walk. It was much later, probably around midnight, when they heard the sounds of a highway. They found the road and hitchhiked back to town, and for three days Brian's father wouldn't even look at his boys.

The creek ran off into the purple edge of the woods, snaked around Up Campus, and then disappeared near the Geary Economics Center, where it would meet the Thatch River about two miles from campus. Sometimes Brian fantasized about following it, jumping in and losing himself in the current and ending up miles away, floating faceup on the Thatch, sailing toward home.

The cool wind blew against his face, and the pink skin of the water shimmered. He tried to focus on its most distant point, out toward the mouth of the woods. Out there, under the canopy of trees, was where he buried it freshman year. The Thing, as he and his family called it. They couldn't even give the object a name; it was just the "Thing," as if actually calling it something would give it credence. Validity. They wanted to keep it obscure, hide it from their thoughts. And so it became, to all of them, the Thing. To this day Brian thought of it as nothing else.

It was just a disturbance of the earth down there, a claw mark in the creek's bank. He came out here every night to check, to make sure that someone hadn't disturbed it. No, it was just as he'd left it, the dirt—

"Brian?"

Startled, he turned to see a girl standing beside him. They were the only two people on the viaduct. Most students were on Up Campus, at one of the frat houses, getting ready for Saturday night.

"Were you . . . ?" she asked.

"No," he said. "I was just looking at the water, at how it . . ." He couldn't explain. Hell, he didn't *need* to explain himself to anyone. Who was she, anyway?

"I'm Mary," she said, noting his confused expression. "I'm in your logic class."

"Ah," said Brian. "Dr. Weirdo."

She looked off, the insult to Professor Williams stinging her. "He's not that bad," she whispered.

"So who did it?" Brian leaned back onto the concrete rail of the viaduct, his back turned to the girl.

"Her father did, of course," Mary said. She wondered if she should lean on the bridge next to him. Was he inviting her over there, next to him? Did he want a long, drawn-out conversation or was he simply being casual, just idly passing the time?

"And he's going to kill her?"

"He thinks he's protecting her," she said.

"But Williams is saying 'murder.' What kind of protection is murder?"

"Have you wondered whether Williams is telling us the truth about everything?"

"Hell yes," Brian said sharply. "He's misdirecting us all the time. That's a given. But there are rules, and that must be one of them. What good is the game if it doesn't have rules. Williams said it himself. The kidnapper is the murderer."

"I guess," she sighed. Defeated.

"Anyway, that whole theory is crap," said Brian, still looking away into the trees. "Mike's the man."

"Mike?" asked Mary playfully. This was her first discussion out of class with anyone about the case, and she found herself enjoying it. She wasn't supposed to meet up with Summer and the Deltas for another hour. She had just been out on campus getting some fresh air and—she had to admit—thinking about Polly and Professor Williams.

"Yes, Mike," Brian said. "Mike told the people at the party that he was going to sleep on the couch, slipped out when no one was paying attention, drove to Polly's house. He broke into her room, took her to some distant location. You know how it is: drunk people can't remember anything anyway. They *thought* they saw Mike on the couch, but was it really Mike?"

"Hmmm," Mary said, placating him.

"Yeah. Hmmm." He was still looking off at that fixed point.

They stood there in the wind with night falling around them. Some of the streetlights along Montgomery were coming on, casting half the viaduct in a blanched, angular white.

Finally Brian said, "I better get going. I'm off to the Deke house to get plastered."

"Oh, yeah," Mary said demurely. "I should be going, too."

He turned to face her. She noticed his eyes: how red they were, how unsettled. It was as if the pupils had been shattered like a dropped plate, skimming off into a thousand different fragments. There was something in them. Disappointment, maybe, or hurt. He looked away. "So you like the Shins?" she asked him, noting his shirt.

"Yeah," he said. "No doubt."

"What's your favorite song?"

He turned away from her again. He didn't really know any of the song names. His roommate had the record, and he knew that he was supposed to like the band because a lot of kids on campus whose majors were the same as Brian's liked them, but it all sounded like noise to him. "The one on the first record," he said.

" 'New Slang,' " Mary said. "That's a great song."

"Yeah, whatever." He said this going away, walking off into the wedges of pale light on Montgomery Street. Mary called after him, telling him that she would see him in class on Monday, but he must not have heard because he didn't say good-bye.

5

He hated these fund-raisers. Hated them. The luminaries would all clump together near the wall and sip scotch, leaving the students out on the dance floor with the wives. It was a sort of social fiefdom, the lords away in money talks and the serfs left to tend the harvest. Dennis Flaherty stood in the corner, ginger ale going flat in a plastic cup, thinking about—well, the only thing he could think about these days.

Her. Elizabeth Orman, the dean's wife.

He'd met Elizabeth in the library that had been dedicated to her husband. He thought she was a reference librarian because she was old—*older*, she liked to correct him when they joked like that—and because she looked as if she knew where things were. He was writing a paper on Alfred Adler, and when he asked her where he could find *Understanding Human Nature*, she asked him what he wanted to know.

Turned out she was a doctoral student, and she knew a lot about Adler. He didn't even need the book after talking to Elizabeth. They sat by one of the east windows and he wrote as she spoke. "Did you know," she said, "that Adler was a neurologist before he was a social scientist? He was interested in how the eye worked, in how we *see* the world. That whole thing—seeing—he would later use in his theories about inferiority. But later, it was us seeing us, not us seeing others. The inward eye, the mind's eye."

And on and on like that. Dennis writing and Elizabeth speaking, long into the evening. He met her there a week later by accident, and they talked again, this time about regular stuff like politics and music (she was a Mingus fan, he discovered). That second time, he started to look at her, really look at her. She was definitely old— *older*, he caught himself. She must have been in her late thirties. But there was something different about her on the second evening they met. It was, Dennis thought, as if she had prepared herself for him. She had unbuttoned the top button of her sweater, and her auburn hair was swept to the side, out of her face. The look of the frazzled graduate student was completely gone. It was clear that she cared.

Elizabeth began calling Dennis her *buddy*. There was a little sexual tension there, he had to admit, but it was fleeting. It would swell up, unannounced, and then taper off for the rest of the afternoon. Dennis would wonder, later, if he had simply imagined it.

It wasn't until his third or fourth afternoon in the library that he learned who she was. And it happened by accident.

"Mrs. Orman," a reference librarian whispered, sticking her head into the reading room where Dennis and Elizabeth were sitting. "Telephone for you."

"Shit. Sorry," Elizabeth said. "I have to take this."

Orman, Dennis thought. *Of course.* Of course. That's why she was given so much respect in the library. Why everyone smiled at her, stepped to the side for her, asked her if she need anything. She was the goddamn old man's wife.

When she returned, he noticed her wedding ring for the first time.

"So," she said. Was there shame in her face?

"So," Dennis said. "Elizabeth Orman."

She said nothing.

"I didn't—" he began.

"I should have told you," she said softly.

He wanted to say, *Of course not, Elizabeth. I just would think that would be one of the first things you'd mention, you know, let it slip out that you were the wife of the most powerful man on campus.* But he said none of those things. What he said was, "It's okay."

"It's not okay."

"Okay," he agreed. "It's not."

That stung her. She turned her face away from him, toward the window. She inhaled loudly, gathering herself.

"As a feminist," she said, "that's not how I announce myself. Do you walk around campus saying, 'Hello, I'm Dennis Flaherty, Savannah's beau'?"

Dennis thought it was interesting how she knew about Savannah Kleppers though he had never spoken about her. Very interesting.

Dennis stayed in DeLane over the summer and interned for a Republican congressman in Cale. He and Elizabeth met only occasionally for the next few months, but even on the occasions they did meet, Dennis had to admit that something was different. Their occasional sexual tension had disappeared altogether, and their conversations were much more antiseptic. She was a completely different person around him now that he knew who she was. Or, more specifically, now that he knew who her husband was.

Since the beginning of September, things had begun to falter badly. She had been distant, preoccupied. Ashamed, probably. The last time he had gone to the library, she hadn't been there. He caught her in the hallway of the Gray Brick Building one day and asked, "Are you mad at me?"

"Of course not," she'd scoffed, and pulled away from him. Then she disappeared down the stairwell.

But there clearly *was* anger in her voice. Dennis was pretty sure, however, that it was not anger at him, but at herself. For she had been deceiving him for those first few meetings, the ones that really counted in Dennis's mind, and she knew it. She knew it and she felt bad about it.

The fund-raiser was a black-tie affair the Taus were putting on for the American Cancer Society. It was held in Carnegie Hall, Winchester's administrative building and the most historic structure on campus. Usually Dennis was able to make it through, smile and grunt while the old men told their stories, but tonight he was feeling particularly out of place. He wanted to leave, but where was he supposed to go? What was he supposed to do? Standing there in Carnegie he pondered these things, wondered if he should just leave Winchester altogether. Maybe transfer to Temple, be closer to his father. Maybe he should . . .

But then he saw Elizabeth across the room. She was looking at him the way she had so many times across the table in the library: passively, almost quizzically, as if there was something about him she couldn't figure out. She walked onto the dance floor. She smiled and he smiled back, the only gesture that he could think to use. It was a forced smile, almost crooked. Then they were dancing to something, some sort of slow waltz, and Elizabeth was saying, "Dennis, I want to have sex with you."

"Yes," he said stupidly. Like a boy.

"I'm sorry for what happened. I should have told you. But I thought you would get—scared."

"Scared?"

"Of Ed. Of getting caught with me. Of what would happen if we were discovered."

"Elizabeth, we were just talking. It was nothing. It was Alfred Adler and the eye."

"Stop it, Dennis. You know it was more than that."

"Know?" he choked. His heart was beating fast, thrumming in his chest. His face was hot, and he felt cold sweat on his chest.

"You know you want to fuck me."

"No," he lied. "Absolutely not."

She was sulking now. He had felt her body stiffen, lilt away from him.

"Why haven't you been there? In the library the last two weeks."

"I've been busy, Dennis. It's not only you. I have work, too. I'm writing my dissertation, remember?"

Over her shoulder, he saw the man staring at him. The inimitable Dean Orman: thirtysome years older than his wife, professor emeritus at Winchester. Orman was one of the most esteemed members of the psychology faculty, best known for his riveting lectures, even though he fumbled for words now and then and forgot his threads and themes. He had studied with Stanley Milgram at Yale in the 1960s, and word was that he had begun a book about Milgram that would redefine the man's legacy.

The waltz finally ended, and Dennis broke from the woman's hold and returned to the other side of the room, where the other Taus were waiting. "You going to screw her or not?" asked Jeremy Price. Price was wearing tuxedo pants and a T-shirt that was airbrushed with a vest, cummerbund, and bow tie.

Dennis said nothing. He wondered how much Price had heard, if he'd been listening in to their conversation.

"Here's what you do," Price said. He got close to Dennis, turned his back on the dance floor, pulled the other boy up by the lapels. "You get her alone and you just *ravish* her. Pound her like a jackhammer. Make it good for you and *horrible* for her. Ha! Pants at your ankles. Buttons skittering across the floor. Make her *hurt*."

"Dennis?"

Dean Orman. He was standing just behind Price, over the boy's shoulder. Dennis had no idea how long the man had been there.

"Huh . . . hello, Dr. Orman," he said. He had met Orman only two or three times before, at similar fund-raisers, and for some reason was always nervous in the old man's presence. Orman knew Dennis's father, had said once of the man that he was a "pioneer in his field." Dennis felt that the only reason Orman approved the use of Carnegie for the Taus was because of his father.

"It's about time for us to be going."

"Of course," Dennis managed. "Is there anything else I can get you?"

"No," the dean began. It was as if he wanted to say something more but could not. Price had slunk back into a dark corner somewhere, leaving Dennis alone with the old man.

The dean had been at Winchester since the beginning, when the school was split in half. He was the first provost of the school. Once, in the late seventies, he had coached its tennis team to a conference championship. He had seen the campus burn and had lived through six different presidents. It was said that any historical discussion of Winchester began and ended with Dean Orman.

But his legend was cemented with the marriage to the wife who was nearly half his age, a graduate student at Winchester he had met on a trip to Morocco. Dennis had heard the story, of course, but he had never heard the woman's name. And now he was caught in something, trapped in this game with Elizabeth. And it *was* a game, Dennis knew that. Why else would she have hidden her ring? Why else would she have given him only her first name? She was seeing how far she could take him, hoping he would cross a line into a place that he couldn't come back from.

Tonight, that line had been crossed.

"What classes are you taking this quarter?" the dean asked. It was just something to say, just filler. Another waltz had begun, and Dennis could see Elizabeth dancing with someone else. But she was looking at him.

"Economics and Finance. Philosophy and the Western World with Douglas. And Logic and Reasoning."

"Logic and Reasoning," said the dean. "Under whom?"

"Williams."

Something changed in the dean's eyes, then. He focused on Dennis more perfectly, let his scotch glass fall to his side. He might have even taken a step forward, closed the gap between them, but Dennis could not be sure.

"How's that going?" he asked. His voice had changed timbre, become more bearing. Dennis realized he was under some kind of spotlight now, suddenly in a sort of interrogation.

"It's . . . interesting," he offered.

"Williams," the dean mused, sounding as if he were thinking to himself now. "Williams is a funny character. I remember the terrible fracas over that book of his. All that mess."

Dennis wanted to hear more. In fact, he badly wanted to hear more, not only because it was taking his mind off Elizabeth but also because he was interested in Williams and his strange class. It was so . . .

Elizabeth was suddenly there, touching her husband's shoulder. "Let's go, Ed," she said curtly, glancing at Dennis. Dennis couldn't read her look.

"Dennis, I'll be seeing you," the dean said. He had lost his train of thought, which was usual for the dean. Some assumed he had the early signs of dementia; most days he would lock himself away in Carnegie and take no visitors.

It wasn't until much later, back in the Tau house with dawn spreading out across the sky and falling sharply on Up Campus, that Dennis remembered what Dean Orman had said about Professor Williams. Even though it was early in the morning and he hadn't rested in nearly twenty-four hours, Dennis could not get to sleep no matter how hard he tried.

6

By Sunday, Mary had finally gotten her mind off Professor Williams and Polly. She and Summer McCoy had gone shopping at the Watermill Mall, and out to eat at an Italian place called Adige. As Summer dropped off Mary at her dorm late in the evening, logic class, and more specifically Professor Williams, was the furthest thing from Mary's mind.

But now, two hours later, she was thinking about him again. What was he doing right now, for instance. He was so . . . mysterious. No office hours. No bio on the website. It was almost as if he, like Polly, needed a set of clues to go with him. Mary opened Paul Auster's *City of Glass*, which she was reading for her only other class that semester, Postmodern Lit and the New Existentialism, which she hated. Mary was taking what the students called a "walk term," which meant you took the minimum six hours. *Walk* came from the idea that with all your given leisure time, you might walk the campus grounds as Winchester's founders had surely done, learning deep and profound lessons from nature. (Mary had noticed that most students, when they were on their walk terms, found their lessons through drinking beer and downloading music illegally.)

Mary lay down on her bed and propped Auster on her knees, trying to take her thoughts off Polly and her creator. Yet the novel's words wouldn't make sense. She would read a sentence and stop, float off somewhere, imagine Williams. She imagined him at home, walking barefoot across the wood floor in his pajamas, staring out a back window, drinking coffee from a cracked mug. She admitted it: she was fascinated by him. So curious, how he had refused to give them anything substantial to work with, how he had led them into those questions. There was something dangerous about it—and it was that danger, that adventure, that had been missing from her experience at Winchester since she and Dennis had broken up.

And this is what Polly's disappearance is, Williams had said, *an intricate puzzle.*

Polly. Williams had tried to make her more real by presenting those weird photographs in class. Mary imagined that transparent Polly standing on the grass, smiling playfully in her summer dress, holding out her arm to block the camera. Where was that grass? Who was the girl, the real girl in the picture? Someone Professor Williams knew? His daughter? And the red-eyed Mike. Mary thought she recognized that couch from somewhere on campus, but she couldn't place it. Was "Mike" a student here? Had Professor Williams taken these photos himself and not told his subjects what they were for?

Mary went to the computer and ran a search. She typed in "Professor L. Williams" and got more than a thousand hits. There were Professor L. Williamses at Southern Oregon University, at DePaul, at East Carolina, at Bard College. She narrowed the search: "Professor L. Williams at Winchester University." Forty hits. She got his bio again, that useless and broken link. She found a couple of program newsletters where he was mentioned as "Dr. Williams."

It was getting late, past 10:00 p.m. now. Mary had an early class on Monday, and she knew that if she didn't get to bed soon she would regret it in the morning. She browsed through a few more links, still only coming up with vague references to Williams by his title and not his name. She needed his name. She didn't know why, but she needed it. She was certain it would help her with Polly's case somehow.

On the third page of results, she found what she was looking for.

It was a press release for an article he had written in 1998. The article was called "The Components of Crime," and the author was Leonard Williams.

Leonard. Mary said it aloud, registered the taste of it in her mouth. It almost made her laugh. Professor Williams was definitely no Leonard, yet there it was on her screen. Undeniable fact. If you would have given her a thousand guesses, Leonard would not have been one of them.

She returned to Google and searched it in full: "Professor Leonard Williams at Winchester University."

Forty-five hits this time, and her heart nearly stopped when she read the title of the first result: "Distinguished Winchester Professor Accused of Plagiarism."

The phone rang.

Breathlessly, Mary picked it up and found herself saying, "Hello?"

"Mary?" It was her mother calling from Kentucky. The line, as it always did, scratched and tweaked across the miles. Mary often wondered if there was an electrical storm, perpetually firing off in the distance somewhere out there, nicking at her mother's and father's *I love yous* and *I miss yous*. Then a strange thought occurred to her: *In a well. The girl sounded as if she was at the bottom of a well.*

I'm here.

Mary closed her eyes, put her head down on the corner of the desk as was her habit when she was nervous about something. She managed to say, "Yeah, Mom. Are you all back home?"

"Who is this?"

"It's me," said Mary. "It's me, Mom."

"You just . . . you don't sound like yourself. It's like—like you're miles away."

At the bottom of a well.

"I'm here, Mom," said Mary, pressing her forehead hard into the desk, the pain spreading across her brow and over her scalp. She didn't want to look at the screen, didn't want to face it. She was afraid of what was there.

"Anyway," said her mother casually. "Your father and I are home.

We just got back. It . . . was . . . magnificent. Mary, you should have seen it. Key West is just beautiful in September. Thank God all those wild kids were gone. We went out to Fort Zachary Taylor and spent the day. We saw Hemingway's home, all those six-toed cats. Anyway. You should get the postcard soon."

"Mmmm," Mary murmured, head still down, eyes shut tight.

"Tell me," her mother said.

"Tell you what?"

"Tell me what's going on."

"There's nothing going on, Mom. Really. Seriously. Everything is fine."

"I can tell by your voice. Something's the matter."

"It's just—" *Dennis*, Mary thought. *Lie to her.* "It's just that I saw Dennis."

"He called you, didn't he? He asked you out again."

"Absolutely not. I haven't really spoken to Dennis since freshman year. He's just—" Mary stopped short. She didn't want to tell her mother about Professor Leonard Williams and this strange class she couldn't get off her mind. Her monitor blacked out into the screen saver, startling Mary for a moment.

"Except what? Tell me."

Mary knew it was futile. Her mother was like a sort of leech for information, a kind of walking, talking, cooking truth serum. "Except he's in one of my classes," Mary said gently.

"That's it!" her mother said. There was nothing her mother enjoyed more than bleeding secrets. Cracking codes. In that way, she was just like her daughter. She would search for kinks in your language, squeeze details out of you, break you across the static-laced distance. "That's it. I figured it out. Harold!" She was calling for Mary's father, who would be off somewhere in the house, getting back to whatever project he was surely in the middle of when they'd left for Key West: fixing the lawn mower, rebuilding the busted computer the neighbors had thrown out. "Harold, Dennis and Mary are taking classes to-gether!" Then, "I feel really good about this, honey. You know I liked Dennis so much even though your father didn't trust him. Tell him—tell him that I don't blame him for what he did. That's just what boys do when they get bored. Will you tell him that, please?"

"I'll tell him, Mom," said Mary.

"Anyway. I better get going. Have to get unpacked and all. Sweetie, listen. I want you to call me if you need anything. Please."

There was silence on the line. It snapped and cracked and scratched like a needle at the end of a record. "Okay," Mary finally said, her eyes still down at the floor. She saw all the great wads of dust under her desk, balls of dirt and hair.

"Good-bye, honey," her mother said.

"Bye, Mom."

It was another minute or two before Mary could look at the screen. Slowly, her heart going mad inside her chest, she read the short article on Leonard Williams's crime.

DISTINGUISHED WINCHESTER PROFESSOR
ACCUSED OF PLAGIARISM

A Winchester University professor, in his fourteenth year at the institution, has been accused of plagiarism. Associate Professor Leonard Williams was accused of lifting multiple passages of John Dawe Brown's famous 1971 book, *The Subliminal Mind*, and placing them, almost word for word, in the text of his pub-lished dissertation *Tragedy and Substance: Logic as a Way of Figuring Out the World*, which was first published in 1986. John Dawe Brown was the author of more than twenty books of philosophy. He taught at Yale University for thirty-five years, beginning in the early 1960s, and recently succumbed to colon cancer. His wife, Loretta Hawkes-Brown, has made no public comment on this incident. Professor Williams has been suspended by the university, with pay, until a special faculty committee can investigate the incident.

Mary finally could feel herself, her legs and knees and her *mind*, barely enough to make her way to bed. By the time she was there, it was after midnight and the chapters of *City of Glass* remained unread for tomorrow's class.

What did it mean? Perhaps it didn't mean anything. Her freshman year humanities professor had said that if you weren't borrowing, then you weren't doing serious work. He said it just like that: "borrowing." But Mary knew there was a difference between that and what Professor Williams had done. He had *stolen*—"lifting multiple passages almost word for word," the article said—entire chunks of text. Mary imagined him with Professor Brown's book open, sitting at his desk and wondering, *Should I?* Or did he feel no compunction? Did Williams, like Polly's father in Mary's theory, act on impulse alone, the knowledge of his reward pressing more forcefully on his mind than the possible risk? Did he even understand the implications of what he was doing, sitting there with that old book open in front of him, holding it with two paperweights perhaps on each side of the spine so he could read the text and type at the same time?

Now, at least, she knew something about Williams. But was it good or bad to have this knowledge? Perhaps it meant that he was capable of anything and his use of the Polly story was the mark of some deeper cruelty. Perhaps the man was unstable and using his students to play out his own twisted obsessions. Or maybe it meant nothing at all. Maybe the incident had been a mistake, something he had long since atoned for and forgotten.

It was these thoughts that finally carried her, sometime much later, into a fitful and dreamless sleep.

FIVE WEEKS LEFT

7

"Logic tells you," Professor Williams was saying on Monday afternoon, "that Mike was the abductor. A criminal background check reveals that he has been busted a few times. Driving while intoxicated. Public intoxication. Possession of marijuana. Kid stuff. But there is something dangerous about him. Something dark and mysterious. Something *inner.* You've seen the picture of the man who is playing him for my experiment. I chose this particular actor because in real life this man is brooding, contemplative. Does he look, to you, like he is capable of this?"

The class was silent for a moment, and then two or three students muttered, "Yes."

"Yes!" Williams said, animated. For the first time he came out behind the podium, but gently, his hands out, easing his way toward them. "Of course. Logic draws a concrete line from Polly to Mike to the abandoned car on Stribbling Road. And your mind—your intuition—will draw an arrow. Intuition fills in blanks for you. If something is *supposed* to fit a certain pattern, then the mind will take you there and you will be biased against any other proposition."

He wrote two words on the board: *invincible ignorance.*

"This is a circular fallacy of the highest order," he said then, placing the marker back in the tray. "X cannot be Y because X clearly *has* to be Z. The mind presents you with rigid—very rigid—maps, and you do not listen to any other suggestions. This is also called, in layman's terms, 'tunnel vision.' It will ruin you in this case."

"What about randomness?" asked Dennis. He was writing on a legal pad that was resting on his briefcase. Mary noticed that he was a bit sunburned, and she wondered if he had been away somewhere for the weekend with his fraternity brothers—or perhaps with Savannah Kleppers.

"What about it?" replied Williams.

"Well, what about someone at the party? A guy sees Polly, he likes her, he calls her late that night and tells her to meet him somewhere off Stribbling Road. She meets him, and he . . ." But Dennis couldn't go on, couldn't say the word.

"And he what, Mr. Flaherty?" asked the professor.

"And he abducts her," Dennis mustered. It was just a whisper, so soft it was nearly just a scratch in his throat.

"Randomness is always a possibility, of course," the professor said. He retreated back behind the podium. "But in how many crimes does someone who is not in the victim's orbit end up being the perpetrator? I'll let you guess on that one."

"Twenty percent of the time," someone said.

"Less," said Williams.

"Ten percent," Mary offered.

"Less."

"Five."

"Two percent of the time," he declared. "Two percent. That means that in five hundred crimes of this manner, about ten random suspects become perpetrators. The odds, then, Mr. Flaherty, are against you." Williams spun on his heel again and faced the board. He wrote two more words below the last: *tu quoque*. "Latin," he explained. " 'You also.' This is a fallacy that suggests that since your theory is poor, then mine is allowed to be poor as well. But there is an inherent problem with wrongness in this class, of course." The professor smiled and leaned forward on the podium. "If you are wrong here, then Polly dies."

Some in the class laughed. For them, obviously, it was becoming a joke. A game. But Mary thought of the article she had read, of Leonard Williams's crime. When she looked at him, she could not fathom someone who had knowingly stolen another scholar's ideas and language. But of course that was invincible ignorance, because she knew that he *had* stolen those words.

"What about the dad?" asked Brian House. He had moved up a row for some reason, and now he was sitting right behind Mary. She wondered if he was just trying to show her up with this question, or maybe he had thought about what she had said on the viaduct Saturday night.

"Ah," Williams exclaimed. "Good old Dad. What about him? He's a schoolteacher. He teaches science at a local elementary school. He's overweight. What else?"

"The man in the transparency—your actor—had a military tattoo on his arm," Dennis said. Mary felt ashamed—she hadn't noticed it in the picture. She suddenly felt as if she was behind the rest of them, slipping away in the current. While she had been chasing down stupid conspiracy theories about Leonard Williams, the rest of the class had been thinking about Polly.

"The last one to see her," said the girl sitting beside Mary.

Mary knew that she better say something, or else the day was going to pass her by and she would be two weeks into a class without any headway. "Watches Letterman," she said.

A few people in back laughed, but Mary had not meant it as a joke. The comment was made in desperation, and again she felt herself flush.

"Good, Ms. Butler," the professor said, and Mary rose her eyes hopefully to meet his. "He watches Letterman. What could this mean? This is an important clue, I think."

"It could mean that he likes Letterman," said Brian wryly.

"Or that he hates Leno," the professor retorted. "But come on. Think here. He is watching Letterman when Polly returns from the going-away party. She watches the show with him and falls asleep and he carries her to bed. What are the possible meanings of that scenario?"

Mary thought. She closed her eyes and tried to find it, to find the truth in the situation. She saw Polly opening the door, coming into the dark house. Polly was a little drunk, stumbling. She put her purse down on the kitchen counter and saw her father. She came into the living room, which was flickering with the light from the TV, and sat beside him on the couch. He put his arm around her. They didn't say anything because they had the kind of relationship where you didn't have to speak. Your actions, your gestures, sounds, and tiny movements, told enough of the story of your day.

"He was waiting for her," she said.

"Why?" Williams asked.

"Because he was worried about Mike."

"Of course," the professor said. He was smiling, proud of her for getting there. "He was waiting for her because of Mike. Because there had—what?—been something going on in the last week before she disappeared. Because he was concerned with the old trouble again. Maybe Mike had been coming around again. Does a guy who teaches elementary school children seem to you like a late-night television fan?"

"No," half the class agreed.

"Are guys with military tattoos normally Letterman fans?"

"No."

"So what was Polly's father doing watching television late that night? Of course, he had to be waiting on her. Which means that Mike may have been—*may have been*—up to his old tricks."

Williams wrote one more word on the board: *retroduction*.

"This is a type of logic that suggests that we can account for a truth based on an observed set of facts. It has been proven, or *observed*, that Polly watched television with her father. It has been observed that Mike and Polly's father had had run-ins in the past, and that, according to a police report, the two men 'hated' each other. It has been observed that Mike physically abused Polly in the past. So we know retroductively, based on Letterman and her father taking Polly to bed, that perhaps he was waiting for her to come in. And thus Mike becomes more of a suspect."

"It doesn't fit," said Dennis then. The familiar light was moving forward, almost to the podium now.

"Mr. Flaherty has an objection!" said Professor Williams. He was still smiling, playing with them, seeing how far they could go with these theories.

"Mike was at the party," Dennis said.

"He was at the party, yes," agreed the professor. "Many people saw him that night. That's what you call a rock-solid alibi. Go on."

Dennis did not know how to go on. Mary could see the doodles and shapes all over his legal pad, boxes and stars and squares. Dennis had the habit—or perhaps the gift—of listening and not listening at the same time, of being there in spirit and off somewhere simultaneously. Whenever they had been at a restaurant eating, Dennis could look off, his eyes darting here and there, while she spoke. When she questioned him about it, saying, "If you were listening to me, what was I just saying?" he could repeat what she'd said word for word.

"Well," he finally said, "this means that Mike could not have abducted Polly."

Another phrase went up on the board: *tainted data*.

"And why was the data tainted?" the professor asked the class.

"Because everybody at that party was drunk," Brian said.

"That's one reason. But there's something else, something that you don't know about yet. What was Polly doing that night? *Where* was she that night?"

"Place," the girl beside Mary said.

"That's right, Ms. Bell. Place. And tonight you will find out just a bit more of this intricate puzzle. Be sure to check your e-mail."

With that, he was through the open door and out of their lives once again.

8

It was not that Dennis Flaherty regretted doing it. Quite the opposite—he wished that he could do it *again*. All day he had been craving her, starving for her as if the woman were some kind of sustenance. The only respite had been Dr. Williams's creepy logic class, but now that he was back in his room at the Tau house, he was feeling it again.

Elizabeth. Somehow her name was more powerful than her body, a body he had roved across for an entire afternoon in the inner sanctum of the old man's yacht. The old man sleeping above deck, the creek and whisper of the river below them, and Elizabeth teaching him things about himself that he had never dreamed could be true.

The day after the fund-raiser she had called him to ask if he would like to go out with her and the dean to the Thatch River. Her voice was even, almost businesslike, yet it was hiding something. "Sure," he said. And then, "What is this, Elizabeth?" But she had already hung up on him. It was done. No turning back now.

They had taken out the old man's cruiser yacht, named *The Dante*, which he kept in a slip at the Rowe County Marina. Because townies would often break into the marina and damage the boats, Dean Orman had been forced to hire his own man, a retired cop called Pig who circled the parking lot and beamed a spotlight down on the slips every couple of hours or so.

It was one of the last hot-weather weekends, and the lake had been crowded with kids on speedboats. The giant wake of pontoons jarred the old man as he fought with the wheel. They had sailed out toward Little Fork, where you could see Winchester University high up in the trees. "This is where we go," Dean Orman explained. "It's quiet here." They took the yacht back in a cove and anchored it there in the shade.

Orman took the *Times* up front, where there was some sun cutting a jagged line across the bow. Dennis and Elizabeth went swimming together. They both knew what was going to happen, had been communicating it silently all morning. When the old man's mouth gaped open, his head tilted back at a strange angle and the *Times* slack on his chest, they climbed back onto the yacht and crept below deck. There was a little room down there. A bed. Satin sheets that were stiff from weeks of disuse. A musty, stained pillow without a pillowcase. Dennis could barely fit on the bed—he lay on his back with his feet flat on the cold plastic of the boat wall. He was naked and soft. He waited. He told himself that he was doing this for a reason, to finish things with her. It was going to be hard and driving and severe. The boat rocked in the current, and with each rock Dennis's heart nearly cracked. The old man must surely be waking, coming downstairs to find them.

She stripped off the wet bathing suit and left it in a heap at her jeweled feet. Suddenly, she was transformed. She had shaved her pussy into a little fine arrow of fuzz. Dennis saw in her nakedness a sort of youth, a kind of playfulness he had never seen in their library meetings. How old was Elizabeth? Thirty-five? Forty? He still didn't know, but she now looked ten years younger than that. She was suddenly achingly beautiful to him, and without really registering what he was doing he was reaching out toward her, touching her, and pulling her down onto him.

But that was the extent of Dennis's power over Elizabeth Orman. His plan, as Jeremy Price had suggested, had been to pin her down, thrust into her a few times, make it as awful as anything she could imagine so that anything between them after today would be moot. But she would have none of that. *She* straddled *him*. And then she began to ride him, her hips matching the sliding, glassy rhythm of the Thatch below them. Dennis wondered: What kind of a woman shaves her pussy? Before he knew it he was coming, losing himself in the frenzied wake, the sloshing sound of the cove now a roar, Elizabeth with her head thrown back on top of him and her tits cupped in her own hands.

Afterward she lay on top of him, both of them bundled together like piles of rope, and listened to the lick of the river. "What about . . . ?" he asked. She put one finger over his lips to hush him. "Don't worry," she breathed, and for some reason he didn't.

Sometime much later Dennis was awakened by the old man yelling his wife's name. Dennis tried to leap up and grab his clothes, but Elizabeth held him to the bed. She mouthed, "Shhh," and slid back into her bathing suit. She paused a moment before she opened the door, gathering herself. And then she went up to her husband, saying—too cheerfully for Dennis's taste—"Yes, darling." Dennis heard him say, "Where's Dennis?" and Elizabeth replied, "Taking a nap." Dennis had his shoulder against the door at that point, fearing that the old man was going to rush below deck in a rage and beat him senseless.

Instead, Dennis heard a splash—someone diving in. And then a second. He put on his trunks and returned to the world. The sun had moved while he slept, and now the cove was almost completely in shadow. When the old man saw him he playfully called, "Jump in!" So Dennis did, and the three of them swam together into the evening, as if nothing had happened.

Now Dennis could not get her off his mind. Her body, her name, her—*rhythm*. She was so different from the unlearned, clumsy Savannah Kleppers. Savannah wanted the lights off and the stereo on, so that others in the house wouldn't hear them. She wanted Dennis on top or else it *burned*. She cried after sex, whether it was good or bad, and her tears would run in streams down his shoulders and chest and he was always afraid to ask her what was wrong, why was she crying, because he was afraid that her answer would somehow have to do with him.

With Elizabeth Orman, though, there was nothing of the sort. Nothing private, nothing emotional, nothing of substance except the raw thrust of pleasure. And so here he was, looking up at his ceiling in the Tau house, thinking of nothing else.

When he couldn't take it anymore, he called her at home, on her private line that she had slipped him on their way back to campus Sunday. At the sound of her voice Dennis almost sank to the floor, his knees weak and his gut hollowed.

"I have to come over," he sighed.

Then he was out on campus, late on a Monday night, walking Montgomery Street. He knew he should have been studying for an economics quiz, but what was done was done. He could no more dam this feeling than he could stop time.

After a weekend with temperatures that topped eighty degrees, the first hint of fall was now descending on Winchester. The wind was sharp, autumn cool, and the autumnalis trees were turning a fierce pink. The first leaves were falling, drifting down in front of the statue, *The Scientist*, which had been dedicated in honor of Dean Orman's lifelong friendship with Stanley Milgram. Dennis walked by the fountain outside Carnegie, which was choked with fallen leaves. A few students were around, their words blasted away by the harsh wind, but none of it registered with Dennis. Not a thing. He could see the lights of the Ormans' from here, their cottage-style home on Grace Hill. Normally he would have driven, but she had told him to come in the side door and cut his headlights in the drive. *Screw it*, he'd thought, *I'll walk*. He didn't trust himself to make it up their steep drive with no light. He imagined himself losing control of the wheel, veering onto the grass, crashing through the old man's front window. What a scandal! It sort of intrigued him, the danger of it all. Dennis the Menace was finally living up to his name.

She let him in the side door. The house was dark; Dennis assumed that the old man had an early bedtime. They tiptoed through the kitchen and stood for a moment kissing in the living room. She was wearing a robe, and she smelled like bathwater and fingernail polish. He felt under the robe, groped her feverishly as if he were in junior high, but she turned away and led him up the stairs. They made their way through a hall, and halfway down she jabbed her red fingernail at a closed door. *The old man.*

Into the guest bedroom then. Another cramped bed. Another solitary, lonely pillow. She didn't so much toss him on the bed as she *unfolded him* there, and again she disrobed. She was glistening in the moonlight that came in through the curtains. He would have come immediately, had she just touched him. It was the same routine: Elizabeth straddling him, pressing down on him, her head thrown back, those red-nailed hands cupping her tits. Too quickly Dennis felt the roil of his body. And then everything was crashing forward and she softly covered his mouth so that he could not cry out.

Later, when she was asleep, he dressed and left the room. The house was creaking, still. He went downstairs, into the dark of the living room. He made his way back the same way he had come, down the stairs and toward the kitchen, and when he turned the corner by the wood burning stove he saw it: a light. Dennis froze, crouched, tried to find another way out, another door.

And then: "Who's there?" It was the old man's voice.

Dennis stayed still, low to the ground, below the light. Strangely, he was calm. It must have been the calm of a soldier, the ease before battle. He did not move until he saw the man's head peeking out at him. "What are you doing there, son?" Dean Orman asked.

"I'm trying to figure out how to escape your house, sir," Dennis answered. He had found that the most brutal honesty worked in these situations much better than embarrassing, fantastical lies. Not that he had ever been in a situation quite like *this* before.

"Come in here."

Dennis went into the kitchen. The old man was eating a sandwich in the nook. He had pulled out a bar stool and had a magazine open on the counter before him. "Know this," he said almost dismissively, his eyes down on the magazine. "You're not the first."

Dennis didn't say anything. He could only stand there, shamefully, and listen. The old man was wearing boxer shorts and a dingy T-shirt, what the Taus might call a "wife beater." He was just an old man; he was supposed to be vulnerable, weak, maybe even half-cocked—but here he was interrogating Dennis.

"There was the boy from England," Dean Orman said ruefully. "The soccer player. There was the kid from California that she was taken with last year. There have been lecturers and such. And now you." He took a bite of the sandwich, licked his fingers, and turned a page in the magazine. "It's just something we do. We agreed on it a long time ago. There is no love in this marriage. There never is at our age. My age. Do you think that those vows are still *applicable*?"

"I don't . . . ," Dennis began.

"Of course not," Dean Orman cut him off. "That's absurd. You get to the point where you can't stand the way she walks, the way she sits on the toilet, the way she mismatches your goddamned socks. This is the way of the world, son. Get used to it." Another bite of the sandwich, another turned page. Dennis wondered if he was done, if that was all there was. But the old man went on: "Of course I have my own . . . *debilitas*. There are two young secretaries that come over on occasion, and Elizabeth watches us although she doesn't like it. She says it's unbecoming. What she really means, of course, is that it's unbecoming of a man my age in the same space, in the same *vicinity*, as two young beauties. Ah yes. Ah well."

Dennis went to the door. He opened it onto the night, and the sharp wind hit him in the face, chilling him to the bone. "Do you love her?" the dean asked.

"No," said Dennis. Too quickly.

"The boy from England did. It was a messy, messy thing. Just awful. The boy crying on the couch, Elizabeth standing there breaking his heart, bringing him Kleenex like some caring mother. It was a scene. I watched it all from the balcony upstairs." He laughed at the memory, shook his head as if to clear it from his thoughts.

"Good-bye, Dr. Orman," Dennis said.

"Wait," the old man called. Dennis stepped back into the kitchen. "I meant to ask you about this class. You mentioned it the other night. With Leonard."

"Dr. Williams, yes," said Dennis. The name was funny to him, unfitting: *Leonard*.

"What do you think about it?"

"It's . . . different," admitted Dennis.

"Yes, I imagine it would be. How do you like him, though, the old boy who teaches it?"

"I don't know how to take him yet. It's still early."

"Let me tell you something about Leonard Williams," the dean said. He lifted his eyes from the bar to Dennis's face for the first time, and there was something serious about the movement, something punctuated and dire. "He is not a nice man. In fact, many of us wanted to get rid of him a few years ago when that whole fiasco began with his book."

"His book?" Dennis asked, remembering what Orman had said at the party.

"Yes. The plagiarism thing. Messy indeed. It almost ruined us all, those of us who had been behind his hiring in the first place. Those of us who granted him tenure. It should have been the end of him, but he has loyal friends in the department, people who will swear by his genius. And he *is* brilliant. I don't think there's any doubt."

"He plays a game in class," Dennis said. He didn't know why he'd said it; it was just something to placate the dean, to win the dean over to his side. *Implicate Williams, cast Williams as a fool*, he thought. *Save yourself.*

"A game?" the old man asked.

"It's very silly. It's—a forensics game. Like a case we have to solve."

"Ah yes," Orman said. "I've heard of it. These puzzles and games—people say he's obsessed with them. Part of his brilliance, I guess. But that's not the question, is it? No. Of course not. We're all brilliant, some more than others. The question is this: what kind of representative is he for this university? And it's been proven, time and again, that he is a dubious one at best. Oh, they think I'm just paranoid. A silly old man. Crazy. They think that I'm just too old fashioned for Williams's teaching practices. But there's something there. Something . . . *off* about the man."

"I've felt it, too," Dennis admitted. He wanted to go on but he was careful about what he said. It was best, his father often said of academia, not to have too many enemies.

"Dennis, I urge you—no, let's make this a demand, considering I have so much leverage over you now. I'm going to demand that you stay away from him. If he asks you to his office, don't go. If you see him out on campus, keep walking. Your parents wouldn't want you to get into trouble on my watch, would they?" The old man smiled sardonically, showing his short, yellow teeth. Dennis nodded and went out into that wind, closing the door gently behind him.

9

Place

As you know, Polly was at a going-away party on the last night she was seen. What you don't know is where this party was or by whom it was given.

The party was on Slade Road, just outside of town. It was given by a man named Tucker "Pig" Stephens. Pig was older than most everybody else at the party. He was considered a "go-to" guy: you went to him for dope, for alcohol if you were underage, for solace when you were depressed or needing.

Pig owned a Harley-Davidson that was customized so that it would roar ferociously as he sped down the highway. He called his bike "the Demon," and he'd painted the snout of a razorback along the sides that seemed to flare in a certain light. During the winter, he kept the bike in a storage facility off I-64 because he was inherently distrustful of all his friends, most of whom were members of a local motorcycle group called the Creeps that Pig also belonged to.

He was well respected by his circle and feared by cops: he had been arrested many times and had served hard time in Montoya State Prison when he was twenty years old for breaking and entering. His criminal record was long, but for the past five years it had been inactive; everyone who knew him claimed that he had turned over a new leaf.

Pig had taken Polly under his wing. He protected her. He considered Mike his younger brother, and often when you saw Pig in town Mike was with him. But Pig had soured on Mike recently. He had been heard saying that if Mike bothered Polly again, he was going to personally see to it that Mike was "put in his place." On the night of Polly's party, the two men were seen arguing by the pool out back. It was late and by that time everyone was drunk. No one could say for sure what the two were arguing about, but most were sure that it had to do with Polly. Pig, a huge man, weighing more than three hundred pounds, put his finger into Mike's chest. Not long afterward, Polly left. Some people who had been standing out on the back deck (Pig lived in a duplex and rented out the top floor to his friends, including, at one point last summer, Mike and Polly) saw Polly leaving shortly after the argument. According to these witnesses, Pig saw her off. He may have even hugged her gently before she got in her car and went home, where her father was waiting.

Mary didn't know what to do with this new information other than the fact that it brought another suspect into the equation: the older father figure, Pig. She imagined him. Pig, fat and volatile, was gentle when he needed to be and fierce when he had to be. What did he say to Mike out by the pool? That he would kill him if he touched Polly again? Was Pig secretly in love with Polly? Had they had an affair, even been in love with each other? When Mike found out about them had he hit Polly, leading her to call the police?

She still had the unread chapters of Auster's *City of Glass* to read as well as the new chapters for tomorrow's class, but she couldn't make herself focus on the words. In the novel, Quinn was filling his red notebook with facts and observations, empirical designs, emotions and feelings. But Mary was not as fortunate: she had very little at this point. She had seen Polly's picture on the transparency but had inexplicably forgotten what she looked like, and now she would be murdered by Mike or Pig or, heaven forbid, her own father. What would Leonard Williams think of this, her forgetfulness?

Suddenly, she was asleep and dreaming. In her dream, Mary saw Williams enter a dimly lit room. There was an overhead projector in the middle of this room. He turned it on. There was nothing on the first sheet, just a yellow wall. Nothing on the second. He shuffled through papers, one by one by one. They were all blank, empty, void yellow squares on a bare wall. Professor Williams was very angry now. His face was red, contorted, veins bulging in his neck. Mary was suddenly there—she saw herself sitting in a chair by the projector. She had dressed formally, for a performance, a presentation of some kind. She buried her face in her hands as Williams went through one blank sheet after another. Then she could feel him looking at her, the heat of his glare. Williams was now completely in control of her. He was her authority and her influence. Williams said something but his voice was muted, sliced off. It was painful even though it was soundless, and she felt herself shrinking from him. Suddenly he was coming toward her, stepping through the projector's light. He was angry, so angry—

She woke in the early gray of the morning. Brown was silent and she knew by the color of the blinds that it was too early for her to get up. But she could not go back to sleep. She had slept unevenly, and her body was stiff when she stood. The floor was cold. It was finally autumn outside, and soon she would have to turn on the heat to shower.

As she did every morning, she checked her e-mail.

There was something she hadn't seen last night. It had been sent just minutes after the Pig clue, but she had forgotten to recheck her messages after reading that one. This one was simply called "Evidence," and Mary tentatively, remembering the hanged man, clicked on it.

There were two attached files in the message. Mary clicked on the first one, and a picture of a red car beside a road appeared. Polly's Civic on Stribbling Road, she assumed.

She clicked on the second one and another photograph loaded on her screen. It looked as if it could have been of a party in one of the frat houses. The foreground was harshly lit by the flash. It was a wider shot of the photo Williams had shown on the transparency that day, the one of Mike sitting on a couch. There was Mike again, his eyes red and his hair mussed.

Sitting beside him, with her arm around his peeling shoulders, was Summer McCoy.

The wind went out of Mary.

What the hell? What were the chances of that? Summer didn't even like frat parties. And this Mike guy was definitely not her type. Yet there she was with her arm around him, her face sun-kissed and a drink in her right hand. Did Summer know Williams? Maybe the photograph was simply random, something Williams had torn from an annual and used.

Yet—what were the chances of the girl in the photo being Summer?

Mary forwarded the message to her best friend.

To: smccoy@winchester.edu
From: mbutler@winchester.edu
Subject: weird stuff

Do you know this guy?

/attached

Mary

Mary waited. She knew she should be reading *City of Glass*, but her mind was whirring. She closed her eyes, rubbed her forehead with her fingers trying to—

Her computer pinged with an incoming message.

To: mbutler@winchester.edu
From: smccoy@winchester.edu
Cc: admin2654@winchester.edu
Subject: Re: weird stuff

****ADMINISTRATIVE WARNING****filtertapspace/winchester servelistaccidentaladministrat/firewall/parse/messageblock*****
ADMINISTRATIVE WARNING****please do not continue sending these messages, you are outside the limits of the school code****
ADMINISTRATIVE WARNING**** ///do not reply to this message!////

What the hell was the "school code"? Mary thought that she may have mistyped Summer's name, so she tried the same message again. And again, she waited. When the ping didn't come, she refreshed her screen—still no message. She stood up and walked around her room. It felt good to stretch her legs. She would have to do some yoga tomorrow. Maybe Summer would—

Her phone rang.

"Summer?" Mary said.

"Is this Mary Butler?" said a sharp, even voice on the other end.

"It is."

"Stop," the man said.

"Stop what?"

"You know what. Stop. Stop sending those e-mails."

"I don't know what you're—"

"Come off it, Mary. We're sitting out here in the Gray Brick Building looking at every e-mail that's sent. With all the shit that's pirated at this school, they pay us twenty bucks an hour to sit out here all night. But what you're doing is . . ."

"What am I doing?"

"The picture. I mean, there's porn and then there's that. You're lucky we don't send this right to the campus police. Or to Dean Orman. It's just sick. I'm sure you think it's a joke, I'm sure you and your girls are laughing it up, but we have to do our job."

"My professor sent this to me," she pleaded with the man. "I didn't know . . . I didn't—"

"Listen, I don't have time for this. If you don't want your Internet privileges taken away, I'd delete that picture immediately. Clean it from your hard drive. Good morning." He hung up.

Mary found the original file again and clicked on it. It would not load this time. All that appeared on her screen were lines of unbroken and meaningless code.

10

The next day Mary was so shaken by seeing Summer in Williams's photograph that she almost didn't go to class. But she needed to ask him what it had meant. The thought crossed her mind that perhaps Williams hadn't even sent the photo. But there was his name in her in-box. Was he trying to impart some message about Mike? Was he trying to give Mary some kind of inside track?

It took everything she had to leave her room, but when she was outside she was glad she had decided to go to class. Surprisingly, after the cool morning, it had turned into one of the nicest days of the month, the sun high and white in the sky, the clouds thin as

gauze. On the yard in front of Brown Hall, some girls were sun-
bathing. They were all on their stomachs with textbooks open at
their noses, studying for the first set of quizzes that were coming up
next week.

As she was entering Seminary, the girl who sat beside Mary in
Williams's class came out the side entrance. "No class today," the girl
told Mary. "There's a note on the door."

Mary stepped into the dim foyer of Seminary. Normally she
would be pleased that her entire afternoon was free—she now had
five chapters in *City of Glass* to read—but today she was anxious to
discuss the photograph—and that weird phone call, too—with
Williams. There were no students in Seminary at this time—it was
too early before the 4:00 p.m. classes and now fifteen minutes after
the last set of classes had ended.

I'll leave a note under his office door, she thought. Even though
Williams had not given them a syllabus with any of his contact information, she was pretty sure his office would be in the philosophy
wing, which was right upstairs, on the top floor of Seminary.

She climbed the three flights of stairs. She passed other students
in the class, including Brian House, who was hopping down the
stairs three at a time. "You hear?" he asked breathlessly. She told him
that she had, but he was already sliding down the rail, letting out a
whoop as he disappeared down the well.

The top floor of Seminary was another world. Professors' offices
lined the halls, and students sat passively outside in uncomfortable
chairs, waiting to be called in. The hum of a Xerox machine punctuated everything. Mary followed the first wall, reading the name-
plates on each door. She went all the way down the hall and around
the corner, toward the west side of the building, which led down a
second set of stairs and into the Orman Library. Near the end of the
hall she found an open door, and as she leaned inside to read the
name, a voice said, "Can I help you?"

Mary started. She backed out of the room as if she had been doing something wrong. Something illegal.

"Are you looking for Dr. Williams?" the voice asked. She peeked in and saw the boy. He was standing by the bookshelves on the far side, a stack of index cards in his hand.

"Yes," she said.

"He's out for the day. Something about his kid." The boy looked back at the shelves, wrote something on one of the cards. Then he looked at Mary and said, "I'm sorry. I'm Troy Hardings. I'll be Dr. Williams's assistant this term." He came toward her and offered his hand, and she shook it. He was tall, reedy, his movements awkward. His hair had been shaved into a buzz, and his scalp was unhealthy and pink. "You need to leave him a note or something?" He nodded toward the paper she had torn and was holding now, limply. "You can just give it to me and I'll make sure he gets it."

"Oh," she said. "Okay." She stepped out into the hall and put the paper to the wall and wrote, *Dr. Williams*, but the surface was bubbled and she could not write smoothly. She went down the hall a bit and sat down on a chair outside a professor's office. She used *City of Glass* as her desktop to write her note. As she was writing, she saw Troy leave the office and walk the opposite way, down the hall, and enter a room just before the exit.

Mary suddenly had a funny idea. She stood and returned to Dr. Williams's office. Troy had turned on just one light, a desk lamp that emitted a pale glow on the shelves. She wanted to look at his books, but she knew she didn't have much time before Troy came back. She put her note—it was a bit unfinished, certainly not all she wanted to say, only the part about Summer McCoy, but none of the other stuff, not the Pig and Polly hypothesis that she'd been thinking about—on his desk, her eyes scanning its surface. What was she looking for? She didn't know. But she couldn't leave. Now that she was here, in his presence, she had to find *something*, didn't she? She'd been brave enough to come this far. There was his mail, for instance. There were a few coffee mugs on the shelves. There was a poster of Einstein on the wall with the heading HE COULDN'T TIE HIS OWN SHOES. But there was nothing of substance that she could see without searching the desk drawers. Quickly she scanned the books—logic texts, philosophy treatises with their spines veined, a whole row of John Locke. But nothing else. She felt ashamed for coming, for—

On the desk, nearly hidden under a stack of envelopes, was a sentence. It was in the cold, distant font of a typewriter. It looked as if it had been written a long time ago; the text was so faded and the page so yellowed that Mary could barely read it. She leaned down to get a better look.

Deanna would be the same age as Polly if not

That was all. The rest of the words were hidden beneath the envelopes. Mary pushed the envelopes aside and leaned in for a closer look.

"What are you doing?" someone said.

It was Troy. He was standing at the door looking at her, arms at his sides, as if he couldn't believe that she would enter the office uninvited.

"I'm just . . . ," she tried. "I was just putting my note on his desk."

"I said," Troy stated flatly, "that if you give it to me, it will get to Dr. Williams. I promise." Then he smiled—it was a stern, rigid gesture.

"There," said Mary, pointing at the note she had laid on his desk.

Troy read the note. He had to spin the paper around so that the words weren't upside down, and when he did this Mary saw the weird tattoo on the back of his hand. It was an *S* and a *P* entangled. The *S* was almost serpentine. Its head was drawn up as if it was ready to strike down on the soft, nearly feminine *P*. Mary thought that whoever did this was talented, and she wanted to ask Troy what it meant.

But then he finished with the note and stood looking at her. His eyes had changed: he was more tentative with her, more cool. "So you're trying to find Polly," he said.

"Yes."

Troy only nodded, but she silently urged him to go on. She badly wanted to know what he knew, but it appeared that he wasn't going to volunteer anything more.

"Do you know him well?" she asked, trying to goad Troy into giving up some information about Williams.

"Not too well. He just called me up this summer and asked me if I would run for him. I'm just a gofer. He wants all these books catalogued before the fall term's out. He wants someone to type some stuff for him. Just the usual crap. It's money, though, so I couldn't pass it up."

"Does he ever talk about Polly?"

"No," Troy said evenly. "That's top secret stuff, man." He laughed, then, a stoner's giggle.

"Did he make it all up?"

"He made most of it up. Except . . ."

"Except what?" she led him.

"Except there was a real case. A long time ago, back in the eighties. This girl went missing and was never found."

"So this girl is Polly?"

"I wouldn't say that. Polly is fiction. She isn't meant to symbolize anything except the illogic that is sometimes in the world. Or at least that's what Leonard says. What, you think she's real or something?" He stared at her. "Uh-uh. It's like they say in the movies: Polly is *based* on a true story."

"I didn't mean it like that," said Mary. Though she wasn't sure if she did or not. In fact, she wasn't sure what she'd meant. "I'm talking about *him*. Missing girls. Vengeful boyfriends. It's not the stuff of academia, if you know what I mean. I was wondering if . . . you know."

"If he has a daughter who was abducted? If he lived through something like this?"

"Well, it just seems so real. There's something personal about it for him."

"They all ask that question. Listen, he just changes her name. When I took his class, she was named Jean. Last fall she was Elizabeth. Same story, same girl, different outcome."

Mary was disappointed. She'd wanted to hear something else, but she didn't know what.

When it was apparent that there was nothing more to say, she thanked Troy and left Dr. Williams's office. As she was leaving, he called down the hall to her, "Watch out for him. He was always misdirecting us."

11

Brian House wanted to get fucked up. Fucked up beyond all recognition, they said. FUBAR. He wanted to lose the world and wake up tomorrow in somebody's bathtub. Currently he was standing out on the balcony of the Deke house, drinking mojitos. Inside, some girl named Brandy tended a makeshift bar that was really just an old door laid between two cinder-block columns. He was already feeling it, that far-off buzz, the zinging collision of all the molecules in the world. When he drank, he got *tuned in*. It was like blowing glass or getting laid: the world softening, darkening, imploding like a breath sucked in and then held.

"Hey," said someone at his shoulder. It was that girl, Tannie or Bonnie or whatever her name was. She was sort of ugly in the face but had a hot body, and she was coming on to him. There was something weird about her, though. The way she talked and walked and moved, as if she were faking everything. Still, it was getting late, and there were no other possibilities that he saw in his immediate future.

They went inside, where the music was pulsing and physical around them, and they danced. She was hiding her face from him for some reason. Was she scarred? Brian tried to look at her, but the mojitos were clouding everything. A song bled out and another came on. It was a slower song, grinding riffs of steel guitar, poetry in the lyrics. She leaned into him and breathed warmly onto his chest. She said something—mumbled, actually—but he couldn't hear anything over the throbbing music.

They were outside again. On the balcony. "Get happy," somebody said, handing him something. Acid. He'd done it before, once. He put it on his tongue and closed his eyes.

They were back inside, sitting on a ratty sofa that smelled as if it had been dragged from a fire. Two girls were sitting Indian-style on the floor, kissing with their tongues. The Dekes had all taken off their shirts and painted symbols on their chests. The paint was peeling in the heat and flaking down to the floor.

They were out on the yard. The Dekes were running naked across the lawn. Somebody was letting off fireworks. Bottle rockets zipped through the air. Soon, it would be term's end and Brian would go home. The thought depressed him. *Home.* He dreaded it, the drive to New York, his mother asking him how he was doing in his classes, his father drinking beer in that pathetic apartment he was renting, the Great Pall of Marcus hanging over them all. The dreary knowledge that nothing could ever be right again. "What's wrong?" the girl asked. Tannie or Bonnie. She was frustratingly difficult to hear. To understand. Or even *see* clearly. He shook his head, told her not to worry about it.

They were on the balcony again. The atmosphere was weird, charred. No one was out there. The world was bending and swerving. The girl was still at his arm, still hiding her face. "What are you doing with your face?" he asked.

"I'm saving myself for you," she said. Or that's what she might have said. He couldn't be sure. The balcony rail was holding him up. Sparks ran across the Deke yard. Naked sparks. Little blurs of men. Tiny men. Scores of them. They wouldn't stop. They were in a race with each other, running toward something fiercely, fighting for some distant finish line.

Later. They were in the art building. Down by the glassblowing kilns. Someone had spread out a blanket on the concrete floor. Brian was on his back, and the girl was on her knees beside him. She was wearing just her bra and panties. She was doing that face thing again, with her chin on her shoulder. Something was *hidden*. "Here," he said, trying to take her face and turn it toward him. But she wouldn't turn. Her dark hair was over one eye, but she looked at him intently with the other. "Who are you?" he asked.

"Polly," the girl said.

"What the fuck did you say?" he asked.

"My name's Polly," the girl said. And then she laughed. It was a mad and desperate cackle, a screech. Someone was in the building with them, firing up a kiln, the growl of the fire echoing off the wide walls. "I've told you that *twice* already."

Whatever the hell she wants, he thought. *I'll play along.*

"How's Mike?" he asked.

"Mike," the girl said. "Goddamn Mike. I wish people would stop bringing him up. I'm through with him. I told them—I love Mike, but he's so . . . *flawed*. It's just the way he is. That's Mike, you know."

Brian let it sink in. He was losing himself here and there, falling into little sharp black trenches every so often. Daylight was coming in through the windows now, and he wondered what time it was.

"Where are you?" he asked the girl. Her face was still on her chin, her eye still on him.

"What are you talking about?"

"I mean where the fuck are you, bitch. Where are you? We're all trying to find you."

"Brian, this is crazy. I don't know—I don't—"

"Stop fucking with me. He sent you here, didn't he? Williams. That's why you're hiding your face. That's why you're scared to show yourself." He was sitting up now, putting his shirt back on, standing up so that he was over her. There was something about the way the girl demurred to him, stayed on her knees below him, that infuriated Brian. "Stand the fuck up!" he shouted. "Get up, goddamn you! You whore. You two-bit whore. You—"

There was somebody watching him. Some guy. Just behind another kiln, standing there with a mug of steaming coffee, looking right at him. That broke his trance. Brian came back to the world, floated down through the rafters and the glass dust and the smoke to the floor of the building. The descent buckled his knees.

"Fuck this," he finally slurred.

And then he walked out, leaving the girl behind.

FOUR WEEKS LEFT

12

"So," Professor Williams said. He was sitting today in a rolling chair in the front of the class. He taken down the podium and had his feet kicked up on the front table. He apologized for missing last week, but he told them that his son had gotten the flu and had to be taken to the pediatrician. *A young son*, thought Mary. *But no pictures in his office.* "Any theories?"

"The name Pig," Dennis Flaherty said.

"Yes?" Williams asked.

"Do you know anyone by that name?"

"There is a man in DeLane named Pig. A former cop. Now he's a night watchman at the marina. He helped me . . . research some of my clues, so I paid homage to him."

"Ah," Dennis said softly. Mary looked down the row at him. She thought he looked tired, different somehow. He caught her stare and held it, tried to impart something to her, but then he quickly looked away, down at the legal pad that he had balanced on his briefcase.

"Anything else?" the professor asked.

"In the pictures of Polly's Civic," said a student behind Mary.

Immediately Mary felt herself flush. She hadn't even looked closely at that one because she had been too focused on the other. Was there a clue in the car photograph, something that she needed to know?

"Yes?"

"There's a railroad track in the right-hand corner," the student went on.

"And?"

"And so that could support a staged crime. Her father could have taken her out to Stribbling Road—"

"Are people still on that?" Dennis sighed.

"—and slipped her away on the train."

"This isn't nineteen twenty-five, Ms. Davies. People still hop boxcars where you're from?"

When the girl fell silent, Mary began to speak. But before she could say anything Dennis said, "I want to go back to the 'Place' clue."

"Go on," Williams led him.

"Pig and Polly had a thing," Dennis said.

"It's interesting, isn't it?" mused the professor. "Here's a guy about fifteen years older than Polly. He clearly—*clearly*—isn't in her class. She's beautiful, he's . . . not." A few people laughed. Williams rolled his chair around here and there but kept his feet kicked up. "She's got a family, whereas Pig grew up on the streets. He's a tough guy. But she sees something in him. What is it?"

"He takes care of her," a girl said from the back row. "He's like a father to her."

"A father," Williams said. "Go on."

"She was drawn to him because she had a rocky relationship with her own dad?"

"The same dad who was waiting up for her the last night she was seen?" he asked. "Try again."

"He protects her." Dennis had picked up the loose thread. "Mike hits her, abuses her, is generally nasty to her. And Pig is there to nurse her back to health. He tends to her wounds, her broken heart."

"Sugar daddy," said Brian. He had his head down and was looking at Williams from the side of his gaze.

"So they were fucking," Williams said. The word jarred the class. Some students giggled nervously. Williams apparently didn't register this strangeness, the ripple it created when a professor used language that was so un-professor-like. "They had an affair. How does this change things?"

The girl from the back again: "Pig fell in love with her."

"And?"

"And he threatened to kill Mike if he touched her again. They were seen arguing by the pool."

"Maybe Polly was obedient to Pig," Williams said.

"How do you mean?" asked Dennis.

"I mean maybe he held some authority over her. Maybe he was demonstrating his authority in everything he did. How he dressed, how he spoke to her. Perhaps he made her afraid to defy him."

"Maybe," Mary said, "he planted the seeds of the abuse in her head."

"That's really interesting, Ms. Butler. And that's pure Milgram."

"Who?" someone asked.

"Stanley Milgram. You haven't seen the statue outside the Orman Library? A dedication to Milgram. He came here in the seventies as a visitor of Dean Orman. He lectured right in this room in February of nineteen seventy-six. Do you just walk past that statue without noticing the inscription? Why must students have such tunnel vision?"

"We have a library?" said a boy in the back. The class laughed, but Williams only grinned and shook his head.

"Milgram conducted behavior experiments at Yale in the sixties,"

Williams continued. "He found that people are willing to go along with anything if an authority figure tells them to do it. Perhaps Pig was Polly's authority figure."

"I don't believe that," said Dennis.

"Let's test it then," Williams said. "What if you were told you were going to fail this class if you didn't, say, stand on your head in the corner. Would you do it?"

"No," Dennis said. Mary saw him blanch—she knew he was lying.

"Okay," the professor continued. "What if someone of tremendous authority at this institution, say Dean Orman, came into this room right now and told you that you would be expelled if you didn't reach across and pull Ms. Butler's hair. Would you do that?"

"Well, it's not *my* head," Dennis said.

"Exactly!" Williams laughed. "Milgram proved that we will go to great lengths to hurt people if we are told to do it by someone of influence. After all, they know best, right? Dean Orman knows best. He is an authority figure, is he not? He is learned, and his education makes him a figure of control."

"The Nazis," Brian said.

"Yes," Williams said. "Milgram was showing that even notions of right and wrong are meaningless when stacked against authority. We are more obedient to another's authority than we are to our own instincts."

Williams stopped speaking. He composed himself, drew in a breath, and went on. "So here we have," the professor said, "two people who have threatened Mike with his life. Polly's father and now this guy, Pig. Mike, it seems, is not the most well-liked individual on the planet. Which proves?"

"Polly is lovable," said Mary.

"Polly is indeed lovable. She is the heroine of this story, after all, and she is counting on you to find her. Some of you have developed an obsession for her already." Mary looked away from him quickly. He wondered what Troy had told him. "Some of you are thinking about this crime when you should be studying for other classes. I know how it is. This is Polly. What you're feeling is the intuition to *save*, to deeply care. This is something that, as a species, we are the only ones capable of feeling. Oh, a mother chimpanzee will save her baby, but only *if the baby is in immediate danger.* Right now, the danger is abstract. You don't know what it is. In fact, the danger is conceptual: I have created it. I have told you that Polly is going to be murdered, and you believe me—in a purely metaphorical sense, of course. And so you have followed me into this narrative until you care, some of you deeply, about what happens to Polly."

Then: "I don't care." It was Brian.

"Oh yes, Mr. House? And why not?"

"Because everybody's going to figure it out anyway. Somebody will get the answer and call someone on the telephone and then we'll all have it."

"But what if nobody figures it out?" Williams asked, and the class went silent.

"Why did you send me a photograph of my friend?" Mary said, cutting the silence sharply. She left out the part about the phone call from the campus police; she wasn't sure what that was about just yet. She didn't tell him that she and Summer had figured it out. The couch was in the basement of the Sigma Nu house.

"It seems, class," the professor said, smiling and swiveling his chair back behind the table again, "that Ms. Butler believes that this class is for her. That she's the only student here. I got your note, by the way."

He said it loudly, aiming it right at the class. The message: Mary Butler is trying to get a leg up on you. She's trying to *sabotage you.*

What had she done that was so wrong? She had simply asked him a question about Summer McCoy. Wouldn't everyone in the class, if they knew Summer like she did, feel that Williams had designed the e-mail specifically for them?

"The picture was just a picture, Mary," Dennis said. "It was just a photograph of a party. I think I know some people in that shot."

"When I send these clues," Williams said, "I am not singling any-one out. We are all receiving the same information."

"But that was my . . ." She couldn't go on. She suddenly felt awful, as if she'd been tricked not just by Williams but by everyone else in Logic and Reasoning 204 as well.

"It's not just about you," Dennis said to no one in particular.

"But he was with her," Mary said quietly. "Mike was with Summer on that couch . . ."

Oh God, oh God, oh God. What have I done? Why did I let it get this far?

She felt herself getting up, walking toward the door. It was not fast; it was more of a methodical walk, determined, head down. Before she was at the door, Professor Williams rolled his chair in front of it. It was the closest she'd been to him. She looked at his scarred face, at his eyes, which were deep and whimsical, and in that constant state of enchanted amusement. She smelled him: cigarette smoke. "Stay," he whispered. There was something stern in his tone, something rough. He was blocking the door fully, with his whole body. "Please . . . let me go," Mary whispered through clenched teeth. She reached out and touched him. She did not mean to push him, she simply wanted to make him realize her discomfort, to let him know that she needed to get outside into the fresh air. But he was so strong that she could not move him. "Stay," he said again, stricter. And though Mary did not want to, she returned to her seat. She felt all the eyes in the class on her, all the mouths ready to erupt with laughter at her expense.

"Those pictures," said Williams, "of course, were meant as artifice. Just to give you a sense of reality. Image makes us understand in a way that narrative cannot. That was the car of a student who is in the PhD program here at Winchester. It's parked beside Highway 72. I wanted it to appear as real as possible. A road you knew, a place you'd seen." He smiled broadly at Mary, trying to win her back, trying to change the tone of his lecture. "The other photo was in the Sig house on a Friday night. Just a former student of mine sitting on a couch. The girl—your friend, Ms. Butler—just happened to be there at the time. Coincidence, nothing more.

"But I do want to apologize to Ms. Butler. I didn't know that the photograph contained someone familiar to her. If I had known that, I would have never sent it." He rolled back to the side, so that he could look at the class as a whole again. Seminary East's light was on his legs and creeping up. "Now that that's out of the way," he continued, "an announcement: there will be a guest speaker on Wednesday."

It wasn't until later, when she was back in her dorm room trying to read the middle section of *City of Glass*, that the thought came to her: *But what is real and what isn't?* Was Polly's father's tattoo real? Williams had referenced it in class, so it must be part of the game. Why were some details meaningful and others mere coincidence? This was what Williams was doing to them. He was intentionally mixing them up, leading them far away from the true source of the crime, decoying them into believing certain things were in play and others were not.

The mystery, then, would have to be figured out by a system of elimination. She must discard all that was false and focus only on the substance of Williams's game. This would not be easy, as it all began and ended with Williams. She had to figure him out, to decipher his tendencies. She had to pay more attention.

13

The next time, to get away from the old man, they went to the Kingsley Hotel in downtown DeLane. Elizabeth had called ahead to reserve the room, told the girl at the desk that people were arriving in town to visit with Dean Orman. They know what you mean when you say "people," she told Dennis. Dignitaries, professors, alumni. It was easy to conceal things in this town, she said: all you had to do was mention *people*, and things were veritably done for you.

The room was impressive. Art nouveau, wrought-iron chandelier bending the light into every corner, Victorian upholstery in the sitting area, and, unfathomably, a flat-screen LCD television mounted on the wall. An impressive Monet replica across from it, hanging over the headboard. It was the nicest hotel Dennis had ever stayed in, and unfortunately the room was his for just three hours. He had a study group back at the Tau house at 8:30 p.m.

Elizabeth was systematic, almost professional, with him. She turned around, still on top of him, and they watched themselves through the cheval mirror that stood at the foot of the bed. Their lovemaking was becoming more polished, less of a rush, and for the first time Dennis felt his mind wander as she rode him. For some reason he thought of Polly, the fake girl that would be murdered if he didn't find her. What would it have been like to be with her? She was wild. She had piercings, Dennis remembered, all over her body. Or maybe she would have been submissive, weak. Vulnerable.

Thinking of Polly, Dennis came in a spasm.

"It wasn't the same," Elizabeth said later. They were lying on the bed, spooning each other, the ceiling fan softly looping above them.

"No," Dennis admitted. Again, that brutal honesty.

"Maybe it's over."

"Probably."

They lay there in silence, the cool air prickling their skin. Dennis thought of the British boy, the one who'd cried in the living room while Dean Orman watched secretly from upstairs. In some ways, he was glad that it had come to this. Ever since his conversation with the dean he had been thinking less of Elizabeth and more about Polly—and, strangely, he didn't mind.

"My mother did this," Elizabeth said.

"This?"

"This thing. What we're doing here. This sneaking around. Deception. Always hiding out, calling on the phone from somewhere and saying she would be late. My father knew about it. This was the sixties, you see. Free love. I once caught them having one of those parties. I was maybe seven years old. I walked downstairs and everyone was naked, all the women with their flabby breasts. Incense in the air. 'Go back upstairs, Lizzie,' my mother said. And I did, just as I was told."

"You're lucky," Dennis joked. "The wildest thing I ever saw was my dad scribbling equations on the windows. He said that he liked to see them from both sides. Mother disagreed."

"You don't understand," Elizabeth said. "It got completely out of control for my mother. She couldn't contain it. She fell in love with an artist, a guy who did lithographing in San Francisco. Finally, she moved out there with him. A few years later, when I was in college, she came back. Broke. Dirty and damaged. She was a completely different person. And still married to Daddy. He took her back, of course. There really wasn't any question. He still loved her, fiercely. He took her back even though my brothers and I warned him not to."

Elizabeth was turned away from him now, speaking into the pillow. Dennis felt her speech wasn't for him. These were things, he knew, that she could never say to Dean Orman. He would look down on her for it, think she was low class, weak and disposable. So, Dennis realized: the same act—the covering of the ring, the omission of her name—had been played with Orman in Morocco. He thought of the dean and Elizabeth in the desert, the sandy wind sweeping across their tent, and all those half-truths being told.

"And a few years later she was dead," Elizabeth went on. "Cervical cancer."

"I'm sorry," Dennis said.

"Don't be. If you had known her you wouldn't have felt anything but a loss, like some sort of phantom pain. At her funeral, no one mentioned her years in San Francisco, those hippie parties. I never told anyone about what I had seen that night. It was just assumed that *these things happen*, you know. They happen. There is no randomness in the world. Everything falls into a certain pattern. My mother—she knew this. She called me once from the West Coast. She said, 'Lizzie, I think I've been cursed.' I didn't say anything. I silently agreed with her, of course. She had been. Cursed with some sort of bitter disease. An obscene pleasure drive. An urge to *fuck* anything that moved. And it killed her. This is what I've inherited from her."

Dennis said nothing. The fan turned and whirred above them. Some children passed in the hall, laughing deliriously. Someone's telephone rang in another room.

"I was married before. Before I met Ed. I was studying at Cleveland State, working toward a master's in psychology. My life was as good as it had ever been. I met this man who was unlike anyone I had ever met: sincere, loving. Magnificent. You would have liked him, Dennis."

"Would I?" Dennis said, just to fill up the space with his own words.

"He was charming and sweet. Just like you. When he fucked me, it was for *my* pleasure, not just his. He didn't want to come on my face or put his finger in my ass or watch me with another woman. He didn't want to jerk off while I danced around in red leather. He was the type who spread roses over the bed. He took me to fancy restaurants all over Cleveland and introduced me to his friends at the office. I felt important, more than somebody's *decoration*."

"Do you feel like a decoration when you're with him?" *Him:* it was their code for Dean Orman.

"Sometimes," Elizabeth said, turning even farther away from Dennis. He couldn't see her eyes anymore, just the back of her hair and the deep crease between her shoulders. He touched her there, wanting her to come back to him, at least so he could see her eyes, but she turned over onto her back and pulled the blanket up to her face. Now she was hidden completely.

"We were married in just a few weeks," she said, her voice muffled in the blanket. "It was nothing, just a civil service with a justice of the peace. We thought our love was above marriage, that it was just something you do, a commitment that was expected by a petty society. Marriage was reserved for the weakhearted, the suspicious. Mike wore blue jeans and I wore a summer dress. My father was there, taking pictures with one of those disposable cameras. We were so happy."

Mike, Dennis thought. He turned the name around in his mind, silently mouthed it.

"Then, as it goes, things changed. Mike started working all the time. He became consumed with this project at work. Months and months of work. My mother's curse would burn inside me, mock me, and for a long time I was sickened with myself. Disgusted by my own body. I dropped out of school and fell into a depression. I hated the fact of my own lust, absolutely hated it. When Mike was home I would ravish him, take him in my mouth and suck out everything he was, leave him raw and bleeding. Afterward, I would apologize and feel guilty about what I had done. But something had changed between us. There was some rift there, some sort of divide."

She turned and glanced at him. Her eyes were slick and wet. Yet something was in them, some hint of a deeper knowledge. *What is she doing?* Dennis wondered. *What is this?*

"The job got to him," Elizabeth said. "He was under pressure all the time to finish a project of some sort. I can't even remember what it was, that's how important it must have been. Something to do with an animal project."

"Animal project?" Dennis asked. "Like dog shows?"

"No, not like that. Mike was in advertising. Now I remember what it was: Pollyanna Pet Food. There was a girl in the advertisement, this pretty blonde, and she was feeding her cats. The problem, if I recall correctly, was that Mike didn't like her. He wanted her to be older, more *set*. A professional type. He didn't want this *bimbo* selling his product. He used that word, *bimbo*. Are you still listening?"

"Yes," Dennis said. She had caught him drifting off. *Mike*. Even though it was a common name, he couldn't stop tossing it around in his head. "Go on."

"He talked about her so much, this actress, that of course I got suspicious. I thought he was fucking her. By that time I was alone all day with nothing to do, and my imagination was free to go wild. Of course I realized how ridiculous it was for me to castigate him for something that may not have even been true.

"But it swelled and built. Blossomed inside me. The hate for this girl I had never seen. The possibilities ran through my mind like a snuff film. Mike on top of her, Mike behind her, Mike in her mouth. It was eating me from the inside out.

"Finally, I couldn't hold it in anymore. When he got home one night I interrogated him about it. 'I know you've been screwing that girl,' I said. 'What girl?' he asked. 'That actress, that bitch.' He was flattened. He told me to calm down. Things escalated. He was hurt, I mean really hurt, by what I'd said. And his pain made my anger swell more, so that I was berating him and berating *myself* at the same time. His fake lust was my real lust, and I was scorning it, screaming at it to stop, to leave me be.

" 'You should calm down right now,' Mike said to me. At some point he changed, became abrasive. But I couldn't calm down. I was crazed, maniacal. My mother, my sex drive, the girl in the commercial—everything was coming to a head and I was powerless to stop it. 'Calm down,' he said again. And when I wouldn't, he smacked me. It wasn't hard. It was just a smack, just a light smack in the face. 'I'm sorry,' he mouthed afterward. We sat on the couch together, and he cried, and I cried, knowing that it was over between us. The artifice of who I was trying to be in our marriage had been broken, and he had discovered my awful curse."

"What did you do then?" Dennis asked. But he already knew. He had already beaten her to that point. Another graduate school, another husband, and now this. Now here, him, Dennis Flaherty, in the Kingsley.

She said, "I went back to Cincinnati. My father was waiting for me that night, watching television. He held me and I went to sleep, and at some point he must have carried me to bed. I woke up the next morning and decided to change things, to change my life. I went to a therapist. The therapist urged me to go back to school, and I did. That's how I ended up at Winchester studying behavioral psychology, and in my second semester here I had a class under Ed. The rest, of course—well, you know the rest."

It took all of Dennis's strength not to say a word. He wasn't even sure what he should say, but he knew there was more there. He knew that Elizabeth would go on if he wanted her to. But he just lay there silently, eyes closed, waiting for her to tell him that it was finally over.

Afterward, she drove him back to the Tau house. It was early evening, a muddy twilight spreading across the campus. The Dekes were marching to the dining hall, the Sigs were out on the yard in their suits and ties, dates on their arms in glittering formal dresses, and the art kilns down the hill at the edge of Up Campus were glowing as they did every night at this time. She dropped him off at the corner of Winchester and Crane, so that the Taus would not see them together. She did not say good-bye; she didn't need to. There was nothing more that needed to be said between them. It was just something that had happened, and now it was over.

When he was back in the room, he thought about all she had said. Mike. Pollyanna Pet Foods. Her father waiting for her when she got home, and how he had carried her to bed. The way she had told him her story, as if she were . . . as if she had rehearsed part of it. As if it were somehow an act.

Dennis opened Word and began to type. He had a theory about Polly, one that had been given to him by Elizabeth Orman. It was really indubitable: he would be ready for Professor Williams.

14

Mary was thinking about Professor Williams's teeth. They were yellowed and crooked and too short. She hadn't noticed them when she was close to him, or rather she hadn't acknowledged it if she had, but now those teeth were all she could think about. How he had grinned at her. *Stay.* Not so much a request as it was a command. His eyes amused and knowing. Testing her.

In *City of Glass*, Quinn was sitting outside the old hotel by then, watching and waiting for Stillman to come out. It was the dawn of his obsession. He was about to lose control, Professor Kiseley had told them in class that week. Things were about to go off the deep end for Quinn.

But what about Mary? How was she doing? She wasn't about to go off the deep end like Quinn, but she . . . she wasn't doing well. Because of her insatiable need to figure the thing out, to understand Williams and his methods, she had allowed herself to become—what had he said about that scientist, Milgram, that day in class? She had allowed herself to lose herself in the class. She couldn't go out without wondering if she was missing something. She couldn't do anything without thinking of Williams. He could do anything now, bend the rules any way he wanted, and she would follow the game.

Now the danger, the adventure she had been craving when the class started was beginning to wear on her. She knew she had to find a way to scale it back, to tone it down, to *chill out*, as her mother would say. Or . . .

Or what? Or she might turn out like Paul Auster's Quinn? Or she might lose herself completely to Williams and become so obsessed with solving his puzzle that she would be able to do nothing else? Because that's what it was about, wasn't it? The need to solve it, to figure it out. To rest her mind.

Just like Dennis. She had gotten the single room not because of trust issues, she knew now. No, she had gotten the single room because she needed that time alone to maybe understand why he had dumped her. It was hard for her to be around anyone except for Summer these days.

And now, two whole years later, she was right back in the same state of mind with Williams and Polly. Frazzled, hurt—but still desperately trying to come up with answers that would put her mind at ease. *It's not you, Mary,* everyone had told her. *It had nothing to do with you.* Move on. Life goes on. This, too, shall pass.

Or would it?

What if you were always just stuck in one place, your mind spinning and unable to go forward like tires clenched in mud, because the answers wouldn't reveal themselves to you? The mind needed answers to satisfy itself. Mary's did. After all, she deserved them. What had she done to bring this on? Accepted a boy's invitation to dinner, signed up for a stupid class? It wasn't enough. She didn't deserve this—what was it? *Torment.* Yes, that's exactly what it was. With Dennis and now again with Williams. Torment. Torture. She didn't deserve it.

Mary had believed that Summer McCoy meant something in that picture, but she did not. The photos were only points of reference. How had she gone so far off track? How had she lost herself? It was such a stupid mistake, to think that what she was doing existed in the real world. It was an exercise. Nothing more, nothing less. Polly was as real as Quinn; that was to say not at all. Her fate was just as important, in the scope of things, as Quinn's survival.

But still. Still. Mary felt that what she was doing was important. She felt Polly—viscerally *felt her.* That meant something. It meant that she was beginning to see Polly as a real person, not just an apparition in Williams's game. Here was a girl who'd been mistreated, wronged by this boy, this Mike. And here was Mary, who'd been similarly mistreated by Dennis. They were two of a kind. Mary felt as if she owed something to Polly. She felt as if she had no choice but to continue in the game until it was finished.

And yet Mary knew that if she got too close to the situation she would lose herself again in it, be embarrassed by Williams and the rest of the class. She had to keep a considerable distance away, she knew now, yet still find Polly.

Find Polly with the understanding that Polly was, alas, not real.

Find Polly.

She logged on to her account and read the latest e-mail from Williams.

Circumstance

Now you know where Polly was on the last night she was seen. And you know who threw the party for her: the brutish yet kind Pig, who was a father figure to Polly. You know that she returned home to her father, watched television, and went to sleep early on the morning of August 2. In fact, you have already been told about the circumstances of Polly's disappearance. But what about *Polly's* circumstance: the facts of her life that may or may not play a part in her disappearance and potential murder?

First, we know that Polly was going away to college. She was planning to major in nursing at Grady Technical College in Piercetown, which is forty miles away from where Polly grew up. The college sits out at the end of a road and overlooks Interstate 64; she had already put some of her things in the U-Stor-It storage facility that was beside campus. She had secured an apartment, where she would be staying with her friend Nicole. For the last two weeks, Polly and Nicole had driven to Piercetown to survey the campus. They partied with some people there and had a good time. Polly was looking forward to going to school, to finally getting started with her life. Nicole dated a man named Lawrence Tripp. Everyone called him Trippy, for short, because he was always high on something. Polly didn't trust him, but she didn't worry about Trippy too much because he and Nicole had been on the outs recently, and Polly was fairly confident that once they moved to Piercetown, Trippy would disappear.

There was also the circumstance of Polly's mother: for the first time in a long while Polly's mother was back in the picture.

Her mother had been gone for almost a year, having left for San Francisco with a lithographer. Now her mother was calling again and Polly was afraid that her mother was going to return and, like she always did, ruin things for her.

And what about Polly's father, Eli? Eli was an elementary school teacher at the Butler School on During Street. He had been teaching for almost thirty years and was on the verge of retirement. He enjoyed his job, but for the past few years things had begun to wear on him. When Polly disappeared, he took a leave of absence. He couldn't imagine himself ever going back. To make matters worse, he had a run-in with an irate parent just a week before Polly disappeared that had left him cynical about the current administration at Butler. This man approached him in the parking lot after school one day and threatened him. Apparently Eli had sent this man's son to the principal's office "for no good reason," as the father put it. As Eli remembered it, the boy had drawn a naked woman on the chalkboard, her legs spread. The father was incensed. Eli, for the first time in a long while, was afraid. He was a large man and could have handled this father easily, but he was timid, shy. Reserved. People referred to him as "quiet." And here was this spark plug of a man with his finger in Eli's face, accusing him of something he clearly didn't do. Eli didn't say anything to the man, just kept walking to his truck. He got in and shut the door, but the man was still there, at the glass. He was spitting mad. Eli pulled out of the parking lot and watched the man recede into the distance. When he was called on the 4th of August by the girl, the girl in the well who had said, "I'm here," his first and immediate thought was this: *The boy's father has her.*

Mary made sure to check the in-box a second time. There was another message there, called "Study Guide." Mary clicked on it.

It was a picture of a dog, one of those big, happy breeds you see on television commercials. Beneath the dog Williams had typed, "Here is Pig's dog, Lady."

Lady was a black Lab.

15

On Tuesday Dennis tried to see Elizabeth, but she wouldn't take his phone calls. When he got the old man he hung up quickly.

He walked around campus, then jogged, then broke out into a full sprint down Montgomery Street. He was in his khakis and blazer, his glasses sliding down his face, his hair smacking his forehead. When he got to the end of the street he stopped, bent over with his hand on his knees, and closed his eyes tightly. It had been a long time since he'd run, years, and it felt good. The muscles in his legs surged with heat. His heart banged in his chest. *Torture yourself, Dennis*, he thought. *Go on*. The stoplight changed, and Dennis started to cross Pride when he heard her behind him.

"I was working."

He faced her. She was wearing a beige trench coat, and her books were slung up on her shoulder. It was true, she had been working: her eyes were tired, blood vessels broken here and there. He reached out for her hand but she pulled away from him.

"There's so much going on," she explained.

Dennis looked off. Evening was falling, and the streetlights were coming to life. "Yeah," he said.

"My dissertation is coming up soon. It's just not right to work all these years and not give it my best."

"What are you writing it on, Elizabeth?" he asked. He looked in her eyes, trying to gauge her. She didn't flinch.

"You know that, Dennis. Caretaking. How human beings take care of one another. How innately human that is."

"Protection," Dennis said.

"Yes."

"Good luck with that."

"Thank you, Dennis."

"I just have one thing to ask you," he said.

"Yes."

"Is the link San Francisco?" he asked. "Or is it Pig?"

Again, there was no movement. No slit of the eyes, nothing. She stared at him. But when she opened her mouth to speak he saw it, just barely, in the way she failed to say anything. In the way her voice just slightly changed timbre.

"I don't know what you're talking about."

He nodded. It was over, then. As quickly as it had begun. He turned back toward the intersection, and when there were no cars coming he broke into a sprint again and felt the roar in his ears. A hundred feet on, when he looked back to see if she was still there, she was. Standing in the same spot. That night he would wonder about it ceaselessly: Had she been crying? Was that movement to her face a tug of the collar over her cheeks to block the wind, or was it something else?

Elizabeth reminded him, standing there, of his father. How strange. How you never could quite figure him out. His posture, his glances. How you would often look back at him after he'd left you somewhere—at school, at a soccer match—and wonder what he was thinking. *Teaching,* he'd told Dennis, *is the greatest learning tool.* And back to his papers he would go. He would shut himself inside his den for hours, and when Dennis's mother said, "Go check on your father," he would peek in to find the man slumped over at his desk, head down, asleep.

It was a long, sleepless night. Dennis had known it was over with Elizabeth before, when she dropped him off after the Kingsley Hotel, but there was a lack of closure. Hadn't she granted it to him? Hadn't she given him what he needed?

Yes. But it was all so backhanded. Underhanded, even. Wrong.

Because he still wanted her. Before she had met him yesterday on Montgomery, he was through with it. Now, suddenly, she crowded his thoughts.

Wrong. It was fucking wrong to do someone the way she had.

There was still a way, he knew. Elizabeth Orman herself had given it to him at the Kingsley. She had given him the trump card, his way back to her. He couldn't get to her by calling her on the phone, just as he couldn't get to his father by knocking on the door of his den and asking to come in. Even with all his honesty and his charm he knew that he would have to find another way back to Elizabeth.

And so Dennis decided to play the card she had given him.

THREE WEEKS LEFT

16

Wednesday's guest speaker was a policeman, introduced simply as Detective Thurman. Thurman stood at the podium and addressed the class with his hands trembling. Professor Williams took a seat with his class and scribbled notes along with his students, pondering Thurman's points here and there, laughing at the man's crude jokes. The detective had an impressive paunch and spoke in a smoker's whisper. His face was just shaved and irritated, and only a mustache, stained from years of nicotine and stress, remained. He had big fat hands that were all nicked up, Mary assumed, from days spent tending his garden. He had brought Professor Williams a huge paper sack of vegetables. *Tomatoes*, he'd scrawled on the bag.

"It's not how you think," he told the class. "Solving crimes ain't the easiest thing in the world. I know you all are smart. I mean, I know Winchester is like Yale and Harvard"—some of them had a laugh at that comment—"but still. It takes a deeper intelligence to solve crimes. They're like locks. You pick the first tumbler, and you feel something slide into place. That's one theory. But there's more. The pin slides in deeper, past the first set of tumblers to the second, and you have to pick them, too. And then there's a third set, way down in the back of the mechanism, almost impossible to get to. You've got a perp? Okay. Does he have an alibi? He does not. Okay. What's his motive? He's got a viable motive? Okay. Can you find the evidence to convict him in court? It's a series of tumblers that you have to go through, and when the last one falls into place the lock slides apart and you can get inside the thing to look around. A lot of people think there's some voilà moment where everything becomes clear. Well, it ain't like that. It just isn't."

Thurman paused then and shuffled through his index cards. His hands were still trembling, those thick knuckles knocking against the podium. "Now," he said, his voice quavering. "I understand you all have a crime to solve. Mr. Williams has asked me not to speak specifically about your assignment. I might, you know, give somebody some *tips*." He laughed, a musical little snort that blared out of one nostril. "But I can talk about missing girls. Lord, I can go on all day about missing girls."

The detective took a sip from the Dasani bottle he had brought with him. Cleared his throat. He was looking at the class now with a glaring intensity, his eyes slick and wet. "There was this one," he said. "Deanna Ward. You all may have heard of her."

Mary sucked in a breath. She'd heard that name before somewhere, but she couldn't remember exactly when. She shut her eyes and tried to recall it.

On Professor Williams's desk. The yellowed paper, the typewritten words:

> Deanna would be the same age as Polly if not

Was this the same girl? Mary opened her eyes again and focused on the detective. She suddenly knew that she should pay close attention to what he said. There was going to be important information divulged today, she thought.

"This is when I was down in Cale, working the homicide beat," the detective went on. "Deanna went missing—oh, 'bout 'eighty-six or so. Young girl. Teenager. Student at Cale Central there. Her momma told me she had eloped with her boyfriend. The whole family seemed unconcerned about it all. Had this 'it'll pass' attitude, you know. Yet they had called the police in, so figure that. Anyway, we didn't think too much of it. We sent one of our detectives out to snoop around, find out if they'd gone to Vegas or somewhere to get hitched. But the boy came back alone. He had just been visiting his dad in Cincinnati and when he came back he was *shocked*. He thought, you see, that the girl had left him for another boy.

"No, wait," Thurman said then, gesturing in the air as if to say, *Wipe that off, clean the slate.* "*Before* then. Before the boyfriend returns, we'd brought the dad in to question him. This guy is a bum. Tattoos all over his body, profane things, Nazi propaganda and all that. He had a tattoo of the solar system on his back. Must have cost him a year's earnings, at least. They called him Stardust. Star. Star had been up in Swani for beating a guy nearly to death a few years before. He was in a motorcycle gang we were surveilling called the Creeps. This was about six months prior to Deanna's disappearance. One of the Creeps had been shot to death during a ride out to Santa Fe, New Mexico, and we were calling them in one by one, you know, interrogating them. We brought Star in and he said something strange, something we didn't really put together until the boyfriend came back and it was clear that something terrible had happened to Deanna.

"Star was talking about their ornaments, the girls who sit on the backs of their bikes and smoke cigarettes and let their hair blow wild while the men look tough in the front. He'd said, 'Johnny Tracer'—which was the guy who'd been shot—'was looking for a girl to ride with, and I said, "I got one for ya. I'm trying to get her off my hands anyways." ' "

Thurman's eyes widened and he breathed in expansively, playing up the drama of it all. "So after the boyfriend returns we call Star back in. He comes in like he owns the place. You know how they do. These bikers and hoods and criminals. They're *above the law.* They're untouchable. So this guy comes in and we ask him again what he'd meant before, which 'girl' he was talking about for dead old Johnny Tracer. And of course he lied. He said it was some girl he'd met at a truck stop, some hook—" Thurman wasn't sure if he should say the word. He looked at Williams anxiously, awaiting clearance. He finally decided on "some trash."

"Tell them about how you caught Star," Williams led the detective. "Tell them the part about Bell City."

Thurman said, "Well, we kept Star on a short leash. Put a man outside the house to watch his every move. For two or three days after Deanna went missing—nothing. Not a peep. He was Honest Abe. I suppose that he knew we had our eye on him, so he was just play-pretending like he was Mr. Common Joe. The guy even went to *church*, if you can believe it, dressed in all black."

"And then?" Williams pushed. It was clear that he was tiring of all the extraneous detail in the man's story.

"And then it happened," Thurman said. "Star got on his bike one morning, real early, just after dawn, and he rode out to Bell City. He stopped a few times on the way, trying to detect a tail, but our guy was good. They played cat and mouse all the way up Highway 72. Finally, Star pulled over to a little dusty trailer right outside of Bell City. The detective stayed back a good distance and watched him through binoculars. Star went in, stayed maybe a half hour, then came outside and drove back to Cale.

"Of course we descended on the place. But get this: there was a girl in there, but it wasn't Deanna. It looked like her. In fact, we thought it was her. We arrested Star and returned the girl to her mother, but the mother told us, 'This isn't my daughter.' And it was true. One of detectives had whispered to me as we drove her from the Bell City trailer that there was something funny about her. She was . . . *hiding her face* somehow. She was disguising herself. The mother was more distraught than before. What a thing! To think that your daughter was going to be returned to you, but you get this . . . counterfeit. So we took the girl in, questioned her. She would only say that she 'knew' Star Ward. She never told us what her relationship was with him. When we asked her about the missing girl, Deanna, she denied knowing a thing about her."

"But she looked just like Deanna, right?" Williams said.

"Right! It was the damndest thing. It struck us all: how similar she looked to Deanna. She was almost an identical copy, except she was . . . different somehow. She would do this thing with her face— I'll always remember it—like *tilt it* to one side and blink at us innocently. It was all very bizarre and crooked, and it still gives me nightmares even now, almost twenty years later."

"Excuse me," someone in the back said. Mary turned and saw Brian House; he was standing up, his hand raised. "Excuse me," he said again.

"Mr. House?" Williams said.

"I have to . . ." Brian sat down, put his face in his hands.

"Are you feeling well?" Williams asked.

"No," Brian said. "I'm not. I'm sorry but I have to go." He stood up again, gathered his things and, with his head down as if he were going to get sick, walked out of Seminary East.

"Go on, Detective," Williams instructed the man when the door was closed.

"We never found that missing girl. Of course the father chopped her up, we all knew that, but we never could prove it. One common theory was that some of the Creeps' rivals took her out to the desert and left her there as a sort of blood capital. But uh-uh. No. You can't convince me that it wasn't Daddy.

"I still think about Deanna. When I retired I would drive the streets down in Cale, looking for that girl. After Star Ward took his family and left for California, they didn't get too many leads about Deanna down at the station. One day I followed the boyfriend— you have to understand, now, that I was off duty by this time and could have gotten in some severe trouble if I'd been found out. He went out to eat. Got gas at the Swifty. Went home and watched TV, and I watched him through the window of his apartment. Nothing. It still haunts me to this day. That one grand failure."

Detective Thurman stopped talking. His eyes were still moist, glinting in Seminary East's steady light. He took another slug of the Dasani. "Questions?" he asked, his voice choked and raw.

The students spent a few minutes asking questions. Thurman answered them clumsily, his language leaning heavily into cliché. When asked why he had gone into the force, he told them that police work was "noble," and that he was just carrying on the legacy of his brother and father, who were also cops. He told them that the key to detective work was "keeping your eye on the ball" and not getting "trapped in a corner." When asked if he had ever fired his gun, he said yes, but only as a last resort. Dennis Flaherty tried to bait him into a question about Polly, but Professor Williams jumped from his seat and announced that time was up.

When the detective had shuffled out of the room, Williams shut the door behind him. Mary braced for an important bit of information.

"There is, you'll be happy to know, some *edutainment* scheduled for this weekend. There is going to be a—how shall I put this and not offend the Square Guard up at Carnegie?—a party at my house on Sunday night."

"A soiree?" asked Dennis jokingly.

"A bash. Montgomery and Pride. Eight o'clock. You can bring a friend."

As usual, a few people convened in the hallway after class. "Are you going?" Dennis asked the girl who sat beside him. "No way," said the girl sharply. It was agreed upon by the group that no one would go to the party, that it was entirely too bizarre a proposition. "He'll get us in there and murder us all," a boy said, laughing, but it was a strangled laugh, nervous and pitchy. "You going?" Dennis asked Mary.

"Of course not," she said. But she was lying. She had already made up her mind about what to wear.

17

*I*t was like she was afraid she was going to reveal herself.

Later that afternoon, Brian was down at the kilns, in the forest of heat. He was thinking about what the detective said, how similar the girl in the story was to the girl he'd met. Polly. He didn't know what it meant, but he knew that he couldn't go back to that class. Were they trying to break him? Make him go crazy? Were they trying to embarrass him? Well, fuck that; he wasn't going back.

Like she was afraid . . .

No.

. . . she was going to reveal herself.

Had Brian met the girl the detective was talking about, the one who'd gone missing—Deanna Ward—at the kilns that night? It was impossible. Why had the girl called herself Polly? Had Williams sent her to him to lie? Another one of his mind-fucks, another cruel twist. It was beginning to haunt him, to tear at him until he felt that he was going to be pulled into two directions by it, one Brian walking toward and one Brian walking away in fear.

What the fuck IS THIS?

He was making his mother another vase, even though she had a house full of them. The last time he had gone home he had found them in a little-used closet, dusting over and untouched. But still— it was the *effort* that mattered.

The Doors blared from the speakers that were mounted in the corners of the kiln room. The building was referred to on campus as Chop Hall, named for the Chinese American sculptor who was the head of the Art Department at Winchester. Dr. Lin was said to practice judo in the building when it emptied every evening, though Brian had never seen him do it. Thus the name "Chop," the suggestion being that if your art was subpar Dr. Lin would have your ass.

Now Dr. Lin was assisting Brian at the kiln. Brian had the blow-pipe and he was gathering the chips of color, greens and blues this time to match his current mood, one of those September hazes he always fell into before the term's end. "Turn!" said Dr. Lin, and Brian spun the pipe and began to blow into it, pushing at the glass, bubbling it into a sphere of fiery orange.

The heat seared at his bare chest. He was covered in grime and sweat. The kiln roared and sucked in the air from the room. Brian found that he could scream, literally *scream*, when the process reached this point and no one would hear him.

"This is the end," Jim Morrison sang above the roar, "beautiful friend. This is the end."

When he had puntied up the vase, Dr. Lin left him. Brian tapped on the pipe and the thing stayed in one piece. There were no crazes or skeins running through it. And it was *ugly*, fierce, more mass than shape. It was perfect. He would call it *Exodus:* the act of leaving, of escaping en masse.

There were so many problems at home. Katie, for instance. She still called him most every night, sent him chintzy postcards from Vassar. She would sign every card *LOVE YOU!* and her aggression had begun to wear Brian down. The tyranny of distance. They had changed him, the nearly seven hundred miles separating Winchester and Vassar College. New York now felt like some distant land, a dreamy place that existed in the beiges and soft greens of Polaroid photographs taken in the 1980s. Since he had been away, his perception of home had changed, become more rigid and obscure. At times, he couldn't even remember his mother's face.

How many girls had there been? Ten? Twelve? It was hard to tell. Some of them he couldn't remember. Some hadn't mattered. A few of them, like the girl he'd met last weekend, the girl who had called herself Polly, hadn't even made sense given the circumstances surrounding the hookup.

He thought of that girl now. She was why he had left class today. Williams was fucking with him, that much was clear. The girl was part of the professor's ruse, part of the whole puzzle. Brian wouldn't even have to tell Katie about her when he got back to Poughkeepsie, so he might as well mark her—this Polly—off the list. Anyway, nothing had happened between them. He could write Katie a letter and explain it all to her. *Dear Katie,* he'd write. *You won't believe what happened to me this weekend.*

It would all be a joke. Yes, he'd kissed that girl. But Katie had kissed a boy last year, a boy named Michael, and Brian didn't care. It happened and he'd gotten over it. Same with this, except . . .

Except what would Williams want to prove by doing that? What was he supposed to do with the information the girl had given him? The more he thought about it, the more pissed off he became. It was his private life that Williams was screwing around with, after all. Was Williams fucked up, some sort of psycho who liked to play with his students' heads? Was he trying to expose Brian somehow, set him up, or possibly—

"House?"

Brian turned around and saw the guy he had seen that night in Chop. "That's me," he said.

"Were you in here last Friday?" the guy asked. Brian remembered: the guy had been drinking coffee; steam had come out of the cup in little wisps.

"I might have been."

"Who was that girl you were with?"

"I have no idea. Just some girl." Brian thought he knew where this was going. "Look, man. We were really drunk. I don't even remember what I said. I—"

"I think I know that girl."

"Oh yeah?" Brian was intrigued now.

"Yeah. She . . . It's funny. This is going to sound crazy, but that girl is *dead*."

Brian stared at the boy. "What are you talking about?"

"At least that's what they told us. She went missing from my hometown a long time ago, back in the eighties, and when I was in school they found her remains out in California somewhere. Near San Francisco. Murdered, you know. Her family had all moved away by that time. But I swear to God, dude—she looked just like the pictures I've seen of her. But the girl you were with was . . . *younger.* It couldn't have been her. The girl from my town would have to be almost forty years old by now. I wanted to stop her, you know, but she looked pretty upset."

Brian, embarrassed, looked away. But then something else occurred to him. "Where you from?"

"Cale, Indiana," the boy said. "Home of the Blue Hens. You know us?"

"No," Brian said, thinking.

"Jason Nettles," the boy said, putting out a color-streaked hand for Brian to shake. "Call me Net. Painting, with a minor in glass."

But Brian had already drifted off. Those tumblers in his mind were falling into place, one by one by one.

Cale. Where the detective had worked. The detective had told a story about a missing girl. Could the girl that Brian brought to the kilns be connected in any way to the detective's story?

Williams, he thought. *Williams is planting it. Setting it up.*

Before he knew it, Brian was jamming his shirt over his head and brushing past the other boy, on the way out of Chop and into the crooked world.

18

That night Mary was back into *City of Glass.* Quinn was decoding Stillman's steps through the city into letters that read *the Tower of Babel.* Mary was finally intrigued by the story. Auster had her, and she was beginning to worry about Quinn's sanity—how he was going to cope with this addiction to Stillman, this obsession for not necessarily solving the puzzle but for the puzzle itself.

It was all familiar to her. Even though she knew now that cracking the code of Williams's class—really cracking, really solving it completely—was going to be impossible because there were too many twists and turns and inconsistencies and false leads, she was going to have to decide on a theory and go with it. Run with it, headlong. There was no other way to placate her mind. Two years ago she had told herself that Dennis had simply changed. (*Boys just change, Mary,* Summer McCoy had told her.) That allowed her some peace, finally.

Now she was going to have to decide on a plan and work through it. Damn the consequences if she was wrong. She had to start working, had to put her mind to the task of finding Polly. Dithering now would only cost her time, and with only three weeks left to find the missing girl, time was something Mary couldn't waste.

"A note to himself?" Quinn was thinking in the book. "A message?"

The phone rang.

"This is Brian," the voice on the other line said. "I've found something."

"Why did you leave class today?" Mary asked.

"Personal reasons. Look, I didn't know who else to call. I found you in the campus directory. I—I thought you would want to hear it."

"Hear what, Brian?"

"That detective? Thurman? He was a fake."

Mary let it sink in. For a second she thought that Brian might be trying to fool her by playing some nasty trick on her. Or, worse, that Williams had somehow gotten to Brian and they were in on the deception together. Perhaps the game—the class, the professor, the students, the Summer McCoy photo—was all some clever hoax at Mary's expense. All this flashed through her mind so fleetingly that she could not grasp it, any of it. It had come and gone before she had had time to register its impact, and then Brian was talking again.

"I called the Cale Police Department. No one had ever heard of him down there, Mary. I checked around. Bell City. DeLane. Shelton. Nothing. No Detective Thurman. No record of him anywhere."

"What does this mean?" she asked. The world was at a roar now on each side of her, *whooshing* across the plane of her perception. So much chaos out there. So much disorder. Randomness.

"It means that Williams is toying with us. It's part of the class."

"It's not against the law, Brian," she said. Taking up for Williams now. Protecting him.

"Not against the law, no, but there must be some ethics regulation. Some policy on the books that prohibits this kind of thing."

He was breathless, ragged, nearly desperate.

"I called around, tried to see what I could do. To—to stop this bullshit. The people in Student Services told me to call Dean Orman, so I did," he said.

"No," she said. Later, she would wonder why she had said it.

"Told him all about it: Polly. The detective. The fake story Thurman had given us. He seemed . . . disturbed by it. Told me that he would have it taken care of. Told me not to meet with Williams if he asked me to his office. If I saw him on the sidewalk, keep walking. Orman sounded as if he had maybe had some *thing* with Williams in the past. It was like he wasn't even surprised by what I was telling him."

Mary told Brian about the plagiarism issue. She told him all that she knew, about the note on Williams's desk and her meeting with Troy Hardings, about the weird phone call she had received from the campus police that night, even how strong Leonard Williams had been blocking her at the classroom door. She could hear his labored, quick breath on the other end of the line following her through the story.

Brian said, "If you saw a note about her and this guy, his assistant—"

"Troy."

"If you saw a note about her, then that must mean—"

"It's true. I went through the EBSCOhost database and found an old article about her. Written by—I've got it printed out here. Written by a guy named Nicholas Bourdoix. August nineteen eighty-six."

"My God, Mary," Brian said. "Why would Williams do this?"

"I really hadn't thought about it," she told him. But that wasn't true. She had given the question considerable thought ever since she'd found the Bourdoix article. Did Williams have something to do with Deanna Ward's disappearance? She found herself thinking about Williams's awful strength again, his tremendous weight pushing against her.

Stay.

"My question is why," Brian said, snapping Mary out of her reverie. "Why is he still at Winchester? Don't you think there's something wrong with him, Mary?"

She didn't answer. She thought of Dennis, for some reason, about when he had gone back with her to Kentucky for Thanksgiving two years ago. Her father had found her late that first night, watching television alone. *Don't you think there's something wrong with him, Mary?* he'd asked. When she had castigated him for saying it, turned her face so that he couldn't see that she was crying, he had softly apologized. A month later Dennis was with Savannah Kleppers.

"I mean, he's mysterious," Brian went on. "The way he talks. The way he acts. There's something forced about him, Mary. Scripted. I know it. I've seen it before. My brother—"

"What?" Mary asked. Something was holding Brian back, some internal boundary he was afraid to cross.

"My brother was an actor. He did Shakespeare, mostly. Some local stuff up in the Hudson Valley. He was brilliant. He'd just landed a commercial when he shot himself."

Neither of them spoke for a few moments. Their silence was broken when some girls screamed with delight out on the quad in front of Brown. It was Friday night, and Mary suddenly had a great urge to be back in Kentucky, at home. It came up on her so quickly she had to choke it down. She was into something, she thought, for the first time, something larger than herself.

"Anyway," said Brian, "I'm not going back to his class."

"You're not?"

"Hell no. That class scares the shit out of me. I made up my mind as the good *detective* was giving his spiel. They can have it. I'll take the F. Polly is just a game anyway, deception on a mass scale."

It's just a game, he'd said. But she'd known that. Hadn't they known that all along? Williams had admitted that it was a logic puzzle on the first day, designed to teach them rational thinking skills. What had changed? A fake detective, a false story? A story about another girl who had gone missing? It was possible that the real world had encroached too far into the ruse and scared them both away. Mary thought of Quinn in *City of Glass*. The mystery had become his life, had turned into something as tangible as a red notebook that he held in his lap and scribbled wild entries into. Ceaselessly, confoundingly, those entries went into the notebook until they made up a record of his obsession and his fall.

"Brian," Mary whispered. And when he didn't answer, she said it louder.

"Yeah," he said. "I'm still here."

"I think Williams is . . ." She closed her eyes, unable to find the word.

"I know what you mean," Brian said.

19

Mary showed up at Professor Williams's house early on Sunday. It was a warm night, and she had walked across the Great Lawn, in front of the Orman Library, and cut back onto Pride Street. It was only a block up. Mary had passed his house many times on her jogs around campus. An unassuming house, nothing really, just some dark brick and a gravel driveway with a pickup truck parked in the front. A dog barking out back, running along a clothesline. It was all normal, quaint even—not in the least what she had expected.

Dennis had called and asked Mary to meet him there. He had spoken to Professor Williams, he told Mary, and there were going to be surprises at the party. Mary imagined it as extra credit, a leg up on the rest of the class. Williams was worried that no one would come, Dennis told Mary, and so he had lined up an exciting evening pertaining to Polly.

Oh, she had fought the urge. With everything in her she had fought it. She thought about Brian House, how distraught he had sounded on the phone. She knew better. As she walked across the lawn that evening, she knew she was wrong and he was right. She was like the girl in the horror movie, opening the door although no one was home. She was *exactly* like that girl. But still she walked, her heels digging in to the moist grass, the leaves above her rattling and dropping into her hair.

Dennis met her at the door and took her jacket. In that one action she knew: he had been speaking with Professor Williams. How else to explain his ease in Williams's home? It was really undeniable. He took the jacket away toward the back of the house, into some dark bedroom. There were a few people buzzing around, drinking beer out of plastic cups. Some Mary recognized from the class and some were unfamiliar. Troy was there. He was talking to one of the girls from the class, and when he saw her he nodded. She gave a little half wave back. A slightly older woman was standing in the kitchen, leaning against the bar, drinking wine. Williams's wife, Mary figured. A little boy, maybe five years old, screeched through the room, the bowl of his yellow hair bouncing on his head like a helmet.

She saw Williams outside on the patio, talking to someone and smoking a cigarette. They were both laughing, heads thrown back, as if nothing in the world were wrong.

"Della Williams," someone behind her said.

Mary turned and the woman from the kitchen was right in front of her. Heavy mauve lipstick, a low-cut blouse—she was beautiful. Too beautiful for Williams. She was younger than the professor by ten or fifteen years, which explained the age of the boy. The dark ringlets of her hair fell gracefully on her shoulders and caught the light. The wineglass, Mary noticed, was mauve all around its circumference, as if the woman had been rotating the glass with each sip.

Mary introduced herself to the woman.

"That's Jacob," Della said, as the screaming boy ran back through the living room at their knees. She smiled as if to say, *What can you do?*

An awkward silence came between them. Mary looked at the floor and noted the vacuum lines were still fresh.

"So, do you have Leonard this semester?" the woman asked.

"Yes," replied Mary. "Logic."

"Ah. The girl."

"Exactly. The girl."

There seemed to be nothing else between them, and just as Mary was planning her escape, he was right there, with his arm around his wife. Williams was wearing a Hawaiian shirt and cargo pants. She smelled bug spray on him and the heavy odor of beer.

"Thanks for coming," he said gently, and she tried to read those words for something deeper. Had he thought she wouldn't come? Perhaps he knew about her discussion with Brian House. But how? Again, there was that lingering gaze he always gave her. Those enchanted, almost astonished eyes.

And then Dennis was at her arm and leading her outside. He drew her a beer out of the keg and she accepted it, and for the first time in many months she drank alcohol. The night was fresh, mystical, the sky high and starless. The dog ran back and forth on its line. She stood close to Dennis, swayed against him in the light breeze.

"How have you been?" he asked, and Mary told him. Stressed from school. Fighting with Paul Auster's *City of Glass* mostly. Dennis brought out something in her, an urge to confide, and if he would have given her a few more minutes she would have unquestionably told him about Brian and Detective Thurman.

But the professor called them all inside, and they crowded around him in his living room. He sat on a rolling stool with his boy on his knee. The boy had a toy truck and was wheeling it across Leonard's thigh. The mother, Della, stood back in the kitchen, drinking the last of her wine. It was all very domestic and placid. Mary was suddenly glad she had come.

"There's been an event," Williams said. The word was underscored, stressed, and uppercased. *Event.* "But first, let me ask all of you a question." The boy rolled the truck off Williams's leg and onto the floor and made a crashing sound, then puffed his cheeks out and blew in a little explosion. "Are any of you disturbed by me?"

"Terrified." It was Troy. He laughed and hummed the theme from *The Twilight Zone.*

"Well," Williams went on, "there have been some complaints. Some uneasy conversations with people up there." He jabbed a thumb toward Carnegie, where all the decisions were made at Winchester.

"They're intimidated by you," Troy said. He had a stern look, and when he drank he kept his eyes rigidly on Williams. Williams was Troy's man, Mary saw then. There was something deep and longstanding between them.

"Maybe so," the professor sighed. "But still, I want to know right now. Do any of you feel threatened by my class? It's been said that I'm conducting . . . experiments. The administration used that word in a letter to me yesterday. Told me to—what was it?—*be careful.* It was written by Dean Orman himself. Winchester letterhead and everything. I detected the faint aroma of horseshit wafting from the envelope slit." Williams chuckled slightly under his breath. "Orman wrote, *Be careful. Your experiments are causing some concern.* I don't know if any of you are concerned about this Polly stuff. Because if you are, we can stop and go to the textbook."

"No, no," they grumbled, fearing the *other* version of Logic and Reasoning 204 they had heard about, the one Dr. Weston taught, where the students memorized Plato and were quizzed every week on the fallacies.

"What about Polly?" Williams asked.

"What about her?" Dennis responded.

"Well, do you think that she is *false* enough?"

Mary turned away. She felt everyone's eyes on her. He was talking about the photograph of Summer again, of course, and suddenly she was ashamed. Thankfully, Dennis picked her up, just as he had done a few times during Williams's class.

"There have been times," he admitted, "when it was as if she was real."

"But mostly you are able to separate what is fake from the rest of your studies?" Williams asked.

No, Mary wanted to say. *Not when a false detective comes into the room and tells a story about a missing girl. Not when the world begins to take on your story's characters.* It was a play within a play, like *Hamlet*, but figuring out which drama was most palpable was the trick.

"Good," he said when no one objected. "Let's get on with it, then." The boy was at his feet now, rolling the truck around through the deep nap of the carpet. Della Williams was in the kitchen washing dishes. Mary felt Dennis beside her, tasted his sweet smell in her drink. "Something's happened," Williams said. "There's been a new development." He stopped, made them wait for it. *"Wooo woooo woooo,"* went the little boy, rolling off toward the kitchen with his truck. "Do you all remember Trippy?"

"Trippy?" someone said from behind Mary.

"Nicole's boyfriend," someone else answered.

"Trippy has been arrested on possession," Williams said.

There were a few ironic hoots and whistles. Someone said, "Shocking," and everyone laughed.

"So Trippy is in jail," the professor told them. "And he has told the detectives something. He has admitted that he knows where Polly is."

Everyone was silent. Pensively, with the trees outside swaying in the wind and making a sound like moving water, they waited.

When it was apparent that Williams wasn't going to continue, someone said, "And?"

"To be continued," he said, and they all groaned.

"So Trippy kidnapped her," Mary said.

"Not necessarily," Williams said. He stood up from the stool, grunting at the sound of his popping knees, and gestured that they could resume whatever they had been doing. The boy appeared again, this time in Della's arms, and Williams ran his hands through his son's fine hair. Mary wanted to approach him, to talk to him about Polly and her dad and all that she had been thinking about, but the professor was suddenly surrounded by a few boys. They were talking Winchester football.

Dennis was at her arm again. "Hey," he said easily. There was something in his eyes, that old gleam. He led her downstairs, where Zero 7 was playing on an old, dusty stereo. There was a spread down here. A vegetable tray, some sandwiches. She and Dennis ate together, sitting side by side on an old couch that smelled of storage. A few people drifted here and there, but they were mostly alone.

"I've been meaning to call you," he said.

Mary wasn't sure where she wanted the conversation to go. There was something in her that still loved Dennis, but he had broken her heart in such an abrupt way that the act had almost been violent.

She still thought about him now and then, of course, but when she did she always caught herself, forced herself to acknowledge that he was never coming back to her.

Yet here he was, in the flesh, in this damp and strange basement. Here he was. Mary almost couldn't believe it. She would not have believed it, probably, were the heat of his body not on her skin.

"It's just that I was crazy," he went on. "That's it. Crazy, Mary. What we had scared me. It was a frightening thing. I had never been in love. You know that. I fought it. Like an idiot, I stifled it until I was the one in control."

Mary wondered, *Is this happening? Am I here, really, in body?*

"So, you're almost at your seminar," he said then, shyly, just like a boy. And it was this boyishness that she had always found charming about Dennis Flaherty—the fact that he could be so innocent, so harmless, yet his intelligence was always there, like some dogged energy that he could reveal just at the precise moment.

They talked. Mary lost track of the time. At first she was nervous—she tucked her hands into the couch cushions, laughed too loudly, kicked off her shoes and slid them with her toes across the rug so that there would be some background noise, something to take his mind off the gigantic beating of her heart—but after a while she fell into a natural pattern with him. It was as if they were together again.

When the sounds from upstairs had slowed, the scrapings and thumpings of footsteps, she knew it had gotten late. But here was Dennis, still on her arm, looking at her. What did he expect from her? He probably expected things to return to normal, to how they'd been two years ago. *No way*, Mary thought. There was no way she could just forget about Savannah Kleppers and all that he had done to hurt Mary two years ago.

"I like you, Mary," he was saying.

She breathed, and she felt him breathe beside her. A dual rhythm.

The old couch puffing out a musty, disused odor from its cushions every time one of them shifted.

"Dennis," she said flatly.

"Yes?" It was almost a whisper, coquettish in a strange way. So harmless.

"I'm going to go home. I'm going to think about this, and I'll call you tomorrow."

He was smiling at her, his eyes soft and pleading. The smile talked, as most of Dennis's gestures did. It said, *Come here.*

"Please," she said, looking away. She felt his gaze, his breath on her neck. She would have given in to it had she sat there for two more minutes. A feeling was building up inside her, that old and lost roil. That urge.

She began to stand up.

Then, perhaps feeling her pulling away, he said, "I know where Polly is."

His words didn't register with her for a moment. He was still looking at her, his stare now active. Then it dawned on Mary what he was propositioning, and the knowledge fell on her like an anvil. Like she had been crushed. Waylaid by it.

Of course. He was trying to get her into bed by telling her the secret.

The goddamned bastard.

She managed to fully stand. Her knees were weak, and she was in that early stage of drunkenness where everything was lurchy and loose. She made her way to the steps, one uneasy step at a time.

"Wait," he called after her.

She kept walking, moving up into the light of Williams's home.

"Mary," he begged. "Your shoes."

Too late, she realized that she had forgotten her shoes. She had kicked them off downstairs, and now they were the property of

Dennis Flaherty. No worries. They were old, anyway, from high school. She would get new ones.

Mary emerged into the living room. A few people still buzzed around. Williams was sitting on one of the leather sofas, his hand gesturing wildly, talking to Troy. "Mary!" he said when he saw her, too loudly, too awkwardly. He got off the sofa and approached her, did a funny little bow. "Thanks for coming," he said. He, too, was a little drunk, his eyes nervous and kinetic. Then he saw her bare toes, and she explained that Dennis had her shoes and he would return them to her.

"Oh," he said. "Okay. I'll see you tomorrow?"

She couldn't focus on him. He was blurred, fuzzy. Swerving. Another awkward moment: she shook his hand. "Well," she managed. And still he smiled that actor's smile. Brian had called it— what had he called it? *Scripted*. Yes, Mary concurred now. There was something fake about it, something positively unreal.

As she was leaving, she thought, *My jacket*. She found her way into the back room. The kid was asleep in the master bedroom, and Della Williams was beside him. She had the television on. The coats were piled up next to the sleeping boy. Mary dug out her jacket and put it on. As she was zipping it the woman turned and looked at her. Della still had her dress on, was still wearing her shoes, buckles and a sensible square heel. Her legs were bare and bruised in various places, Mary noticed.

"Good-bye," she said.

"Bye," Mary replied.

"I wanted to give someone this," Della Williams said anxiously, "but I could never decide who." She revealed a slip of paper, its edges soft and moist from her hand. "Don't read it until you're outside."

Mary knew what that meant: *Don't let him see it*.

She left the house and ran across Montgomery Street and back onto campus, the bottoms of her feet slapping the pavement. She ran across the grass of the Great Lawn, sticks tearing at her stockings, the grass wet and cold on her toes. When she was under a security light, in the alleyway that ran beside the Orman Library and opened up onto the viaduct, she unfolded the slip of paper the woman had given her.

None of this is real, it read. *I AM NOT HIS WIFE.*

TWO WEEKS LEFT

20

Actors.

On Monday afternoon, Brian House went out looking for them. When Jason Nettles told him about Cale, his first thought had been, *That's how I can find the girl from the party.* But the more he thought about it, the more he felt like driving to Cale might reveal them all. Detective Thurman, the Polly he'd met, maybe even Williams himself. He now knew that he had been tricked. They had all been tricked. The boundary between Logic and Reasoning 204 and the real world had been altered by Williams, reconstituted by the man's deception. Brian had found himself wondering if any of it was genuine—his other professors, people he met at parties (he had not even dared hit on a girl after the Polly incident in Chop), even his roommate. Always, wherever he went, he felt this uneasiness, this fear that the world was coming unglued on him and turning inside out, its mechanisms becoming exposed like the sharp springs of an old mattress biting through the foam.

Brian wondered, not for the first time, if this is what Marcus had felt. Brian had called his brother from Winchester the day before Marcus killed himself. "I'm feeling great," he had told Brian. But there was something under there, veiled and throbbing. Brian could still hear it, that old hurt, in his brother's voice. "Got another audition tomorrow," Marcus said. It was a commercial for car insurance and would pay him enough to keep his studio apartment in Brooklyn. It was a conversation between two brothers that should have been full of hope, but Brian hung up the phone with a feeling of dread. *Marcus was acting.*

Now here he was, trying to uncover another conspiracy. He could not help but feel that they were somehow linked, a cruel joke played only on him. The world was transparent, see-through *by design.* Marcus had given him clues: sending Brian boxes of his old clothes, his talk—no, his obsession—with bridges, stopping along the way from Kingston to Poughkeepsie one evening two summers ago with Brian, standing on the edge of the Route 9 bridge that overlooked the Hudson River, and asking when he got back in the car, "How high do you think it is?" And that last phone call, so plainly deceptive, an attempt to inform Brian of what was about to happen.

But he didn't see it back then, of course. By that evening he wasn't thinking about that phone call. In fact he **was** out with a girl named Cara Bright, doing shots at her apartment off campus. The next day his mother's call woke him.

"Brian," she said. And he knew.

It crushed his father. His father fell into a grief fugue, slow-eyed and despondent, and Brian had to push him through the motions at Marcus's funeral. His father: sitting on the couch, three days removed, mouthing something silently. His father: refusing to eat, stomping through the house at two o'clock and three o'clock in the morning. His father: waking Brian one night and asking, "Do you know where Marcus's old twelve-speed went?" The two of them then went outside, into the garage, and at first Brian just wanted to placate the old man but then, when the bicycle didn't appear, it became a test, as if finding the bike would bring Marcus back. They searched till dawn, crashing through old computers and tools and boxes of junk, slinging stuff here and there, turning the place upside down in an attempt to find it.

They never did, of course. It became the Mystery of Marcus's Old Bike. And soon thereafter, just a couple of weeks or so, with Brian now back at Winchester even though he didn't want to be, his father left his mother with a note that read, simply, *I can't take this anymore.*

Nothing Brian had begun since Marcus died had been finished. He left everything half-closed and incomplete: Katie and his mother, blown-glass vases that should have been cylindrical but had turned out, even as he cared for them and jacked them with care, flat and lumpy right before his eyes. The world dripping, melting, coming down around him. There was nothing he could do.

Or maybe there was. Brian had begun to think of Williams's class as his way of salvaging something, as a sort of strange redemption. He had failed with Marcus, refused to see the signs of his brother's illness that were right in front of him. Nothing had happened in his life since. Not really. He had grieved, come back to school, gone through the motions of a life. But now, here, he was finally presented with something. A challenge. In recent nights the obsession had been so fierce that he had had to pace his dorm room to allay it.

It had been a long time since he'd driven around town. His truck had been sitting outside Davis Hall, unstarted, for the better part of the fall quarter. It was good to roll down the windows and listen to the radio. It was good to be alone. He was listening to Johnny Cash, his father's music. He tried to get the guys in Davis to try it, but of course it went over their heads. Now, in the rocking wind, Brian turned it up.

Actually, he didn't know what he would do once he uncovered Williams's game. He didn't want to think about that right now. It just felt good to get out, to wander around. He drove down Montgomery and hit Pride Street. He drove past Professor Williams's house slowly, trying to catch a glimpse of the man. There was no one home except the dog, which madly ran back and forth on its line. He headed out onto Turner Street, and then Highway 72 toward Cale. He was on the Rowe County line before he knew where he was going. The wind blasted into the cabin, obliterated everything, every thought he had. Katie. His mother. Going home. It was gone, all of it, in the wind.

Brian knew Cale. He had gone there on a few beer runs. Because Rowe County was dry, the students had to drive the twenty or so miles into Cale to one of the many liquor stores that operated right on the county line, which Winchester students referred to as the Border.

Cale was two wide expanses of farmland sandwiching the town proper. Brian kept on Highway 72 through Cale to the other side of the city limits, where he saw a sign that read BELL CITY 36. He remembered Detective Thurman's lecture: Bell City is where the girl was found, the girl in the trailer who looked like Deanna.

Thinking of that girl, Brian got an idea.

He followed the signs to Cale Central High School just off 72. School was in session, of course, on this Monday. The cars glinted across the parking lot, and a phys ed class was taking laps around the track. The school was one of those old buildings, unchanged since the 1960s. It was like a scar on the land, low and squat as if it had been pancaked flat. A flag snapped in the wind as Brian walked toward the front doors. The sign on the front lawn showed a toothy, sneering blue hen, its wing raised in a threatening gesture. WELCOME BACK, the marquee read.

When he entered the school, a sense of nostalgia overtook him. Cale High was exactly like all the other schools he had ever been in. The floor waxed and shiny, a few students wandering here and there. Echoing off the walls was the deep thud of a basketball being bounced.

In the foyer, he searched the trophy cases. He was looking for some kind of a shrine to the girl who had attended the school years ago. As he was looking at the dusty trophies, some so old their etchings had gone black, a voice behind him said, "Can I help you?"

He turned to find a young woman, not much older than he was. She was wearing a name badge that read MRS. SUMNER.

"I'm here researching a class," Brian said, which was an admonition resting perfectly between truth and lie. "And I was just looking for something, a memorial maybe, for that girl who went missing."

"Deanna Ward?" she asked, as if it was part of the Cale cultural mythology, as if she had said the name a thousand times before. It implied something larger, an entire multitudinous history in itself.

"Yes," said Brian.

"You would want to talk to Bethany Cavendish. She was kin to Deanna. She'll be in room 213 after school lets out."

Brian waited until the final bell rang at 2:15 p.m. and then he went upstairs to see Bethany Cavendish. She was a short, thin, masculine woman. He found her grading papers in a science room. She was wearing a Cale Blue Hens shirt that had been chemical stained in several spots, and her lab goggles were pushed up into her short, spiky hair. When Brian shook her hand, the woman gripped hard and pumped.

"Deanna was in trouble a lot," Bethany said when they were sitting. They sat at one of the desks beside a window. "I had to go down to Mr. Phillips's almost every week and talk them out of expelling her. I wouldn't have done that if I didn't love her momma, Wendy. Such a sweet woman. My cousin, you know. One of the only Cavendishes who came back to Cale. I felt so sorry for her, having to put up with Deanna and that man of hers at the same time."

She said it bluntly, almost spitting the word at Brian: *man.*

"Deanna disappeared on August first. This was twenty years ago now, back in 'eighty-six. Everybody thought she'd run off and got married to Daniel Jones. They were both in a funny kind of love. Danny was older, and Deanna had fallen for him hard. I mean, like, *hard*. I had her in Chemistry II that semester, and all her day would consist of was doodling Danny's name all over her notebooks and skin. She would leave school like a human mural, all hearts and '4evers' and declarations of undying love. It was disturbing to watch, really. It was obsession more than anything."

"They thought Danny had something to do with it at first, didn't they?" Brian asked.

"At first. But we all knew. We all knew who was responsible."

"Her father?" Brian asked.

"Uh-huh. Star. That was Deanna's daddy. He was accused of that crime out in New Mexico. They thought he'd shot a man and dumped him out in the desert. He probably did, knowing Star. He started out as Stardust, you know, then he became Star. He was into astronomy, telescopes and all that. He got interested in how what we're seeing when we look up could be the beginning of the universe."

"The Big Bang," Brian said.

"He even had stars custom painted on his bike, which cost him and Wendy a pretty penny they didn't have. He was tatted up with the universe, the whole solar system sketched and labeled on his back and arms. She told me that tattoo had cost almost two thousand dollars. I let him borrow some of my equipment one time, some cheap telescopes I had, and of course he never brought them back. That's the way he was."

"Did he kill the man you talked about? In New Mexico?"

"I believe so. No, let me rephrase that: I *know* so. Star was as dangerous as they come. I have no idea what sweet Wendy was doing with him. He'd probably taken her out on his bike one night and named all the constellations, and she thought he was something. That's how it always goes in Cale. These girls, smart as tacks and pretty as they come, get swept under by these no-count boys. That's the legacy of this town. Nothing else to do here, I guess, except run off with some crazy. She should have stayed at Winchester when she was there, but of course she got pregnant and dropped out."

"She was a student at Winchester?"

"Should have been class of 'sixty-six, but it never turned out like that. She got pregnant and moved out here to Cale, and the rest is . . ."

"Yes," Brian said, leading her.

"Anyway, they were all over Star for his New Mexico stuff. I heard they almost had that murder pinned on him, but then Deanna ran off. And suddenly all of Cale was in a frenzy, and we sort of forgot about Star. *I* never forgot about him, though. I always thought he had killed that girl and hid her somewhere out on his property."

"His own daughter." Brian said it more to himself than to Bethany Cavendish. He was thinking of Polly's father, of Mary Butler's wild theory. He wondered now if Mary was right.

"When I told anybody this," the teacher said, "they looked at me like I was sick. It almost goes beyond the human capacity to understand, how a father would kill his own daughter and hide the body. But people don't know the whole story. This was not your normal, run-of-the-mill dude. He was bitter to the core. Evil. I wouldn't have put anything past him. Not anything.

"And when Danny came back from Cincinnati without Deanna, it turned into a full-fledged crisis in Cale. The *Indianapolis Star* ran a front-page story about it. There was pressure on the sheriff to make an arrest, even if Deanna was still missing, and so they focused on Star. He admitted to something when they brought him in as a suspect for the New Mexico shooting, something about having a girl that he wanted to have taken off his hands. This is the way the Creeps were with girls: they used them, beat them, spit on them, and just left them damaged by the side of the road somewhere. This is how it was with Wendy. For all intents and purposes, Star had left her. She was back there in that old crappy house off During Street, taking care of the two little ones, mourning Deanna."

During Street, he thought. Where Polly lived. Suddenly the two narratives were running perfectly together, and Brian knew he'd come to the right place. He was beginning to see what Professor Williams was doing: leading them to Deanna Ward's killer by creating this game—this logic puzzle—starring a girl called Polly. *But why? There is no logic*, Brian reminded himself. *Only randomness.*

"I went to see her one day. She was broken up by it. Assaulted. A beaten woman. But Wendy wouldn't give Star up. I pressed her on that. I wanted her to say that he did it, you know, to have it all over with. But she wouldn't. She said she was horrified at the thought. She told me that Star had some flaws but he wasn't as bad as all of us thought."

"The police were on him, though," Brian interjected. "They tailed him out to Bell City."

"Yes. The cops followed Star. And I guess they found this little girl. He was keeping her out in Bell City in this trailer, and they raided it and arrested Star, and thinking the girl was Deanna, they took her back to Wendy. But it wasn't the right girl. I never could figure that, how the police could do something so stupid. I talked to a newspaper writer about it, a few years ago. Nick Bourdoix. He ate breakfast at the McDonald's every morning, and I finally got up the nerve to talk to him."

Nick Bourdoix. Brian couldn't remember where he'd heard that name, but it was familiar.

"Bourdoix said that the girl had been dressed up to look like Deanna. Same hair color. Same clothes. Said she'd been scripted into answering their questions. She lived with her aunt and uncle in Bell City, and police were on those two for a while. Thought they'd been coaching this girl, you know. When the cops asked the girl if she was Deanna, she'd said she was. They never knew what it meant. I never did, either."

"She said she was Deanna?"

"That's how I heard it. She told them she was Deanna, she looked like Deanna, and so obviously they thought . . ." She stopped speaking. She took off her glasses and wiped her eyes with the back of her hand. "But still, you can't do that. You can't make mistakes like that. It's just inhuman."

"What happened to Star?" Brian asked.

"They had to let him go, of course. They had nothing on him. He and Wendy and the two boys moved out to San Francisco, where his family's from. And Deanna was never found. I kept telling them: I said, 'Dig around the old house on During Street, down by the river. She's there somewhere, in that field, out by where he kept all the parts of his old motorcycles.' There's no doubt in my mind that she's there."

"The house is still out there." It wasn't a question. He was thinking of Williams's transparencies, of Polly's house. Williams had been there to take those pictures. Brian thought about driving by Deanna Ward's house to see it for himself.

"I drive by it sometimes. Think about getting out and poking around. A family lives there now, an elderly couple. The Collinses. I knocked on the door one day and they let me in. I didn't tell them what I was there for, and they didn't ask. I guess they were just happy to have somebody to talk to. I didn't tell them the history of that place, about the girl who had gone missing. I suppose they knew. We just talked, like me and you are doing right now, but the whole time I was wondering how I could get outside and dig up their field."

"Are they still living there?"

"I don't know. That was five years ago. I still think about her. And Wendy, too. There was a rumor a few years ago that Deanna had been found dead out in California. But it wasn't true. Just kids spreading tales. I fantasize sometimes—that she's still out there, that Wendy will come back to Cale and buy her mother's old house. With what money, I don't know. But I envision it, the mother and the girl living out there so happy, with the past all behind them."

Bethany Cavendish stopped speaking again. Her hands were shaking, her rings scuffing the table a bit. She looked away, out the window and down to the football field, where the team was hitting, forming lines and rushing across and knocking each other flat to the ground.

"Is this for the school newspaper?" she asked.

Brian told her that he was writing a paper on unsolved crimes.

"They come over here sometimes," she said. "Students from Winchester. They're interested in it. I guess in the fact that it's unsolved. They want answers to everything, as if there *are* answers to everything. You young idealists. I know: I believed the world was perfectly rational when I was young, when Wendy and I were students at Winchester. We commuted every Tuesday and Thursday night in her daddy's old Chevrolet." Brian tried to imagine this woman at Winchester, walking over the viaduct, partying on Up Campus. He couldn't. "There was that book that one of their professors wrote a few years ago."

"Book?"

"Yeah, some true-crime nonsense. It made him a lot of money, though, I guess. It was called *A Disappearance in the Fields*. 'The Fields' referring to, I suppose, cornfields. I don't know. It was all a shot at Cale, at how backward we are. I thought it was damn insulting, but it got everybody interested in Deanna again. He came to Cale High to speak. This funny man who looked like an insurance salesman."

"What was his name?" asked Brian, thinking, *Actors. Actors.* His heart felt squeezed, tightened and strummed like a rubber band.

"Williams, I believe. Leon Williams. He's still teaching over there as far as I know. I heard they reprimanded him for the book, though. A good Presbyterian school having a professor who is interested in the abduction of young girls is a no-no, I suppose. I heard he was planning a follow-up to *A Disappearance in the Fields*—some new information or something. But that was three or four years ago and a book never came."

He's planning a follow-up, Brian thought. *Some new information.*

"I tried to get into contact with him. Wrote him an e-mail telling him about the stretch of dirt over at During Street, but he never responded. Never even sent me a thank-you note for my information."

"He's probably busy," said Brian sarcastically.

"Yeah. Anyway, you should check out the book sometime. He knew a lot more than I know about Deanna, that's for sure. The details. The sights and sounds. It was almost like—you're going to think this is crazy, but it was like this guy, this professor—it was like he was *there*."

21

Williams sent the next clue early this time, on Monday afternoon, two hours before Logic and Reasoning 204 began.

Motive

Whenever one is attempting to solve a crime, one of the first questions that must be asked is this: What was the motive of your suspect? Motive asks the fundamental question, *Why?*

Because it is not enough to suspect someone of committing the crime; in a court of law there has to be a clear and identifiable motive that suggests—either implicitly or explicitly—why this person is the culprit. In the disappearance of Polly, there are five main suspects that we have encountered along the way: Mike, the abusive boyfriend; Pig, the protective father figure; Eli, Polly's biological father; Trippy, the boyfriend of Polly's friend Nicole; and the man who approached Eli at the elementary school, the vindictive father. Let's look now at the possible motives for each man.

MIKE: We can say without any hesitation that Mike was abusive toward Polly. He hit her on more than one occasion, and the police had to investigate a domestic disturbance once at Mike's apartment in Needlebush. Mike's motive is clear: he is obsessive about Polly. Polly is going away to Grady Tech in the fall, and Mike knows that he is going to lose her. If he can't have her, then nobody should. He has been heard in town talking about what a "bitch" Polly is. He has been threatened by Pig at Polly's going-away party, and everyone assumes that Pig has warned Mike to stay away from her. Mike is a loose cannon. He drinks too much, smokes too much dope, is finding himself losing control in the weeks leading up to Polly's leaving.

PIG: Pig's motive is less clear than Mike's, of course, but there are still some inconsistencies of character that could be investigated. First, Pig is almost forty years old. He considers himself a father type to Polly, but many have observed that Pig's relationship with Polly borders on the unhealthy. Pig has not dated a woman for over a year, and many of his closest friends assume that he is waiting for Mike to step out of the picture so that he can have Polly. Because you have been told that Polly is to be murdered in the next two weeks, you know that *if* Pig has abducted her then his incentive to do so has to be malevolent—as does his motive. One theory is this: Pig feels that Polly will never give up Mike. He is tired of waiting for her to come to a decision, tired of seeing her be harmed. In his mind, Polly is harming herself with her indecision. Pig has a criminal record that is at least as long as Mike's, and there are more violent marks in his record. He is quick with his temper. Perhaps he has abducted Polly and, in a fit of jealous rage, has demanded that she leave Mike. Perhaps Polly has refused to do this, and so Pig has given her an ultimatum. An ultimatum that will run out when the term ends next Wednesday. Nine days.

ELI: Eli is the most mysterious of our characters. He seems like the perfect family man: his wife has left him for a West Coast artist, and he has taken on the challenge of raising a teenage girl on his own. We know that he has threatened Mike in the past, so he is aware of the disputes between the lovers. We also know that Eli was waiting for Polly to return from the party, and that when she went to sleep he carried her to bed. Eli was the last person to see Polly before she was abducted. A motive here could be, simply, malice. Eli could possibly see something in his daughter that he saw in his wife: the same flightiness, the same inability to be content. In his despondency over his wife's leaving, he could possibly be to the point where he is at his end, ready to take it out on the only person who is readily available to him. Eli's colleagues say that he has walked around for the past few months in a fog. They are all worried about him. He is not, for all intents and purposes, the same man he was before his wife left. "I wonder sometimes if he's not just going to snap," one of his colleagues said. "Fly off the handle and just smack one of those kids. He lets them just run all over him. I watch him sometimes, although he doesn't see me. I'll observe from the open doorway of his classroom. The kids are going *crazy.* And there's Eli in the middle of it, reading from the chapter, the noise of the classroom making it impossible for anyone to hear. Mr. Dry, our principal, asked Eli about it once, but Eli said that he was fine. But everybody knows he's not. We all know that he hurts inside. You can see it on him: the pain. It's indescribable, really."

TRIPPY: Trippy is engaged to Nicole. They are all friends with Pig, and after Mike and Polly moved out of the upstairs apartment at Pig's house, Nicole and Trippy moved in. Trippy is a two-bit criminal. He has a drug habit that borders on severe, and it is not an exaggeration to say that Polly worries that he is going to kill Nicole. Nicole has told Trippy, in one of their arguments, that Polly doesn't like him. She has also told him that she and Polly are going to be staying in an apartment near Grady Tech next semester. So a motive here is clear: Trippy abducted Polly to save his relationship with Nicole, which would clearly end if Polly and Nicole rented the apartment near Grady Tech. In the weeks before she was abducted, Trippy was becoming more volatile toward Polly. It started as playful ribbing, but turned malevolent in the week or so before the going-away party. The group of friends went together to the swimming hole on Porch Creek one day, and Trippy repeatedly asked Polly to jump from the highest rock into the creek, even though he knew—everyone knows— that Polly is afraid of the rocks. Trippy kept on until Polly was in tears, and indignantly she climbed the muddy bank up to the rock. Terrified, she jumped. Trippy's manic laughter followed her all the way down until she crashed, feet first, into the water. Polly told Pig about this incident, and he told her to "stay away from him."

THE MAN AT THE SCHOOL: The man at the school has a clear motive: he abducted Polly because of the perceived slight toward his son. Yet a motive, to be admissible in court, must be grounded in reality. Is it realistic to say that this man, who may have been simply angry about his son being punished, would have taken things to such a severe level as to abduct a girl and be willing to murder her? What else do we know about this man? Very little, right now. All we know is that he had a confrontation with Eli, and when the mysterious phone call was made on August 4, Eli's first thought was of this man.

Mary clicked on the second e-mail, which was titled "What About That Phone Call?" Inside the message, there was a sound clip. When she clicked on the link, a female voice emanated from her computer's speakers. "I'm . . . here." A faraway voice. Polly. Mary dragged the play bar back, held it, let it go again.

I'm . . . here.

22

"Let's talk about Polly," Professor Williams said on Monday afternoon.

"You first," Dennis Flaherty replied. A joke. Everyone laughed but Mary. For the past day, after she received the note from the woman playing Della Williams at the party, she had been anxious. She could not shake the fear that *everyone* was a potential player in this game. She went through the line at the dining hall and felt the servers' eyes on her. She listened to the students in her lit class talk about Auster and Quinn, and she wondered if *City of Glass* was somehow part of Williams's plan. She felt as if it was reaching a critical point now, this game, racing toward its climax. She was a week and a half away from the deadline and she had still not found any hard evidence. In a lot of ways, she felt that she wasn't at all closer to solving the case than she had been in the first week of class.

"Okay," agreed Williams. "What do you think Polly is feeling right now? Imagine her. Everybody close your eyes and imagine her." They sat thinking about this fictional girl and her possible emotional state.

"She's scared," said someone in the back. Mary turned and saw that it was the girl who usually sat beside Brian House who had spoken. His seat was empty.

"She would be, wouldn't she?" asked Williams softly. "So close now to the end. Just nine days away." They all felt it in the classroom, the jarring concussion of the words: *nine days*. "Where is she?"

"She's in a cellar, I think."

"In a cellar." Williams. "She can't see out. He has her tied up. How does she eat? How does she live?"

"He brings her water and food every day." Dennis Flaherty. "Maybe he feeds her like she is a child. Maybe he takes care of her."

Eli, thought Mary.

"Does she scream for help?"

"Often." Mary now. She was beginning to feel the exercise; she saw the girl, trapped and struggling, the ropes burning her arms, the air heavy and choked with dust. She awaited him, the man who opened the door every afternoon and entered to feed her. What else did he do? Wash her face for her? Was he gentle with her? Did he tell her that there were only a few days left unless someone found her, or did she know that she was going to be murdered?

"Trippy says she's in a storage facility, just off of Interstate 64 in Piercetown."

"That's where that college is," said someone. "Grady Tech."

Mary opened her eyes. She felt it: the electricity, the closeness of vital information. It was right there, behind Williams's closed eyes. If she could only know what he knew then she could find Polly.

She wasn't being logical enough. She knew that. She wasn't seeing the thing the way it was presented. She had been playing wild cards this whole time when she should have been safer. *Not anymore*, she thought.

"If Trippy knows where she is, then that limits our suspects," she said, her voice definite and rigid.

"It does, doesn't it," Williams agreed.

"Mike or Pig," someone else said.

"Or Trippy himself," put in Dennis Flaherty.

Wait, she thought.

Williams had given it to her. Yes. It was right there in front of her.

Interstate 64.

That's where that college is. Grady Tech.

Suddenly, with startling clarity, it came to her. It was there before she knew it, flashing across her mind. She realized that she had always known it, she had just needed the slightest provocation to give her the proof.

"The bike," Mary said.

"Ms. Butler?"

"The motorcycle. Pig's. He kept it in a storage facility off Interstate 64. That's where Polly is."

Everyone in the class now was wide-eyed. They were all looking straight at her. She felt the buzz of success, the nearly electric whistle in her ears. She was suddenly euphoric. She almost couldn't contain it: it ricocheted within her, snapped this way and that and made her, for the first time that term, *alive* with the possibilities her discovery had presented.

"Motive?" asked Williams slyly. But she could see it in his eyes: she had broken him. She had tied the clues together and had given him his man.

"Obsession," Dennis Flaherty replied, still looking at Mary. His eyes said all she needed to know: *Well done, Mary.*

"Yes," Williams said. He was disoriented, looking away. Mary had shocked him, and now he didn't know how to carry on with the class. "Well. Check your e-mail tonight. There might be a little more information about Polly there. We will review for our final exam on Wednesday, and we will take the exam next week." With that, he walked out of the classroom. Even his walk was hesitant, disturbed somehow. None of the students moved from their seats; they sat listening to his footsteps recede down the hallway toward the stairs that would lead him up to his office.

Afterward, as the others stood in the hallway and talked, Mary again stood off to the side. They were all pleased, chattering excitedly as if they had received their final marks in the class. Now, of course, everyone would receive an A for Logic and Reasoning 204. "Mary, you trumped my theory," Dennis Flaherty said, faux hurt in his voice. "I thought for sure it was Mike." They all agreed. Everyone had thought it was Mike, the boyfriend, the most obvious of the suspects. Williams seemed, they said, like someone who would be big on obvious misdirection—present something so apparent that everyone would discredit it because of its simplicity. It *had* to turn out to be Mike in the end, they had all thought. But Mary had seen through his ruse and connected the storage facility to Pig. "Did you see how he walked out of class?" said one girl. "It was like he was an angry child." And Williams *had* looked like a child, stunned and pouting. Mary should have been pleased, but something was bothering her. She stood with her laptop clutched to her chest, her mind wandering.

Dennis walked her back to the Tau house for her shoes. He apologized for Saturday night, claimed that she had misinterpreted what he'd actually said. "It was just a thing you say, you know," said Dennis, looking at the sidewalk. "It turned out to be the wrong thing, though." It was drizzling in one of those sideways manners, coming down cold against their faces. Mary should have been happy, and at first she had been. But seeing Williams walk out of the room had disturbed her for some reason.

An act.

"Is something wrong?" Dennis asked her. She didn't say anything, but yes—something was wrong. Something was very wrong, but of course she couldn't tell Dennis. He left her in the great room of the frat house, which was nearly empty. At 5:00 p.m. everyone was out to the dining commons or on a beer run to the Border. Someone was playing Oasis in an upstairs room. She could smell the moistness of marijuana in the air. She looked around the room. There were bookshelves built into one wall. Instead of books, the Taus had lined the shelves with DVDs and CDs, many of them pirated from the Internet and labeled with crude, markered covers. She rifled through some of the movies—action flicks, the Austin Powers films, directors' cuts of kung fu movies—and as she was doing this she saw something etched on the back wall of the shelf. She leaned closer, squinting so that the image became clear in the shadow.

She had seen the image before. It was a serpentine *S* and the soft *P* tangled together. It had been *carved* into the shelf. Mary traced her finger over it, felt the harshness of the cut rubbing across her finger.

Troy Hardings's hand. His tattoo.

She wanted to get closer, to look—

"Ready?" Dennis asked. She spun around as if she had been caught stealing. He was holding her shoes.

He walked her back to Brown. He was quiet the entire way, and Mary found herself feeling sorry for him. "I didn't know Troy Hardings was a Tau," she said.

"Who?" Dennis asked.

"Troy. Professor Williams's gofer."

"I don't know who that is."

Mary thought about this. She wondered what it meant, that aggressive *S* and the passive *P* tangled up in a casual dance. And then something absurd came into her mind. A bizarre thought.

Save Polly.

Perhaps a Tau had taken Williams's class long ago and had etched the symbol on the wall. Maybe Troy Hardings saw the image there at a party one night and liked the way it looked so much that he tattooed himself with it.

Maybe, Mary thought. But still—there was something about the image that frightened her. She didn't like how the feminine *P* was being squeezed and taunted by the more masculine *S*. There was something cultish about the image, something mockingly boyish. It was an inside joke. She tried to imagine Dennis tattooing himself with the image, sneering at the needle as it bit into his flesh—but the thought was so ludicrous that it fell apart.

Later, back at Brown Hall, she took the elevator up to her room and sat at her desk, watching the rain slant off the room's only window.

Later, when it got dark and the rain began to fall harder, she checked her e-mail. There was a message in the box titled "Where Is She?" Mary opened the message and another photograph appeared on the screen, this one of a U-Stor-It beside a busy freeway.

That was the only message, which meant that Williams was admitting Polly's location and her abductor.

But still there was that feeling inside Mary, that incomplete feeling. It was the same feeling she had gotten in high school when the teacher left the room one day during an exam, and the students had taken out their textbooks from under their desks, furiously paging through them to find the answers.

Her victory, then, if it could even be called that, had been Pyrrhic. Finding Polly had been *too easy*.

23

A Disappearance in the Fields had been checked out of the Orman Library. Brian knew what that meant: someone else in the class had beaten him to it. But there was still hope. He searched the computerized card catalog and found that the public library had a copy of the book. He drove there, Johnny Cash howling "Ring of Fire" on the stereo, with the rain falling hard on his windshield.

As he drove, Brian thought of Deanna Ward. And he thought of her doppelgänger, the girl from the trailer in Bell City.

It struck us all: how similar she looked to Deanna, the man playing Detective Thurman had told the class. *She was almost an identical copy, except she was . . . different somehow.*

By Monday afternoon, as the rest of the logic class was meeting in Seminary East and Mary was solving Polly's disappearance, Brian was working on another vase for his mother at the kilns. He was trying to get his mind off Polly.

But by that night he was thinking of the book Bethany Cavendish had told him about earlier in the day. The thought of it was like a hunger pang. He couldn't shake it no matter what he did. He went back to Chop, started a second glass vase, but before he could get the blowpipe into the kiln he was thinking about the book again.

The thing was this: he had possibly played a small part in this drama. By meeting the girl named Polly at the Deke party, he had intervened in the mythology that Leonard Williams had created. And shouldn't he be interested in something that he had personally been involved in, Brian rationalized in front of the glowing kiln, no matter how indirectly?

And what about the second narrative, the real one? Shouldn't he be interested in Deanna Ward, a girl who had been missing for twenty years?

He had decided to check the public library, and now, powerless against this urge to find out more, he drove down Pride Street and into the town proper. There was no one in the library when he went in except the librarian, and Brian found the book easily. It had been moved down from its spot on the shelf and was leaning apart from the other books, making it apparent that someone had been there before him. The title was printed large across the front in bold red letters to give the effect of blood writing. On the back, Leonard Williams smiled at him. It was a younger, more polished Williams. His face was thinner, and he had a fine trace of a mustache. The book had been published in 1995 by Winchester University Press. *"Leon Williams is a professor at Winchester University in DeLane, Indiana,"* the bio on the inside jacket read. "A Disappearance in the Fields *is his first book. He lives in DeLane with his wife."*

As Brian was checking out the book, the librarian, an older woman who taught a study skills class at the university, looked at him curiously. Immediately, without hesitation, he thought: *Actor.*

"Do you reat much true crime?" she asked conversationally, her accent thick and difficult to place.

"No," he said. "I'm just reading this one for a class."

"Oh. This is a goot one. He came here for a reating once. Williams. Right after it was published? Ya. He set he had some 'new information,' but he couldn't give it to us. Promised a new book in the spring. That was almost five years ago."

Brian took out *A Disappearance in the Fields* and drove back toward campus. He turned right out of the library onto Pride, which was one way in downtown DeLane, and followed it all the way to the bypass and hit Highway 72—the quickest way back to campus. The highway drops down and turns onto Montgomery Street, which winds around the Thatch River and then rises a hill to Winchester.

As he was turning onto Montgomery, he saw a figure crouched in the undergrowth to his right. At first he thought it had been a trick of the light. An animal, probably. But before he could speed up the thing rose and stepped out of the undergrowth. It had one arm up, signaling him to stop. *A woman.*

Brian stopped the truck and eased onto the shoulder. He rolled down the passenger window. The woman leaned into the cab and said breathlessly, "You've got to help me." The woman was familiar to him, somehow, but he couldn't place her. Had he seen her around Winchester? It was so dark with the dense clouds masking the moon.

Brian, before he knew what he was doing, unlocked the door and the woman climbed in. She was wearing a cocktail dress that was torn, and her face was scratched and bloodied. Her fingernails were black with mud. He drove toward Winchester and listened to the woman's harsh, labored breath. She looked straight ahead, never at him, her eyes wide open with shock.

"What happened to you?" he finally asked. "Do you want me to take you to the hospital?"

The woman shook her head softly. The wind was whistling through the cab, and it chilled Brian to the bone. The woman, even though her arms were bare, did not seem to notice.

"Here," she said, pointing at Turner Avenue. They drove straight down Turner, the street that skirted the southern edge of campus.

He stopped at the light in front of the Gray Brick Building and a few students crossed the street. The woman, who had not spoken more than that one word since he picked her up, said, "I told him not to. I told him not to. I *told him.*" She was crying now. Brian noticed a nick on her temple that was oozing blood. The driver in the car behind him blew his horn, and Brian looked up to see that the light had turned green. The woman had her face buried in her hands now, and he asked, "Who? Who hurt you?" She shook her head again, trying to regain control of herself. She gestured for him to turn onto Pride. "My husband owns a boat," she said, and suddenly Brian realized who she was. "And there's a man who watches it for us. This . . . former cop. Here." Brian made a right onto Pride Street. "He drives by every now and then and just keeps the kids away." She stopped, pointed to a side road for Brian to turn onto. "Tonight I was on the boat, just cleaning some stuff up, you know. Getting it ready for some people who are coming by next weekend. And he came onto the boat. I didn't know who it was at first. I tried to get him off me, but he wouldn't. He kept *tearing* at me, *ripping* at my face. He was in a rage. He was . . . he was impossible to stop. He covered my eyes and took me out somewhere, to this . . . room or something. I don't know. I couldn't see anything. No one came. I was there for what seemed like hours, and no one came.

"And then he came back. He came back and he took the blindfold off and I saw that I was in this garage. There was a motorcycle there, all these stray parts laying around. He said that he would kill me if I told anyone what he had done. He said . . ." She wept then, just a little jagged sob, into her hands.

"I don't want my husband to know," she told Brian. "He'll kill him if he finds out. He'll just murder him." She flicked her wrist toward a steep side road that spurred off Pride Street, and they sat in front of her house, the engine running. All the lights were on inside, and apparently the old man was waiting inside. Brian felt immovable, heavy with fear. He managed to ask if she needed help getting inside. "It's okay," she whispered. She got out of the truck and closed the door behind her. Through the open window she thanked him. The night was harsh, too dark somehow. Elizabeth Orman's black, ragged dress disappeared up the walk and then she appeared again when the front door opened, inside the slice of light from the living room. Then she was gone.

24

Mary was sleeping when Brian knocked on her door. It had to be after eleven o'clock at night, maybe later. She bolted upright, banging her head on the bar that ran beneath the top bed. (She had kept the bunks because it was a school rule to have bunk beds in every dorm room. "Just in case," one of the deans had told her indignantly, "something happens and you have to take on a mate.")

She found Brian pacing nervously in the hall. "Something's happened," he told her when she opened the door.

Inside, she made him some of the cheap Lipton tea that she drank. He didn't touch it. His attention was elsewhere. He wouldn't sit for long, even though she had pulled up a chair for him. All he could do was walk, pace the room, and shake his head as if to clear it of unwanted thoughts.

"First," he said. "Williams wrote a book about that girl, the one that detective told us about. Deanna."

"What?"

"Yeah," said Brian. "But here's the interesting part." Brian took the book out of his bag and handed it to Mary. He handled it as if it were electric, as if the thing held some deadly power. The cover of *A Disappearance in the Fields* showed a house bordering cornfields and a pitch-black, ominous sky. It was written by Leon Williams.

"Look in it," he said. "Flip through it."

She did.

As the pages crept across her thumb, she felt her heart pattering with the same uneven, clipped rhythm as it had earlier in the day, when she was close to finding Polly.

There were only sentences on the first few pages. The rest of the pages were nonsense, two words appearing back to back for the entirety of the book: *for the*. Page after page of those two words: *for the for the for the for the.*

"Why?" was all she could say.

"I don't know," Brian admitted.

"Could be a mistake. Could be that the publisher made an error."

"I thought of that. So I drove all the way out to Cale Community College. They were closed. Had to beg the reference librarian to let me in. Same thing in that book. A few pages of text and then"—he flipped through the book as Mary had done, marveling at the thing—"this. Two books with mistakes this severe? No way."

"What does it mean, Brian?"

"I think it's Williams," he said. "I think he's doing this. He's trying to see how far we'll go with it. Trying to lead us off track. It's all part of the class."

Mary thought about that explanation. "But," she told him, "the class ended."

"What?"

"I figured it out. Williams said something about a storage facility, and I remembered one of the earlier clues. It's Pig. Pig has Polly."

Brian looked distraught, as if he could not quite understand what she had just told him.

"There's one other thing, though," she said.

"What is it?"

"It's just that—"

"Tell me, Mary."

"It's just that it was so *easy*. It was like Williams wanted us to have the answer. After all this, after all these games, why would he just *tell us* the answer?"

"Maybe it wasn't the answer," Brian said.

"What do you mean?"

"I mean maybe there's more. Maybe there's a whole other level to this thing."

Mary considered that. Her tea steamed in her face, and she kept her mug there, feeling the warmth on her eyes.

"But you could tell," she said. "You could tell that I had cracked it, Brian. The way he talked. The way he walked out of the room. It was like he was . . . like he was *shocked*."

"You said it yourself, Mary," Brian urged. "You said that it didn't feel right. It doesn't to me either. What about this girl, Deanna Ward? What about his book? What parts do they play?"

"Did you know that his wife wrote me a note? Saying that she wasn't—that none of it was real?"

"A note?"

"At the party Sunday night."

"You went to the party?"

"Yes," Mary said. She felt herself blush; she was ashamed for not having told him. "She was trying to tell me something, Brian," she continued. "She was trying to get me involved, and I didn't listen to her. I thought it was all part of the hoax. But now . . . now I don't know."

Again, she was beginning to feel the familiar uneasiness that she had felt all along. She was beginning to slip back into it, like Quinn with Stillman in *City of Glass*, and no matter how she fought it now it was coming on, forcing her to rethink all that she had believed to be true just seven hours earlier.

"What do we do?" she asked him.

"We've got to stop the class. It's madness that he's been allowed to go on this long anyway."

"Dean Orman," she said. "We go to his office tomorrow morning and tell him what we know. We show him the book."

Brian said nothing. She felt in his silence something else, some other pressing issue that he wanted to tell her but hadn't yet.

"What, Brian?" she prodded him.

Brian sat down across from her. She pulled two folding chairs up to the card table she used to eat her dinner when she cooked in Brown. He didn't sit so much as he *crashed* down, the chair creaking a little under him. He exhaled loudly and rubbed his face with both hands as if to wipe away some of what he had seen. "Orman's wife," he said. "Elizabeth? I picked her up tonight in the bushes down by the Thatch River. She'd been beaten by someone."

"You can't be serious."

"As a heart attack. Listen, she told me not to tell anyone. She said Orman would kill the guy if I told. So we have to keep that quiet until I can figure out something else. I really don't think—Mary, I don't think that was part of the game. I think she was telling the truth. She looked awful."

"Oh God," Mary said. She felt tears in her eyes, the heat of anxiety in the pit of her stomach. She closed her eyes and tried to will herself not to cry. "Oh no. Oh God."

"Mary," Brian said gently. "Here." And then his arm was around her. They were hugging each other, but strangely there was nothing romantic about it. It was just something you did, a healing act. She felt his heat and she stayed there in his chest until he pulled away, and when she was standing up on her own she didn't regret what she'd done.

He lay on the top bunk and she took the bottom. Mary knew that he wasn't sleeping by his uneven breath, by the way he could not be still. Like him, her rest was labored, erratic. "Brian," she said. It was late, sometime after midnight. A siren passed outside, screamed down Pride Street. "Did you know that Williams has an assistant?"

25

They found Troy in the online campus directory. Beside his name they saw the familiar lightning bolt, which meant that he was online. "Let's e-mail him," Brian said.

"You mean now?"

"Hell yeah, now. I want to see what he knows."

Slowly, still pacing the room, Brian dictated the message to Mary.

To: thardings@winchester.edu
From: mbutler@winchester.edu
Subject: Professor Williams

Troy,

We found Williams's book, *A Disappearance in the Fields.* A very fine book. A masterpiece. We were wondering—did Williams write that himself, or did he have help from someone in the Philosophy Department? By the way, it was Pig. I guess you know that by now.

M

They waited. Mary refreshed her screen a few times, hoping that Troy would get the e-mail and respond to it immediately. Brian made himself another mug of tea in the microwave. Down on the quad, a fire burned—the every-Monday bonfire of the Delta girls, who were notorious for showing up to their early classes smelling of smoke and with their hands stained with soot.

"Maybe he's working on a paper," Brian said.

Mary felt the first signs of exhaustion coming on. It descended on her suddenly, pulling her down toward the floor. If she could just lie down, if she could just—

"Mary." Brian was pushing her shoulder, waking her. She looked at him. Blinked. He pointed at the screen, and she saw a message from Troy in her in-box.

To: mbutler@winchester.edu
From: thardings@winchester.edu
Subject: Belated Congratulations

M,

Congrats on the solve! I solved the one in the spring of '04, and it was a great moment. They were all talking about it today in the department. Leonard thought he was going to fool you all this time, but I guess not.

And yes, I have read Leonard's book. I'm not into true crime, but *A Disappearance . . .* is one of the classics of that genre. A shame it never got the recognition it deserved. That girl, Deanna Ward, she's still missing, you know. Leonard thought he got some new leads a few years ago, but they turned out to be dead ends.

All the best,
Troy

"Why would he lie?" Brian asked.

"Why is anyone lying? Why is the woman at the high school lying, making up a story about a fake book? It's part of the game, Brian. Obviously Troy is playing it, too." She still felt the buzz of sleep in her head, that flagging sensation of late-night fatigue.

"Ask him," Brian said.

"What are you talking about?"

"I mean, ask him. Tell him that the book's a fake. See what he says."

Mary would have never done it had she not been drunk with fatigue. She had spent her life sidestepping such confrontations, but tonight she was feeling bold, ready to tear down Williams's game and get to the heart of this thing that had been plaguing her for the last month.

To: thardings@winchester.edu
From: mbutler@winchester.edu
Subject: One More Thing

Troy,

The book's a fake. A friend and I have secured two copies, and both of them have text on exactly twenty-five pages, an introduction by "Leon Williams," and then nothing for the rest of the book. When we Google *A Disappearance in the Fields*, we get nothing. No Amazon listing, nothing in the Library of Congress database. Winchester University Press hasn't published anything for the last twenty-five years. We want to know exactly what this is and we want it to stop. You and Williams are playing a dangerous game.

M.

Now she felt sped up, her senses awake and aware and her heart mashing through her chest. Brian was pacing again. Outside, the orange flames of the Deltas' fire licked up toward the sky. Mary stared at the screen. She refreshed. Nothing. She drummed her fingers, all the nails bitten to the quick, on her desk. Refreshed again. Nothing. Where was he? Maybe they had scared him off. Maybe they had driven him away. Was it possible that Troy was calling Williams right now and asking what he should do? She expected a call from the "campus police" any minute, another admonition to stop what she was doing. Maybe—

Another message appeared in her box.

To: mbutler@winchester.edu
From: thardings@winchester.edu
Subject: Re: One More Thing

M.,

You and your "friend" don't know what you are getting into here.

Troy

Upon reading it, Brian murmured, "Fuck him," under his breath. With some force, he took the mouse from Mary and clicked Compose. Then he began to type.

To: thardings@winchester.edu
From: mbutler@winchester.edu
Subject: The Game

Troy,

Apparently you don't understand. What's going on here is a criminal enterprise. We have spoken to a woman from Cale High School who has told us the story about Deanna Ward. Leonard Williams has brought in a man impersonating a former police officer, and that man told the class a story about the same girl. Now we have found a book about that girl that was apparently "written" by this Leon character, and the book is a fake. We have already contacted Dean Orman, and he has personally told us that he is keeping Williams on a "short leash." His words. You all do not seem to understand the complexity of this thing. You are dealing with real people, real events, and it doesn't seem to faze you one bit. Now, I suggest you tell us what you know before I come over to Perkins Hall.

It took only a matter of minutes for the next message to appear in her box.

To: mbutler@winchester.edu
From: thardings@winchester.edu
Subject: Re: The Game

M. (or whomever),

I assume that I am not speaking to Mary Butler anymore. It's not the most feminine thing to do, threatening to beat someone up at 12:15 a.m. Anyway. As for your concerns:

This is not a "game," as you seem to think. What's happening now is bigger than anything you have ever experienced before. Suffice it to say that you or your girlfriend have NOTHING to do with any of this. You are just bystanders, mere extras. You will be used when your time comes, but do not think for one moment that you have any central role in this. Don't fool yourselves. You are simply being played right now, and when these six weeks are over you will go back to your lonely, simple lives as college students. You say, "You all do not seem to understand the complexity of this thing." No, it is YOU who do not understand the complexity of this. But you soon will.

As for Dean Orman, we are not the least worried about him. We have—how shall I say it—*dominion* over the dean.

Good night.

Troy

They both sat, staring at the monitor. Neither of them quite believed what they had just read. What was this "happening" that Troy had referred to, Mary wondered. But no sooner had she asked the question than Troy's lightning bolt disappeared, signaling that he was offline.

Back in their beds again, Mary asked Brian, "Do you think we're in danger?"

At first he didn't answer. And then he said, "I don't know what to think anymore."

According to the clock, it was after 3:30 a.m. by the time she went to sleep. She knew that Brian was awake because he was still tossing above her on the top bunk, and even though she was afraid she closed her eyes and an impenetrable weight closed in over her. The last thing she thought was, *What if Brian is in on it?*

26

Mary walked into Seminary East that Wednesday expecting to review for the exam that Williams was giving next week.

But Williams was late. As they waited, a few students talked about their other classes or gossiped about the goings-on around campus. Dennis Flaherty opened his briefcase and took out his economics text and began to highlight a chapter. The girl beside Mary filed her nails. Brian was still boycotting the class, and his back-row seat remained empty.

Five minutes passed, and there was discussion about how long they should give Williams before they abandoned the classroom. "Knowing Williams," someone said, "he's scheduled a field trip and hasn't told anyone." They all had a laugh over that. But Mary was concerned. She could not help but wonder if her and Brian's discussion with Troy Hardings had something to do with the professor's lateness.

At 4:20 p.m., Dean Orman walked into the room. As always, he was overdressed, with his three-piece suit and Cole Haan loafers. The wind had ripped him apart; his orange hair was disheveled and the ridiculous flower he wore in his lapel was almost shredded to nothing.

Orman took Williams's place at the podium. He looked small up there, tiny. He sighed, as if he were about to deliver some devastating piece of news to the class. Mary could not help but think of the man's wife and what Brian had said about her, and she wondered if Dean Orman had found out about what had happened to her.

"As a dean," Orman began, "it's never easy to inform a class that something will . . . impede the process of learning. 'In delay there lies no plenty,' as Shakespeare said. But what's done is done, and it is now my duty to inform you about what has happened."

Orman steeled himself. Mary thought, *Williams is dead. They've killed him.* But she had no earthly idea about who "they" might be, nor could she summon in her mind any possible situation that would pit *Williams* as the victim in this whole thing.

"Your professor is gone," the dean said. Mary felt nothing. No fear. No confusion. She was void. Bankrupt of anything like empathy or wonder about why he had left. It, like everything else in Logic and Reasoning 204, was just a fact of the narrative, an irreversible plot detail that was simply a trope in the twisted, bizarre script Williams had written for them. "He was not in his office this morning," said the dean, "and all his things had been cleaned out. This is a . . . a disturbing turn of events, to say the least. But rest assured we are trying to find Dr. Williams as we speak, and when we do we will get a full disclosure of why he chose to leave campus a week before the six weeks' end."

Now Williams had become a player in his own game. There was really no question. He was inside the drama, and Mary suddenly wondered if it was over or if it had just begun. She wished Brian were here to help her with this new turn of events.

"If you need anything," Dean Orman was saying, "all you have to do is come to Student Services and talk to Wanda. She will be happy to assist you with any questions you have. And of course you will all be reimbursed for this class and awarded the full three credits."

Afterward, Mary immediately went to find Brian. He was in the Orman Library, sitting at a table in the back. He was staring out a

window, a textbook open in front of him. He had still not recov-
ered from Monday night and their discussion with Troy Hardings, it
appeared.

"Williams is gone," she told him.

He blinked at her. "You're kidding."

"Cleaned out his office. Orman came to class to break the news."

"Troy must have told him about our discussion."

Mary didn't say anything, but her silence betrayed her. She knew
as well as Brian did that the two events could not be isolated. As
Williams had told them so long ago, randomness was not the rule
but rather the exception to the rule.

"What do we do now?" he asked.

"We could find Hardings and ask him about it. Find out what's
going on. Threaten him in some way."

"Already did it," Brian said somberly. "His roommate said he went
home for the week. I had a chat with him earlier. He wasn't
very . . . forthcoming."

"Of course he wasn't."

They sat in the silence of the library, thinking about what they
should do next. It seemed they were at the end now, at the apex of
the game, yet neither of them was quite sure how to proceed.

And then something dawned on her, something so obvious that
Mary wondered why she had not thought about it before now.

"Dennis Flaherty," she said.

"Dennis the Menace?" asked Brian skeptically.

"Let's go visit him. He owes me one, anyway."

Dennis Flaherty was grilling hot dogs on the Tau house roof. He
was wearing a tank top and rubber flip-flops, and Mary thought he
looked like somebody's dad. "Mary Butler!" he greeted her, with too
much enthusiasm in his voice.

"We're here to talk about Williams," Mary told him.

Dennis looked at Brian, a puzzled expression on his face. "Yeah, what a thing, huh?" he asked, turning one of the wieners. "You gonna join us for dinner?"

"We don't buy our friends," replied Brian. There was a moment of charged hesitation between the two boys, and finally Dennis broke it by looking down, smirking at the grill.

Mary stepped between them. "What happened to him, Dennis?"

"Why are you asking me?" he asked, shock in his voice. "I'm just as surprised as you are."

"I know you were talking to him. I could tell when we were— when we spoke at his house that night."

"What are you talking about?" He shut the grill's lid and hung his spatula on the side. The Taus had a gigantic Weber, a veritable legend on campus, and they had been forced to chain it to the house itself to keep the Dekes from stealing it.

"Cut the shit, Dennis." Brian took a step toward Dennis, his finger jabbing accusingly toward the other boy. "We're not playing a game anymore." But of course that was the problem: they *were* playing a game. It was all part of Williams's game, and that was what made it so confoundingly difficult to understand.

"I talked to him once," Dennis said, looking off the roof, toward Up Campus, where some students were staging a protest about the tuition hike that was about to come into effect. The protesters walked slowly across the viaduct, their signs bobbing in the air above them. "Maybe twice. We just talked about Polly. About the class. It was nothing. Look, if you two think that I may have had something to do with Williams skipping town—"

"It's not that," Mary said sharply. "It's just that there are other things. Things you don't know about yet."

"What other things, Mary?"

Brian produced the book. He showed it to Dennis carefully, as if

it contained a terrible secret. Brian flipped through the book, paus-
ing on some of the pages as if a story could be told in the nonsense
language.

"What the hell is it?" Dennis asked.

"It's Williams's book about the girl, Deanna. The girl from Cale
that detective talked about."

"Except it's not a book," Dennis said flatly, as if he was still trying
to grasp the concept of the two words—*for the for the for the for the
for the*—on those pages.

"Right," Brian put in. "This is why I believe—we believe—that
this is all part of some kind of . . . *ploy* on Williams's part." Brian explained it all to Dennis: uncovering the detective, Brian's trip to
Cale High and his discussion with Bethany Cavendish, the cryptic
phrase Mary had seen on that typed page in Williams's office, Della
Williams's note to Mary on the night of the party, and finally his and
Mary's e-mails to Troy Hardings.

"Shit," whispered Dennis. He opened the Weber and transferred
the hot dogs to a plastic plate. For a few moments he was silent,
contemplating what he had heard. "So you think Williams had
something to do with this girl in Cale?"

It was the first time anyone had expressed it in words. Yet it had
been there, unspoken between Brian and Mary, from the moment he
had showed up at Brown late two nights before. Bethany Cavendish
had told Brian, *It was as if he was there.* An innocuous admonition at
the time, but now, looking back with all the information they had
gathered in the last day, it carried an undeniable weight.

"I think so," Brian said.

The knowledge of what they were involved with now fell on
them, and they stood silently on the hot roof of the Tau house, contemplating their roles in what was happening.

"What do we do?" Dennis asked. His brothers were at the door
asking for the food, and he passed the plate inside.

Brian and Mary had already spoken about it on the way to the Tau house. They had decided that there was no other way around it, that if they wanted this thing to stop they had to go the whole way, and to do that they must get to the root of it. They must find a missing girl, again, for a second time, and then Williams's role might be revealed. Mary had already resigned herself to the fact that she would not be going home this weekend to study as she had promised; in fact, she had already called and told her mother. When her mom asked if Dennis was somehow involved in Mary's decision to stay at school, Mary had neither confirmed or denied it.

"We have to find her," she told Dennis now, referring for the first time not to Polly but to Deanna Ward.

27

That night, he met Elizabeth at the Cossack, a little bar on the border of DeLane and Cale. She was already drunk. He slid across from her and she looked at him, her glare unfocused, sloppy. "What's wrong with you?" he asked. They had been talking again in the library, and while Dennis had to admit it wasn't like before, there was still a certain charge to it. She was at least acknowledging him again, looking at him and considering his thoughts.

"Nothing," she slurred. "This—this damned dissertation." The word was dirty on her tongue, a swear.

"So, I'm going to be busy these next few days," he told her.

She only nodded heavily.

"I'm going with some friends of mine on a trip," he said.

Again, that slow nod. She knew all of this, of course, but he was making sure. Making sure she knew so that she would remember when he returned, so that maybe—maybe that old energy would return. Who knew: maybe that would be his reward. In just a week, he had gone from angry at her—the kind of anger that is unhealthy, vile—to something else. Something like desperation. Yes, he admitted it: he was *desperate* for Elizabeth now that she had turned him away. Dennis stayed awake at night thinking of ways to bring her back.

They were silent for a moment. And then she said, "I got a tattoo." When Dennis didn't say anything, she continued, "Want to see?"

He stared at her as she tore back a square of gauze and showed him the back of her hand. "Isn't it cool? You ever seen anything like that?"

"No," he lied. "No I haven't."

In the blood-dotted ink he saw an S and a P, entangled.

Cale & Bell City

ONE WEEK LEFT

28

They had planned the Cale trip for Saturday, but it turned out that Dennis had a mandatory charity event with the Taus, so they postponed it until early the next week. Brian and Mary spent the weekend sitting in her room at Brown, anxiously waiting on a call from Dennis. They played Uno, their hands moistening the deck until it was so slick that it could not be shuffled. They watched re-runs of *Seinfeld* and *Friends* and Mary's entire DVD collection: *Persuasion, Elizabeth*, Mel Gibson's *Hamlet*. They listened to Mary's CDs, falling asleep here and there to the Weepies and Cat Power and the Arcade Fire. They spoke to each other in short, clipped phrases about anything not related to Deanna Ward.

On Sunday afternoon, Mary checked her mail at the campus post office and found a crude package in the box. It was a mangled manila envelope that had been taped and lined with a series of months-old *Attn*'s on the outside. Her name was the last in the line: *M. Butler*.

Mary waited until she returned to Brown Hall to open it. Inside, she found a VHS tape. Someone had written on the white strip in the middle of the tape, *This might help.*

She pulled out her old VCR from under the bed and plugged it in. She and Brian sat in front of the television and waited for an image to appear. The film was grainy. Lines ran through the wavering picture, making it difficult to see what was happening.

But Mary had seen this film once before. It had been freshman year, in Dr. Wade's Psychology 101: The Milgram Experiments.

The experimenter was asking the subject a question. This man, Mary knew, was being paid by Milgram to scream when the participant pushed the buttons on the "shock generator." When the subject answered a question incorrectly, the participant said, "You will now get a shock of one hundred and five volts," and he pushed a button on the machine. The subject in the next room cried out in mock pain. The participant said, "Just how far can you go on this thing?"

The scientist, who was also one of Milgram's actors, said, "As far as is necessary."

The participant said, "What do you mean 'as far as is necessary'?"

"To complete the test," the scientist said.

The participant continued. The next time the subject answered incorrectly, the participant pushed a button and said, "One hundred and fifty volts."

Again, the subject cried out. "Get me out of here!" the man shouted. "I told you I have heart problems. My heart's starting to bother me now."

"It is essential that you continue," the scientist told the participant.

The screen went black. But there was still audio coming from the television, a scratching sound that resembled someone rubbing fabric over a microphone.

A man's voice said, "I don't—"

"Bring it here," another man said sharply. "Bring it the hell over here."

"Can't," the first man said.

"Listen, she's got—"

"Deanna. Call her Deanna."

"Whatever. Listen. She's not doing good. It's her breathing. It's her color."

"Like chalk."

"What?"

"Like sidewalk chalk. That's what she looks like. I used to play with it at my grandma's house. We'd draw hopscotch on the sidewalks, and—"

"Listen to me. Would you shut up and listen to me? We need to do something. We need to—"

"Turn it off," Mary whispered, and when Brian didn't hear her she began to shout, "Turn it off! Turn it off! Please turn it off!"

Later, they sat in her room and ate lukewarm soup. They hadn't spoken about the tape or the weird audio at the end. "Did you recognize the voices?" Mary asked.

"No. They sounded like they were . . . inside something. An airport hangar. Or a—"

"Cave," she said. "It sounded like a cave. The echo."

"Yeah," he said, turning his soupspoon over and letting the broth drip into the bowl.

"So how old was the audio on that tape?" asked Mary.

"It sounded old," Brian said. "Years. It was . . . scratchy."

"But what if it wasn't? What if she's still there in that place? What if whoever sent the tape was trying to tell us something, trying to lead us to her? She's sick, Brian. You heard it. She's not . . . not breathing right. Should we take it to the police?"

"There's no"—he picked up the package the tape had come in and studied it—"return address here. I don't know what they would do with it. What does it say, anyway? It's meaningless."

Mary said nothing, only stared blankly out the window and down to the quad.

"He was testing evil," Brian finally said.

Mary didn't say anything. Her soup steamed in her face; she closed her eyes and felt its warmth on her lids.

"Milgram," he went on. "Williams didn't mention that part in class."

"I know," she said.

"The participant would go as far as the scientist would tell him to go. He was afraid of the scientist. He was . . ."

"Obedient," Mary whispered.

"Yeah, obedient. Most of them went so far that the screams stopped in the other room. Milgram's subject was playing dead. And still the participant would go on."

Mary was looking off, through the open window and down to the quad. She shook her head. It was all elusive, so abstract but entirely cruel. She didn't know what it meant, yet she had a notion about what it *could* mean.

"Did Williams send it?" he asked.

"I don't think so," she told Brian. "I think somebody's trying to warn us about him."

"Orman," Brian said. "Orman studied with Milgram at Yale. Maybe he's trying to tell us something about Williams."

"But what about Deanna?" Mary asked.

Yes, what about Deanna? It was the only part of this she could verify; she had the documentation to prove it. What was unclear was how Williams's story, and how Williams himself, connected with Deanna Ward. Until Mary could somehow find the answer to that question, all else—Williams's puzzles, Brian's story about Elizabeth Orman, and now this mysterious tape—would be inconsequential.

29

They left on Tuesday afternoon, one day before the deadline Williams had given them. They drove to Cale, unsure of where they would go once they got there. Mary had the idea that they would find Bethany Cavendish again, but it was decided among them that Cavendish was possibly a part of Williams's game, since she had put Brian on the trail of the book that was not a book. Dennis thought they should drive out to Bell City to ask around about the girl who had been returned to Wendy Ward, the girl who had been mistaken for Deanna.

But that was for later, they decided. They had to ask a few questions in Cale first, because Cale was where it had all begun. Mary suggested that they go to the house on During Street, where the elderly couple lived (if Cavendish could be trusted with even this information), and the boys agreed that it was probably the best place to start.

They drove Dennis Flaherty's Lexus, and Mary felt a kind of nostalgia the whole way there. She had spent time in this car. There: she had reached across and taken Dennis's hand one night on the way back from a play in Indianapolis. And there: he had kissed her, pulling her across the seat toward him. They were confusing memories, and she had to look out the window, at the blurring scenery, to get it out of her mind.

They got lost on the back roads of Cale. Brian had the map spread across his lap in the backseat, and he and Dennis had a spat when it was determined that they'd missed their turn and gone five miles out of their way. Dennis, sighing in an exaggerated manner, turned the Lexus around in a gravel turnabout and made his way back into town.

Finally, they found During Street, its sign bent and nearly shrouded by a weeping willow that was growing beside the road. If there is such a place as the "backwoods," they were there. During Street was a tree-shrouded lane, and from the road you could see the blue expanse of the Thatch River. The vegetation was thick— river foliage, dark leaves and dark soil, kudzu falling in torrents all around. A few cabins, probably only used in the summer, were falling into disrepair here and there.

Brian claimed that he would know the couple's house by the field that Bethany Cavendish had described to him. And there it was, just ahead on the right, a simple Cape Cod with an American flag flying out front.

"Polly's house," Mary said, referring to the transparency they had seen in Williams's class the first week.

An old man answered the door. Dennis, because he looked the part of a salesman, was appointed their speaker. "We were wondering," Dennis said through the mesh of the screen door, "if you wouldn't mind talking to us for a few minutes about the girl who used to live here." Although Brian would not have used such honesty, Dennis's tactic seemed to work. The old man opened the door for them and let them inside.

"We find some of her stuff sometimes," an old woman explained once they were sitting at the kitchen table. Her name was Edna Collins. She fixed them instant coffee and they sat around the table, drinking and listening. The couple, just as Bethany Cavendish had said, was happy to see them. *Lonely*, Mary thought. *They're just aching for company.*

"People come by here all the time," the old man said. "Tourists. Taking pictures. This is a famous site, isn't it, Edna? We're local celebrities." He laughed—a hearty, deep laugh that was larger than his small frame.

"Just the other day I found a doll out in the field. I told Norman,

'I bet you it come from that girl.' We find little things like that all the time out in that field—trinkets, toys, all sorts of objects. Possessions she may have had. All down the hillside, down to the river, we find stuff. Why, I bet you could go out there right now and find enough to fill a house."

"They hide out there sometimes," the old man put in. "Kids. We'll see them out there in the field with their flashlights. God knows what they're doing. Once they were having some kind of ceremony, some evil thing. *Wicca*, I reckon they call it. I went out there with my gun and told them to stop. We don't mind pictures being taken of the house. We knew what we were getting into when we moved in. But I have to draw the line when you're bringing Satan onto my property."

"She was so sweet," Edna said. "I never did meet her, of course, but I've seen pictures. Just a little thing. Deanna. Such a sweet name. How old? Seventeen? Eighteen? Such a tragedy. Even now we look for things from our front porch. We watch to see if there's anything suspicious going on. I always thought they could have taken her down to the river, slipped away in the quiet, you know. How easy that would have been."

They, thought Mary.

"Do you know this man?" Brian asked, showing Edna the photograph of Williams that was on the back of *A Disappearance in the Fields*. They all watched the woman for anything, any tic of deception, but she studied the photo seriously, pulling her bifocals down and pondering it as if the picture were of a long-lost relative she was trying to place in the family tree.

"I don't suppose I do," she said. She handed the book over to her husband, and he also said that he didn't recognize Williams. As far as Mary could tell, they were both sincere.

When they began talking again, reminiscing about their years in the home, Mary excused herself. She followed Edna's directions to the bathroom, shut the door, and looked at herself in the mirror. Her eyes were dark, and her hair, always unruly, the curl prone to frizz and flyaways, was wilder than usual. She turned on the faucet and splashed some water on her bare face. She heard the whir of a motor-boat down the hill on the Thatch, and she wondered about Dean Orman's wife again and her story of being accosted on the boat. *Does it all fit together?* she wondered. *Is the river the connecting theme?*

She left the bathroom and walked down the hallway toward the kitchen. She could hear Edna in there, talking about a family re-union they were planning to have if they could find all the family. She stopped at the end of the hall and looked at the pictures Edna had hung: nieces and nephews, Mary assumed, daughters and sons, all of them light-haired and fair-skinned. She felt a breeze at her feet, and she turned to see if the front door had come open. It hadn't. "It was just fantastic," Edna was saying in the kitchen off to Mary's left. "And they had a fireworks exhibit after the show." Mary looked at these relatives, the kids gap-toothed and their parents too polished somehow, too perfect. One girl was wearing a Cale Central High shirt, and the picture looked to have been taken in the 1980s. Mary assumed that it was Edna and Norman's daughter, as she showed up in later pictures with her family. She wondered if this girl had gone to school with Deanna Ward.

Then she felt it, that breeze again against her ankles. It was cool and sharp, definitely outdoor air. She walked back down the hall-way, trying to find its source. She stood outside the first door and registered it, stiff, against her feet.

Mary cracked open the door and peered in.

The room was empty. The windows were blindless and raised an inch or two, and the walls were half-painted. Paint cans rested here and there around the room. Swaths of blue tarpaulin were laid out on the floor, yet there was no carpet to protect, just the bare board lying across two-by-fours.

Mary shut the door and went to the next room. She opened that door and found the same thing. A bare room, paint cans. There was no tarpaulin here, and the painting had not yet begun. Some stray paper blew around in the breeze. Mary felt her heart tugging at her again, pleading to her to get out of this, to stop it somehow.

She went to the third room. The carpet had been stored in this room, wide rolls of it that were still in their cellophane. She was just about to step inside when she heard a voice behind her: "What are you doing?"

It was Norman Collins. He was looking at her solemnly, as if he were disappointed in her.

Laughter exploded from the kitchen.

"I was just—" Mary began, but she couldn't go on. Lying had never been easy for her. She dealt in truth, and that is what had drawn her to Dennis in the first place.

"We're doing some work," Norman explained. His steely eyes were still on her, probing. He smelled like the outside, like sun and breeze, like her own grandfather.

"I like the paint," Mary managed. He nodded, still searching her with his eyes, his jaw tensing as he breathed.

He was about to say something more when Dennis appeared in the hallway. "I think it's time that we go," he said. Mary slipped by Norman and went to the door, and the three of them thanked the Collinses and walked down the landing steps to the Lexus. Mary could feel Norman watching her walk away, and her heart boomed with each step she took. She got in the car and exhaled loudly, sinking down in the seat beside Dennis.

"What's wrong?" Brian asked from the back. His hand was on Mary's shoulder, and she liked it there, liked the comfort it afforded her.

She told them about the fake rooms and Norman finding her. She hadn't trusted his look, that curious gaze he had given her. She thought he knew something that he hadn't told them.

"Maybe they were really doing a renovation," Dennis said.

"Come on, Dennis," Brian huffed. "Where do they live? That house is tiny. If all the rooms are bare, where do they sleep?"

"What is it, then?" Dennis came back. "They knew we were coming? They just happened to be there when we arrived in a . . . in a fake house? And are they in on this, too? Williams killed Polly—"

"Deanna," Mary corrected him.

"—and they're all trying to cover for him? The woman at the school. Cavendish. This Troy guy at Winchester. The fake wife. Now this old couple. How big is this thing?"

"That's what we've been asking," Brian said flatly.

"How is he doing it?" asked Dennis. "These people are forty miles apart. How is he conducting it on the fly? What, are the Collinses his relatives? Has he paid them to lie for him? Is he trying to—"

Mary had it before Dennis did. She sat up straight and asked, "Is he trying to lead us to something?"

They all thought about that for a moment. The car rolled out During and hit the chip and seal of the connecting road, and Dennis drove back toward Highway 72.

"Maybe Williams didn't have anything to do with Deanna," she said, "but he knows who did. Maybe the deadline . . . maybe it's still applicable."

"The deadline?" Brian asked.

"Tomorrow," she said. "The class was going to end tomorrow. I think something is going to happen."

"But Deanna Ward disappeared twenty years ago, Mary," Dennis said.

"I just think . . ." She trailed off. Her mind was spinning. The answer was somewhere out there; the meaning of all this could be divined, if she could just concentrate hard enough, if she could just focus . . .

"He knows who did it," she said.

"Why would he do that?" Brian now. "To withhold evidence like that is criminal, isn't it? I mean, it makes Williams as culpable as anyone in this thing. In that case he's an accomplice. If he has information, like Bethany Cavendish said, then why not just *say it?*"

"Puzzles," Dennis said. His eyes were on the road, and the sunlight glinted harshly against his sunglasses.

"What?" Brian urged him on.

"He loves puzzles. You should see his study. He had these ancient puzzles from China. They're called tangrams. You cut out these shapes, these silhouettes, and you place them in the puzzle. He had made some . . . weird ones."

"What do you mean 'weird'?" asked Brian.

"I mean some of them were lurid. Some had decapitated heads. Naked bodies. Rapes. They were disgusting. He saw me looking at them and put them away in a closet, but I had already seen enough."

None of them said a word. The road trundled beneath them, kicking up gravel against the undercarriage. Dennis met the intersection of Highway 72 and took a right. Toward Bell City.

"So are you saying that Williams is leading us through this just because he likes puzzles?" Mary asked. "I don't know if I buy that or not."

"What's the other scenario?" Dennis wanted to know. "That Williams is Deanna's abductor? Do either of you believe that?"

Mary thought of his strength when she had pushed him that day in class. His tremendous strength. Did he abduct Deanna Ward and was he now, almost twenty years later, leading them on a wild chase to find her? Or was he intentionally leading them off base, putting up foils to their plan, placing "actors" here and there to drive them away from the truth?

Motive, she then thought. *What would the motive be for playing this game?*

"Well," Dennis said, "I don't believe it. I think what Mary said earlier was right: Williams knows who took Deanna Ward. This is all part of his game."

"Aren't games supposed to be fun?" asked Brian, his voice determined and lacing. "There's nothing fun about a missing girl."

"I'm telling you," Dennis said, "Williams didn't do this. I spoke to him. I know if someone is telling the truth, and he was genuine when he said that Polly was a logic puzzle and nothing more. This other thing, Deanna—I don't know what that is, but I can assure you that Williams is trying to tell us something. Maybe he can't say it the way he wants to say it. Maybe there's someone who knows the truth, and Williams is trying to tell us what he knows without alerting this other person."

Mary thought of the deadline again. She thought of Deanna Ward, and if this could possibly be about her. In a way, it made perfect sense. No wonder Williams's logic game had been so easy: he was just preparing them for the real test.

She thought about the deadline and what it must mean. As they drove across Cale and toward Bell City, she realized that they had only twenty-four hours to locate Leonard Williams and find out what he knew.

30

Bell City is one of the poorest communities in the state of Indiana. It has about five thousand residents and rests on the border of Martin County. It became famous years ago for a basketball game played at Bloomington, where Bell East High School beat number-one-ranked Cale High for a shot at its first-ever state championship.

There is a sign commemorating that feat as you pass into the Bell City limits. It has been dented, pocked by thrown rocks, and nearly torn off its post, surely by Cale residents still bitter about a game that was played almost thirty years ago.

In Bell City there is a Dairy Queen, a bait and tackle shop, and the local high school and junior high. There are a variety of churches, most of them Baptist, some of them falling into disorder along the side of Highway 72. The road in Bell City becomes cracked and pitted because the asphalt has not been tended to in so long. The three of them were entering, it appeared, a ghost town.

They were looking for the girl who had been mistakenly taken to Wendy Ward that fateful day. The police had trailed Deanna's father, Star, to the trailer and arrested him on site. Yet the girl had turned out not to be Deanna. Brian was particularly interested in driving the twenty-five extra miles to see this trailer, though he couldn't tell them exactly what he expected to find.

Dennis stopped for directions at a gas station just outside of downtown. He went inside while Brian put gas in the Lexus. When Dennis returned, he said the attendant had told him to drive to Gary's Diner because apparently Gary was the guy you asked if you had questions of particular importance. The diner was right beside the courthouse, which they saw up on a hill, its dome rising out of the tree line like some sort of battlement. They would probably be able to find somebody there, the attendant said, someone they could talk to about Deanna Ward.

The town proper was nearly dead. There was a furniture store that was open across from the courthouse, and two men were carrying out sofas while others were pinning red sales tags to the upholstery. The three parked at the courthouse and walked the three blocks to Gary's Diner, their jackets tied around their waists and the high sun beating down on their faces.

There were no cars in the parking lot, and the waitresses were all outside the diner, leaning against a picket fence that blocked the patrons' view of the funeral parlor next door. They were all sharing a cigarette, passing it down the line and taking deep drags with their eyes closed. It was an unseasonably hot day in early October, the trees all aflame with wild color.

The women didn't move when they saw the three students coming. They just stood there in a row by that white fence and continued to smoke their cigarette. They were wearing pink, frilly uniforms straight out of the 1950s. It was a different kind of pink, a pink that was softer and more subtle than anything you see today. Mary felt as if she had stepped back in time. Everything was unreal, beginning with Brian's story of the book last week, to Professor Williams's disappearance. And now here she was, in this strange little town, trying to find answers to a question she didn't even know how to phrase.

"How are you doing today, ladies?" Dennis asked the waitresses. Always the charmer.

"We're okay," one of them said dubiously.

"We've just got a couple of questions for you, if you don't mind."

A tall black woman who had assumed the role of spokeswoman nodded.

"We heard about a kidnapping that happened years ago out in Cale. We were just wondering—"

"Deanna," the girl said quickly.

"So you've heard of her?"

"Who hasn't?"

"Wasn't there some tie to Bell City? Something about a girl in a trailer home out on the outskirts of town that looked like Deanna?"

The waitresses looked at each other. Their glances were telling—

they were communicating apprehension among one another, silently wondering how much they should tell these outsiders.

"You'll have to ask Gary about that," the woman said.

"Gary?"

"He's the boss here. He knows everybody in Bell. He'd be able to tell you anything you wanted to know."

"Gary here right now?" asked Brian.

"He's on vacation," the woman said, stubbing out the cigarette on the fence. "Daytona Beach. Be back next week."

"We don't—" Dennis began, but Mary cut him off. She could see where this was going, and for all Dennis's charm he wasn't going to get answers from these girls. She stepped in front of Dennis and smiled at the girl.

"Listen," she said. "We've got this class. We're students down in Winchester. You know how it is. We've all got a paper do this week about the Deanna Ward case, and we need to just drive by that trailer to look at it. For inspiration, you know."

"I'm at Cale Community," said one woman. "Taking twelve hours this semester."

"I always wanted to go to Winchester," the black woman said. "But I couldn't afford it. I made a three-point-five in high school. Got accepted and everything. But the money, you know . . ." She trailed off. Then she looked at Mary, her eyes steady with some deep knowledge. "You're talking about Polly," she said.

Mary felt the breath go out of her. Brian, who was just beside her, took her arm involuntarily, the way you brace yourself as you're falling. "Polly?" Mary managed to say.

"The girl the cops found in the trailer. A lot of people said she looked just like Deanna. She was a few years in front of me in school. Everybody said she was a witch. You know. You know how they do. They get to talking about you and they just don't want to stop. Well, after that thing with Deanna, everybody started talking about Polly like she was some *spirit*. My mom knew her aunt and uncle. That's who she lived with out there on Upper Stretch Road. They finally had to move away from here out to DeLane. Couldn't take it anymore, I guess." The woman paused, looked off in the distance. "I think in a strange way a lot of people *blamed* Polly for Deanna's disappearance. I don't know what that was about. Just because they looked alike? Just because they were both young and pretty? Please. Some people in this town are so backwards. It ain't like Winchester."

With nothing more to ask, the three thanked the waitresses and returned to the Lexus. The day was still and smooth, a few clouds drifted lazily across the sky. Dennis opened all the doors, and they waited as the seats cooled. They felt it now. They were close, close enough where they were nearly one step removed from Deanna Ward.

"What does this mean?" Brian finally asked.

That Williams is the culprit here, Mary thought but didn't say. She didn't want to get into that again, because it was clear that Dennis didn't agree with her theory. She didn't feel like arguing with him, at least not until she knew a little bit more.

"It means that we have to go out to Upper Stretch Road to find that trailer," Dennis said.

"But you heard her, Dennis," Mary said. "They moved away. Polly's gone."

"I think he's leading us there, Mary," Brian said plaintively. "I think we're supposed to go. The detective talked about the trailer, Bethany Cavendish did, and now that waitress."

Mary remained silent. She couldn't debate the point that it seemed as if Williams was, in fact, leading them to the trailer for some reason. She thought about that old comic strip of the carrot on a string leading the mule. This is what she felt like: led, played, not in control of anything she did.

Just as Dennis was bending into the driver's seat, Brian said, "Wait. I have something to tell you." They both looked at him. Mary braced herself for some acknowledgment that Brian had been in on it all along, or that Brian knew where Williams was but had not told them for some reason. But he only said, his voice soft and hesitant, "I met Polly."

"You what?" Dennis asked.

"It was two weeks ago. I'd had too much to drink. This girl started following me around, and we ended up"—diverting his eyes from Mary now, refusing to look at her—"down in Chop Hall, by the kilns. She told me her name was Polly, and of course I didn't believe her. I think I got mad. Irate. I screamed at her. I thought she was part of this, you know. I thought Williams had sent her there to show me up. The next day, this guy told me the story of Deanna Ward."

"How old would Polly be?" asked Mary.

"Thirty-five?" Dennis guessed. "Forty?"

"It was hard to tell," Brian said. "She looked—she looked young. But she was hiding her face. Her hair was over one eye and she kept turning to the side, like she was afraid she was going to reveal herself. Look, guys, I didn't know what it meant. I would have told you if"—he looked at Mary, shame in his face—"if I thought it meant something."

Mary couldn't stifle the laughter that was in her throat then. She let it out and it crashed out into the air like an animal uncaged, her soul finally, after weeks of pressure, finding release in what Brian had said.

"What?" he asked, reddening.

She couldn't answer. She only laughed, and when they were in the car and heading toward Upper Stretch Road, she was still laughing, giggling every now and then into her fist. "Shit," she heard Brian mutter. But then he was laughing, too, and then Dennis, until they couldn't contain themselves anymore.

How silly! thought Mary. *Everything* means *something.*

31

Upper Stretch Road was a sinking stretch of highway in northern Martin County. If they had felt as if they were in the backwoods at the Collinses' house on During Street, then now they were beyond the pale of civilization. Rusted car hulks burned orange under the sun out in front lawns. A group of children, many of them in diapers, played inside the carcass of an old Cale school bus. The road was just a whisper now, nonexistent, pitted and damaged and crumbling down the hillside.

They drove for two or three miles. They were beginning to wonder if they had missed it when the forest to their right opened up and they saw the trailer. It was in a sad shape, dilapidated and caving, its facade red with rust. The color gave the impression of blood, and Mary could not help but feel that she was entering into the final chapter of Williams's game. What would it be like, to find a lost girl? But what if the girl was dead and Williams had killed her? There were still so many questions—but there was something about this abandoned trailer out in this expanse of nothingness. An answer was in there. She knew it.

They got out of the Lexus and stomped through the high grass. The trailer had been set up on cinder blocks, and every time the wind blew the whole thing creaked, as if it were going to tip over and break apart into a thousand pieces. The sky was graying up now, and a little mist was beginning to fall. The grass swayed at their knees, and wisps of oak seed blew here and there, white as snow.

"Look," Brian said, dragging up the remains of a tricycle out of the muck. The significance was clear: these are the things that had belonged to Polly. Finally, she was more than a misty apparition they were trying to find for credit in some stupid class. She was real, and they were standing outside the place where she had grown up.

They walked around to the back. An old children's pool was there, turned upside down. A swing set without the swings. The ground here and there had been burned, and Mary thought about what Edna Collins had said about kids building fires on their property. It seemed that the same activities went on at this trailer, and suddenly Mary felt sad for Polly, that the girl had unwillingly caused all of this. And for what? Just because she bore a striking resemblance to a missing girl from Cale? There had to be more than that.

"Over here," Dennis called.

He was standing on a small embankment that overlooked a stream. At the bottom of the embankment was a motorcycle. Its wheels were missing but the bike was otherwise intact. "What is that?" Brian said, pointing. They strained to see. "There," he directed them, "painted on the side of the bike."

"It looks like . . . stars," Mary said.

"It's his," Brian said unequivocally. "Deanna's father's motorcycle."

They went back to the trailer and looked in the dirty windows, swiping away the grime that had accumulated on the panes with their sleeves. There was no furniture inside. The walls and floor were stripped bare, and in one corner there was a lump of rags and trash. There was something about the lump, though, something angular and strange—

The lump *moved*.

Mary jumped back from the window. "What the hell is that?"

asked Brian, who was standing next to her on a milk crate, looking in the kitchen window.

Mary looked back inside. The man was sitting up now, rubbing his eyes as if he were just waking up from a long sleep.

The mist had turned into a light rain, which now slanted down and ticked off the window, striking Mary sharply on the cheeks. She was too afraid to run or move or do much of anything but stare at the man. *This,* she thought. *This is where it ends.*

"What?" she said aloud. She didn't know why she had said it, but it was the word that had come out, choked and broken like a gasp.

From across the room where he lay the man looked at her. He looked right at her. The window was so streaked that it looked as if the inside of the trailer was the inside of a lung, or a storm cloud— everything was blurred and stretched. The man got up and took a few steps toward the window.

"What the hell does he want?" Brian asked. He was suddenly at her arm, squeezing it, priming her maybe for a mad dash to the car.

The man slid open the window. It broke and cracked away from the nails that held it down to the rotted sill. The man leaned out as if he were serving them from a drive thru window. "Afternoon," he said.

Mary felt his hot breath on her face. She *tasted* him—his breath was dirty, as if he had been eating soil. His teeth were ruined, and little wisps of oily hair splayed out on both sides of his head. But there was something attractive about the man, something Mary couldn't identify. He had been someone's lover once, a long time ago.

"You the folks here about Polly?" he asked.

Mary nodded. She was still locked in place, immobile.

"Sharon called me from the diner. That's my girl. Said there were some kids down from DeLane looking into the Deanna Ward thing. Anyway. Said I might know something about that. I said, 'Yes ma'am, I certainly do. Or I know someone who does.'"

"Who would that be?" Dennis asked.

"He's at the Wobble Inn. That's down on Rattlesnake Ridge, out there by I-64. You just take Upper Stretch all the way to its end and take a right on Hopper Road. You'll be on the ridge then. Follow the signs toward the interstate. The inn is up on the right-hand side, just a mile off the freeway. You can hear the rumble of the semitrucks from there."

"Who are we supposed to see at the inn?" Brian this time.

"You'll know him. Tends bar there nights. You tell him Marco sent you, and he'll tell you everything he knows. Which is a lot, let me tell you. The boy is like a goddamned encyclopedia on Deanna Ward. Some folks said he might have been involved in it, but that ain't the truth. He's just curious, you know, like you all."

The man smiled his ruined smile again. "I don't want you all thinking I'm some crazy," he said.

"No." Dennis again, assuring the man. "Not at all."

"It ain't like I live here or nothin'. This is just . . . *temporary*. Just until I get on my feet and Sharon gets her own place. Look, I got it nice in here. Hot plate. Cell phone. I'm twenty-first century, baby." Mary saw that he was trying to convince himself more than them. The man did an odd little bow then and leaned back into the shadows of the trailer. Slowly, as if favoring a hurt leg, he returned to that corner, where he curled up among his rags and old quilts.

Then the sky opened up and the rain came flat across the wind into their eyes and faces. "Run!" Dennis said, and they all dashed for the Lexus. Inside, the rain crashed against the windshield and their breath steamed every surface, making it impossible to see. For a few minutes they sat in the car without speaking. *The inn is just a mile off the freeway*, Mary thought. There was something to that statement but she didn't know what. She decided to let it be until she could articulate it; she had found in the last six weeks that there were "private" thoughts, such as her curiosity about Summer McCoy in the

Mike photograph and the call from the campus police, and there were more shared thoughts, possible facts that she needed someone to check. Confusing the two, she knew, would only get her into trouble.

"Are we ready?" Dennis asked when the rain had slacked a bit.

"I guess," Mary said, too soft for anyone to hear.

They set off down Upper Stretch Road, toward the Wobble Inn.

32

The bartender was a member of MENSA. He was telling them about his many failed attempts to get a degree, how the "establishment" had robbed him every time. When Dennis asked what his interests were, he said, "How much time do you have?" He began to list them: seventeenth-century poetry, fluid mechanics, string theory, game theory, chaos theory. He looked at them squarely, gauging their level of intimidation. Brian sipped his Diet Coke. "Anyway," the man said, wiping down a glass with the long towel he had draped over his shoulder, "none of it is applicable to the real world. I guess that's why I'm here." He spread his arms so they could behold it, this dark little dive off to the side of a rarely traveled stretch of two-lane highway. There were four or five people there, all men, and they were huddled in a back corner playing Texas Hold 'Em. Mary wondered if the man on Upper Stretch Road had somehow led them astray.

They were trying to bide their time with the bartender, disarm him somehow so they could ask about Polly. He was going on now about one of his theories—the one where there were multiple galaxies "pancaked," as he explained it, on top of one another. "It's a certainty that there is extraterrestrial life in this model," he said, his tone deftly serious. And then he leaned closer to them, his finger pointed toward Dennis's chest. "An absolute certainty."

Brian was getting anxious. His foot was tapping below the bar, and he was down to the water in his Coke. The men in the back fell into sudden laughter, the sound like a shot in the close acoustics of the tavern. "Did you know Polly?" he finally asked.

The man stared at them. He wiped out another glass and placed it on a high shelf, his eyes never leaving Brian's. "Sure," he said, his voice calm now and searing. "Everybody did."

"Did she come in here?" Dennis went on.

"She was just a kid when she left Bell City. Nineteen or twenty. This wasn't her kind of place."

"Where did you know her from?" asked Dennis.

"I knew her aunt and uncle. They lived out on Upper Stretch Road."

The bartender was being difficult. He was stubbing up, closing them out of some information that Mary could see he had. He was leery of them, she knew, suspicious of these questions. Just the name, the word itself—*Polly*—must have sent a charge through the residents of Bell City.

"What kind of girl was she?" Dennis tried.

"Nice," the man said. "Sweet girl. Got involved in some stuff, you know. We all did. Made mistakes. Regretted them. Lived to see another day. It happens. Otherwise, she was just an average teenager."

"Stuff?" asked Brian.

He was still looking at them, his gaze almost hot. He shook his head, then; laughed a little. The lights behind the bar were severe, probably on a mandate from the county because bad light led to fake identification scandals that a place like the Wobble Inn surely couldn't afford. The man's face was lit harshly in the glow.

He knows something, Mary thought. *It's right there. If I could just get him to open up. If I could just—*

"Marco sent us," she said, smiling at the man.

"Marco?"

"We saw him earlier today," Brian put in, moving his stool in closer so that the bartender could refill his soda.

"Damn, Marco knows more about it than I do," the owner said, spritzering the drink into Brian's glass.

"But Marco's not here," Mary said coolly.

The bartender blinked. His eyes finally disengaged from them, and he took a step away from the bar. "Look," he said, "everything I know is just secondhand. I got it all from Marco, anyway, so I'm not sure why he sent you to me. But if you're really interested, there's some stuff that will make your toes curl."

"Such as?" Dennis asked.

"Such as: the girl was abandoned by her real mother and father. She was staying with the aunt and uncle because she had nowhere else to go. And these were good people, like I said, but they didn't know nothin' about raising a girl. They wanted to do what was best for Polly, but she got wild. She fell in with the Creeps. Dom Frederick started seeing Polly—and now, keep in mind, Dom was thirty-four and Polly was all of seventeen—and he was a member of that gang. Of course, that's how she met Star, Deanna's daddy."

"What kind of a relationship did she have with Star?" asked Brian, urging the man forward, his foot now going crazy beneath the bar.

"Different people said different things, you know? Marco and Star went to school together down in Cale, and so Marco knew those folks pretty well. Star was fresh on the girl, I do know that. He came in here one night about that time talking sweet about her. We'd just opened. This was right before Deanna"—Mary began to see that people in these parts labeled periods of time according to that divide, Before Deanna and After Deanna—"and nobody knew a thing about what was going to happen. We were all just ignorant of it, you know, like the man standing on the bridge watching the storm coming on, and then in a few minutes lightning strikes and *zap!* The guy's hit. He's charred because he didn't have enough sense to get off the bridge, poor bastard." The bartender paused in his story, looked back toward the men playing cards. They had stopped to listen to him. He was commanding attention now. He had the floor and he didn't intend to give it up. "Marco says that Star was seeing Polly's aunt, but who knows. Who knows why he came around here. I never did really believe that he and Polly . . . you know. This guy could have had any woman in Martin County. What business would he have with this little girl?"

"Some people say Polly looked like his daughter," Brian said.

"If by 'looked like' you mean that they were both teenage girls, then 'some people' are right. That's about the extent of it. I saw Polly all the time around Bell, and I saw pictures of Deanna of course on the news when it happened, and there wasn't much of a resemblance. The police fucked that one up. They said he confessed to it and everything. I never believed that. If he confessed to it, then why didn't they arrest him?"

"Maybe the confession wasn't about Deanna," Dennis offered.

"You mean that New Mexico bullshit?" the bartender said. "No, there's something more to this. I'm not a conspiracy theorist"— though, clearly, he was—"but come on. Any idiot can see that Polly was not Deanna Ward."

He stopped talking and poured himself a beer. His hands were shaking a little, and it was obvious that the story had rattled him. The men in the back resumed their game. *No*, thought Mary. *There's more. There's something that he left out.*

"That's about all I know," he said, his voice scratchy now and nearly gone.

"Thank you," Dennis said.

They turned to leave. As they were walking out of the bar, Mary whispered to Brian, "There's more to find here. He didn't tell us anything that we didn't already know. The guy—Marco—said that we would get our answers from this guy."

"That's all he's got, Mary," Brian said. They reached the door and opened it. The world outside had the thick and heavy smell of rain. As Marco had said, she could hear the nearby echo of eighteen-wheelers surging down I-64. The trees dripped, and somewhere nearby a creek rushed noisily down through the hollow on its way toward the Thatch River.

A sudden thought came to Mary. She stopped at the door, one foot outside.

"Do you have the book?" she asked Brian. He removed it from his pocket, just as he had done for Dennis that day on the Tau roof.

She returned to the bar and got the bartender's attention. "Yeah?" he asked, clearly disturbed to see her again.

"Have you ever seen this man?" Mary asked, holding the book into the bar light so the bartender could see Leonard Williams on the back flap.

The man's eyes widened. "Oh yeah," he said. "I've seen him. That's Polly's uncle."

33

I t was late when they made it back onto Highway 72. It began to rain again, harder even than before, and when Dennis could not see the road any longer he pulled into a Days Inn, the students deciding to stay overnight in Cale. They pooled together all the money in their pockets, sixty-five dollars exactly, and got the cheapest room at the hotel.

There was an uncomfortable moment when Brian and Mary were in the room together and Dennis, who had sprinted to be the first in the bathroom, was changing. They were all wet from their run from the car, and Brian and Mary looked at each other warily, their clothes dripping on the carpet. Finally, when it was clear that Dennis was showering, they turned their backs on each other and got undressed, putting on some golf clothes that Dennis had in the trunk of the Lexus. Mary wore a long PING oxford and her underwear, and before Brian could turn around she dove into the bed so that he could not see her. Brian had put on a pair of bright-colored, checkered shorts, and he stood by the mirror shirtless, looking at himself. Mary had to laugh at the sight of it, and she lost it when Dennis appeared from the bathroom wearing pants in an identical pattern. He and Brian climbed into bed together as if they were twins, regarding each other suspiciously and creating a boundary down the middle of the bed with pillows so their skin couldn't touch during the night.

When the lights were off, Mary said, "What next?"

The boys shifted in their bed. A car passed in the parking lot and spread a white arc of light into the room, blanching the walls.

"What are our choices?" Brian asked, his voice muffled in the pillow.

"We could go back to Winchester," she said, "and tell people what we know. We could tell Dean Orman, get the folks at Carnegie to take action."

"But what do we know?" Dennis asked skeptically.

"We know that Williams was Polly's uncle," replied Mary. "We know that Polly and Deanna Ward were connected somehow, not just because they looked alike, but also because Deanna's father was driving out to Bell City to see Polly. In that way, we have Williams tied to the missing girl. We have the telephone call from the campus cops, which was clearly rigged by Williams. We have Williams's 'wife' giving me that note, and then the weirdness at the Collinses' house on During Street."

"And Troy," Brian put in. "We've got Troy Hardings admitting to a conspiracy over e-mail."

"It's not enough," Dennis offered. He kicked off the covers, and Mary could see his plaid legs doing bicycle kicks in the bed. Mary remembered this tic. When he was nervous, Dennis always lay on the floor and began his bicycle routine. Sometimes he would go for a half hour or more; it made her tired just watching him. "They'll just ask what we were doing, wasting our time in Cale looking for a girl the police have been searching for for at least twenty years. I shouldn't even be out here on this—this wild *chase*. Christ, Mary, I've got an exam tomorrow."

It was the first time Mary had thought about her other class. She had her lit class in the morning. They were wrapping up *City of Glass*, and she didn't want to miss their last discussion of the novella. But right now, it certainly wasn't looking good that she would get back to Winchester in time to make it.

"We might as well go to the police if we're going to go that route," Dennis scoffed then.

"Maybe we should," she said diffidently.

"And tell them what? Tell them that we have all these fake leads and this fake book and that we think we might be a part of an intricate game with a professor from the university who has disappeared off the face of the planet? They'll laugh us right out of the station. None of it makes sense, Mary. None of it makes a damn bit of sense."

They lay there, each of them looking up at the dark ceiling. She had to agree with him, of course. *Sense* was not a word that could be rationally applied to their situation at the moment. Across the room, Dennis churned his legs and counted under his breath.

"What do you think, Brian?" Mary asked. Over on his side of the bed, he was quiet.

"I don't know," he sighed. Mary knew that, like her, he was exhausting himself from turning all the complexities of the game around and around in his mind. "I seriously . . . I seriously think about hurting him."

"Hurting who?" Dennis asked.

"Williams. At all this shit he's caused. I haven't slept in a week. I can't—I can't seem to get my mind off it. If I could get to him and demand answers, you know. Even if he told us Deanna was dead, then that would at least be something."

"She's not dead," Mary said softly.

"It makes me wonder about Dean Orman's wife," said Brian.

Dennis stopped kicking. "What does?" he asked.

"This," Brian replied. "All this. After seeing her that night, I just wonder if she was part of this thing or if Williams was somehow . . ." He trailed off, couldn't define the thought.

"That night?" Dennis asked.

"I saw her out on Montgomery Street. By the Thatch River. She'd been beaten. She said that something had happened between her and the guy that looked after their boat for them. A former cop, she said. She wouldn't let me tell the dean because she was afraid Orman would kill the guy."

"Pig," Dennis whispered.

Brian bolted upright in the bed. "What did you say?" he asked Dennis.

"The guy who looks after their boat," Dennis said. "He's called Pig. That's where Williams got his name for the bad guy in his Polly story."

On her side of the room, Mary tried to figure it out. She worked it around in her head, fused the two narratives, Polly's and Deanna Ward's, and now this third narrative that starred Dean Orman's wife and the former police officer called Pig. But she couldn't come up with anything. It was all a muddle, jumbled, like the bar owner's theory of the pancaked universes. What was real, what was fake, what was part of the game and what wasn't? She lay back down and shut her eyes.

"How could it all be related?" She realized, too late, that she had said it aloud.

"I don't know," Brian replied. "But I just have a feeling now, after all we've seen today, that it was too coincidental. Too freakish, you know. How could Elizabeth Orman have been there just as I was driving back to campus? It was like she—like she was *waiting* for me."

"We have to go to the police," Mary said.

"No." Dennis now, speaking in such a hushed voice that it was barely above a whisper.

"What do you mean 'no'?" Mary said angrily.

"I mean no. Out of the question. It's too soon, Mary."

"People's lives could be in danger, Dennis. This is going beyond some—what did you call it?—some *tangram*. This is real life here." She realized she had stood up, and she was approaching him across the bedroom. Her underwear was showing, but she didn't care. She was losing control of herself, of her emotions; she was past the tipping point now. She was so angry—at Williams, at Dennis, at Polly for getting involved in all this somehow. She wanted it all to go back to normal, to when it was just a class. But somewhere along the way they had crossed some imaginary boundary and things had spilled over into the real.

"I know Elizabeth Orman," Dennis said. Mary stopped. She knew what he meant by his voice, by the seemingly innocuous word *know*, and the thought of it deflated her, sent her back to her bed where she collapsed face down into the pillow.

"What do you mean?" Brian asked.

"I mean I knew her. I'm familiar with her. Listen . . ." Dennis began the bicycle thing again. Mary could not listen to him. There was a roar through her entire body, a piercing noise that filled her with an old, familiar ache. "Listen," he said again, his legs kicking madly and his breath chopped and labored, "there's something I haven't told you. I figured it out by . . . by the San Francisco thing."

"The San Francisco thing?" Brian asked.

"Well, that wasn't first but that cemented it in my mind," Dennis said. "Polly's mother left and went away to San Francisco. Elizabeth told me a story about her mother running off to San Francisco with this guy. That's when I figured out the link between Williams and Elizabeth Orman."

34

Dennis Flaherty told them about Elizabeth Orman. He didn't tell them all of it, of course, just bits and pieces. He told them about the boat, and about his reasons for going to the Thatch that day. He told them about their relationship, and some of what she had told him at the Kingsley Hotel. He told them about speaking to Dean Orman that night at the house on the hill. And then he told them his secret: Elizabeth Orman used to see Leonard Williams.

"It was a few years ago," Dennis explained. "She didn't think anything of it, you know. Just a fling, to her. But Williams was smitten with her. He fell in love with her, I think. When she tried to break it off, he wasn't happy. He started getting crazy. Sending her flowers every day. Showing up at their home and just standing outside, watching her. She got scared. She finally told Dr. Orman, and the dean was furious. He confronted Williams at a faculty meeting. It got real bad. Drama. The two men almost came to blows, right there on the third floor of the Carnegie Building. Williams was reprimanded, put on some kind of suspension. They sent him overseas to teach. Sort of to get him out of the way, you know? When he came back, the dean got worried about him again. That's when he hired this guy, this former cop, to watch after his boat. He was afraid Williams was going to deface it or something. Apparently he'd threatened to set it on fire. This former cop, of course—his name is Pig Stephens."

"Do you think he's part of this thing?" Brian asked.

"No," Dennis said. "I think that Williams put Pig into his narrative just to get a dig in at the Ormans. He was into irony like that. A coal black sense of humor. He told me about Elizabeth when we talked. Was real forthcoming. He claimed the affair was nothing but Dean Orman, who had always been intimidated by him, made it into something much more than it really was. But . . ."

"What?" Brian urged.

"But I don't know what this means. I don't know why Pig would hurt Elizabeth. Unless, you know, unless it's just random. Unless it's just a random thing and Pig just flew off the handle one night. Hell, I don't know."

"Williams says there is no randomness," Brian said, sarcasm thick in his voice. "Everything happens for a reason."

The two boys laughed at that, but Mary had stopped hearing them. She could only think of Dennis and Elizabeth Orman. The image kept flashing through her mind, the sickening image of the two of them together. It shouldn't have bothered her. She knew that. She and Dennis had had a thing once, a long time ago—freshman year, for goodness sake—and now they were through. At least she thought so. Hoped so. But still the image was there, dogging her, teasing her. She shut her eyes against it but that only made it stronger, more vivid. Suddenly she wanted to be home, away from this mess, this game. She felt hot tears in her eyes, and she had no choice but to let them come.

35

In the morning Mary found Brian outside on their little balcony, sitting on a plastic chair and looking out at the bustling traffic moving down Highway 72. She took a seat beside him, and they silently watched the gray Wednesday morning shift in the early, diffuse sunlight. "We're at the end, aren't we?" she asked him.

"Six weeks to the day," Brian replied. "Williams's deadline."

Neither of them knew exactly what it meant. But something was going to happen today—something horrible, perhaps. They just had to figure out what it was. That was the only way they could stop it: by going back, back to the clues Williams had supplied them regarding Polly.

Polly is Deanna. Deanna is Polly.

When they had all showered, they decided to return to Cale Central. Even if Bethany Cavendish was a player—an actor—in this thing, she might be able to lead them somewhere they hadn't been. The book was the key, Dennis offered. If they could understand the book, then they could understand it all. So it was decided. He would go in to talk to Bethany Cavendish this time, show her the book, and try to get an answer from her about what it was, what it meant.

They arrived before 8:00 a.m. School had yet to begin. Students were pulling into the parking lot in their converted cars, trucks that rode low to the ground and had been painted outrageous colors, sports cars that were blinding with chrome. Brian and Mary waited for Dennis outside, under that manic American flag. "What do you think about him?" Brian asked Mary.

"Him?"

"Dennis. You like him?"

"I dated him once," she said. There was no reason to keep it from him now.

"I know," Brian said.

They let that hang between them. Mary sat on the curb and Brian kicked pebbles around the parking lot. It was now 8:15. Dr. Kiseley's lit class would have started by now back at Winchester. They would be discussing the book *City of Glass*, pondering on Quinn's last days, talking about the symbolic meaning of the red notebook that the main character used to document his life. Existentialism and all that. The meaning of *real*. "To write it down is to make it become real," Kiseley had told them. "What Quinn is doing is fighting off the idea of the interior. By writing in the red notebook, he is admitting that he is invested in facts and not the imagination. In this way, he is bringing into the world the details of his own demise."

"I could tell by the way you two acted together," Brian was saying. "It's nothing. Don't worry about it. We all have our own past. I don't begrudge you for it." He smiled, cuffed her on the arm playfully.

Mary looked away, her face hot. "It was . . ." She didn't know what word to use. *Nothing* probably, but she was sure Brian would see through the lie.

Out of her periphery she saw two students leave the school grounds. They were walking briskly, their heads down, going toward the woods beside the school. *Playing hooky*, thought Mary. One of them had a shock of white-blond hair. When he turned, checking to see if anyone was following him, Mary recognized him immediately.

He was in one of the pictures at the Collinses' house. One of the grandsons.

"I know that kid," she told Brian.

He looked over, but the boys had already gone down the hill and were out of sight.

At first, she didn't know what to think. But the longer they sat there, she began to wonder if this was not another test. Was Williams trying to tell them something else? Another plot twist, maybe?

She told Brian that she would be right back and jogged over to the edge of the woods. She looked into the dark trees, to the clearing that seemed to open up at the bottom of the hill, but she couldn't see the boys. A light fog had descended, pulled down like a cloak through the tree line. Mary took a few steps into the woods, but she still couldn't see the boys. "Hello?" she called. *It's no use,* she thought. *They're gone by now. All the way out to the highway.* She could hear I-64 out in the distance, the rock of those big trucks passing through Cale on their way to Indianapolis.

But then—a noise. Just off to her right.

Mary turned and saw something darting. Some presence. A boy, crouched and low.

"Are you there?" she called.

Again she saw something move, low to the ground. Then she saw him, just up ahead to her right. That white hair. Standing in the reeds of fog, the boy was like an apparition.

"What are you doing?" she called.

Nothing. Silence. The forest moved in the wind.

"Are you there?"

"What the fuck do you want, lady?" one of the boys asked.

"I just wanted to see if you knew anything about Polly."

"Who the hell is Polly?"

Mary felt ashamed. It was getting to her now, all this chasing and uncovering. It was making her paranoid.

"Sorry," she muttered, and she walked back out of the woods. Brian and Dennis were in the car when she got back. She slid into the front seat of the Lexus and they left Cale Central. On the service road that took them back to Highway 72 she saw him again. It was just him this time, the white-haired boy. He was standing on the shoulder of the road and watching the car pass. She was afraid to look in his eyes, afraid that she might see something that would make her want to go back and ask more questions.

36

"Bethany Cavendish is in on it," Dennis announced. They were eating breakfast at a Denny's near the high school. Mary had missed her lit class and now Dennis had missed his economics exam. It was becoming clear that they would all pay dearly for this little excursion. "She got all nervous. Started walking around the room, you know. Looking out the windows, like she was afraid someone might break in on us. She said that she didn't know a thing about the book."

"What do you mean?" Brian asked incredulously.

"She says that it had to be just a mistake. A printing malfunction."

"Did you tell her about the book in Cale?"

"Of course. She said the same thing: printer malfunction. She said that the two books in DeLane and the one in Cale would have been shipped by the same company. Probably all the books in this part of the state would have the same glitch. But she was lying." Dennis took a bite of his scrambled eggs. Mary was having toast (her appetite was almost nonexistent), and Brian wasn't eating at all. Only Dennis seemed to have the composure to feed himself.

"What did she say when you asked her about Polly?"

"She told me the same thing she told you. That she didn't really know anything about Polly. She said that Wendy and Star had left

Cale about six months after Deanna disappeared, and now they were living somewhere near San Francisco. She knew there was a girl out in Bell City who looked like Deanna, but she just thought it had something to do with Star. Said that the man was a sleaze-ball. Scum."

So they hadn't found out anything more than they had yesterday. They weren't necessarily back to square one, but they were close. Mary knew that they would have to return to Winchester in the afternoon, and if they returned without finding out what part Leonard Williams played in the Deanna Ward abduction, then why had they even come to Bell City and Cale in the first place?

"Do you think that girl you met at the kilns is still on campus, Brian?" she asked.

"I don't know," he said. "I guess we could go back and find out. She wasn't a student, because I looked her up. I asked some of the Dekes if they had seen me with her, but they were all drunk and couldn't remember anything. She had just—*appeared* there. It's like she was searching me out."

They thought about that as Dennis read the newspaper at the table. When he came to the story in the Local section about Williams's sudden departure, he read it aloud to them. They already knew everything in the story: that Williams had left before the se-mester ended, that Williams taught logic and philosophy courses at the school, that his office had been cleaned out. There was a state-ment by Dean Orman that read, "We are very concerned with these goings-on. We will get to the bottom of this. The first thing, of course, is to find out if Dr. Williams is well. Then we will get to the business of discovering why he chose to leave Winchester before the term was out."

"Why did he leave?" Brian asked. He was drinking slowly from a glass of water, a few sips here and there. Mary noticed that he was as frazzled as she was, maybe even more so.

"You said it yourself," Dennis said. "He left because he knew you all had gotten to Troy Hardings."

"But Troy offered up the information about the book himself," replied Mary. "It wasn't like we were threatening him or anything. Well, actually Brian did threaten him. But that's beside the point. He clearly wasn't afraid of us. He could have just denied that the book was genuine, like Bethany Cavendish did. He could have just remained silent and not responded to our e-mails."

"Maybe Williams and this Troy Hardings character were trying to tell us something," Dennis tried. "By just disappearing like that, maybe they were trying to bring it to a head. They were trying to force our hand in some way. Trying to show us that the game was really just beginning."

Mary thought, *The game.* Had the first five weeks of the course been simply a test, a sort of exhibition, for the real thing that was happening right now in Cale? How were Williams's "clues" a part of this? She recalled that hanged man from the syllabus, and wondered who Williams imagined under the velvet hood. She thought about the red Honda Civic and the railroad tracks that the professor had strangely digitally imposed into the image. The house that had turned out to be a real house on During Street, the house where Deanna Ward lived before she disappeared. The dog, that black Labrador that had apparently belonged to Pig. And finally the U-Stor-It facility out by I-64 where Williams's Polly had been kept.

What's there? Mary wondered. *What are we supposed to find? Something we aren't seeing because we're suddenly too close to the situation?*

She put a couple of dollars down on the table and went to the bathroom. She washed her face and stood before the mirror, breathing deeply, trying to balance herself. She looked awful. Depleted and exhausted. *Horrible.*

When she came out of the bathroom the kid was standing there.

He had on a big coat, too heavy for this time of year, and his white hair was long and in his eyes. He had been younger in the photos she had seen: a school picture with his smile gapped by missing teeth, and then later, with his mother and father and younger siblings in a family shot.

"What do you want?" she asked.

The boy continued to look at her. He was sizing her up, trying to gauge her intent.

"That name you said before," he said. "That girl."

"Polly?"

"Yeah. I know who she is."

37

His name was Paul. They took him to the Cale Community Park, which had been his destination anyway. He said that some friends were meeting there. School, to him, was just a waste of his time. None of it mattered. The teachers sucked, and he got picked on all the time by the jocks. He was a frail kid, tiny in that big jacket, and Mary could see how he would be a favorite of the bullies at Cale Central. She had gone to Holy Cross in Louisville, and even at that Catholic school there were kids like Paul, kids who were the brunt of jokes, too scrawny to take up for themselves. Kids who had become bitter toward the system, and toward any adult. Paul's clothes, his look, his *face*, even, asked the question: *Why don't you help me? Why didn't you help me?*

"My grandparents live in the house where that girl lived," Paul told them. "Deanna. The one who went missing from Cale. Two or three years ago my friend Tony and me heard about this other girl, the one who looked like Deanna. My friends at school are dogging me all the time, you know, trying to have me get my grandparents to let them come over and have a séance. Sometimes we go over there in the field beside their house and smoke cigarettes. Drink wine coolers and stuff. My girlfriend, Therese, is big on that spiritual stuff. We took a Ouija board out there once and the thing started going crazy. It freaked us all out."

"You're lucky you didn't get shot," Mary said.

"Oh, Papa wouldn't shoot anybody," the boy said. "His shotgun isn't even loaded. Anyway. Tony told me his older brother went to school out at Bell East with this girl who looked just like Deanna. It didn't really mean anything to me until I started doing some research. In the computers at the library one day I looked her up on the computer. Saw a picture of her. They could have been the same girl. Polly and Deanna. Deanna and Polly. I started thinking about it, you know. Started wondering where it was leading."

I know exactly how you feel, thought Mary.

"Well, one day me and Tony were bored and we decided to go out to Bell City to try to find out about this girl. This woman, I mean. We asked around, and someone said she was living down on Rattlesnake Ridge with some guy. Her family had left Bell City, but Polly hadn't liked it so she came back. This was just down the road from that old bar, the Wobble Inn. Tony—he's older than me, you know, out of school—we drove over there and talked to them. Acted like we were just interested in buying a car this guy had for sale, this red Honda. I kept looking at the woman, kept trying to place her, and man, was she *weird*. Kept hiding her face from me, turning it to one side so that I couldn't, like, get a good look at her. It was almost like she was wearing a disguise.

"Of course I thought it was Deanna. Tony did, too. We got back to school and told a few people, and you know how that goes.

Everybody wanted to see this woman. They'd all heard about her, back when it happened, back when their parents were in school. But it was like another chapter was opening now, and we had started it. We thought we were going to hit it big, solve this old crime and get famous, but it never turned out like that. Polly, or Deanna, or whoever the hell she was, left Bell City. It made the papers. Polly's aunt and uncle even made a statement, said that it was ridiculous to suggest she and Deanna were the same person. They'd raised her from when she was a little girl. Her uncle even wrote a book about Deanna, I heard. Or at least that's what Mrs. Sumner says at school. I never read it."

"I don't recommend it," Brian said bitterly. "It's boring."

"So anyway, it blew over. We never did go back there to that house in Bell City. We were too scared to. My mom and dad got a letter from someone, a real heated thing, saying we had opened up old wounds that should have never been opened. It wasn't too long after that that someone started that rumor about Deanna's remains being found out in California, but I never believed it. I think she's still out there somewhere, and I think if you can find Polly you'll find Deanna."

Mary looked at this scrawny boy, trying to register what he had said. Some girls played tennis up on the park courts, laughing at every missed hit. The playground was empty, the swings blowing back and forth, their rusted chains squeaking. She could not get her mind off something Paul had said, some bit of information that was almost buried in there.

The car. A red Honda.

Mary knew that they would have to return to Bell City to find the house Polly had stayed in when she returned to Bell City with her red car. The car would not be there, of course—not now. But this is where they needed to go, Mary knew that much. Once again, they were being led. The kid lit a wrinkled cigarette, and the smoke caught in the wind and trailed away across the field off to their right.

A car pulled up then, an old Bondo'd Mustang that was packed with kids who looked just like Paul except for the white hair. He said good-bye and piled in the car, and the kids disappeared down a little dirt road into the heart of the park.

"Where now?" asked Dennis. But of course he already knew.

38

The house on Rattlesnake Ridge was easy to see. It was just up the hill from the Wobble Inn on a little switchback-heavy road named St. Louis Street. Through the trees you could see the top of the inn where they had questioned the bartender just twelve hours ago.

The house was dilapidated and probably empty, but Dennis knocked on the door anyway. "Nobody's home," he said. They all stood around the car, waiting for some divine inspiration. It was after 11:00 a.m. They had missed all of their classes now, and still they hadn't made any progress since last night.

"Let's go down the hill to the bar," Brian said. Mary shrugged. They didn't have anything better to do.

There were no cars parked at the Wobble Inn today. The place had a desolate air, empty and ominous. Brian tried the front door, but it was locked. "Closed?" he asked. They looked in the streaky front windows, and saw that there were no tables inside as there had been last night. The booth where the men had played poker was gone. The bar itself had been torn out. Wires swung from the ceiling where the beer lights had hung.

"What the hell?" Dennis asked.

Mary felt that constriction in her heart again, just as she had at the Collinses' yesterday. Things were beginning to move, the pattern was revealing itself. They had to figure out the pattern before this afternoon, before Williams's deadline expired.

"Let's go to the back," Brian said. They went around the building. The back doors were locked, too. When they looked inside, it was the same thing. Emptiness. No tables, no bar stools. Nothing except the floorboards and the bare walls.

"What should we do?" Mary asked. She was feeling an anxiety like she had never felt. It poured down on her, opened her up from the inside out. She felt every notion of the world, every lick of the wind and every beam of heat from the sun. The spin of the planet, too, under her feet. She felt it, all of it, and in a strange way it was exhilarating.

"Hey!" someone shouted from up on the hill.

They all turned. He was standing in the trees, halfway down, holding himself in position by a sapling. Coming toward them.

The bartender.

"What's going on?" Dennis called. "We came back to talk to you!"

The man didn't say anything. He turned and began to claw up the hill. Fast, faster—grabbing trees as he went, turning up the fallen leaves with his boot heels as he tried to find his footing on the loose dirt.

"There's a car up there," Brian said.

There was. They could see the top of it from where they stood, parked in front of the empty house they'd just been to on St. Louis Street.

My God, Mary thought. *He's coming for us.*

Before she could say anything, Brian was pulling her and they were running toward Dennis's car. They got in and Dennis fought with the keys. "Hurry!" Brian shouted. He kept looking behind them, out the back window, for the car they had seen. Dennis finally found the right key and shoved it into the ignition. He started the car and put it in gear, and they spun out of the Wobble Inn's parking lot, throwing a cloud of gravel behind them.

"There he is!" Brian shouted. Mary turned to see it: the car was pulling off St. Louis and speeding toward them. There were two men in the front seat.

"Oh Christ, oh Christ," Dennis was saying.

The ridge dropped away on either side of the car, and at some points along the road there was no guardrail. Mary looked to her right and saw the tops of the trees. It was the same thing on the other side. Behind the Lexus, the car was gaining on them quickly but Dennis didn't seem to be driving very fast.

"Faster, Dennis!" Brian shouted.

"I'm going as fast as I can!" Dennis came back at him. His voice was high pitched, girlish almost. "Do you want to end up down at the bottom of the ravine?" Things were breaking down fast now, churning toward a boiling point. Mary cursed herself for getting into this, for coming out to Cale and Bell City in the first place. She should be at Winchester, or at home, even, back in Kentucky where everything was safe.

The car was a silver, rusted Mazda RX7. It was right on their bumper now. Mary could see the two men's faces. The bartender was driving, and the man in the passenger's seat was the man from the trailer. Marco. Their stares were placid. Businesslike. As she stared at them, Marco raised a video camera to his eye. She could see its pulsing red light. *My God*, she thought, *they're filming us.* The camera struck an awful fear in Mary, and she turned around and put her face in her hands.

"The interstate," Dennis said.

She looked up in time to see it whizzing by her on the right-hand side: the sign for I-64. *Straight ahead.*

Dennis drove toward it. The ridge opened up into a straight stretch, and he put on the gas. But the car behind them stayed on their tail, and Brian slunk down in the seat. He was praying under his breath.

"There!" Dennis shouted.

Mary looked ahead of them. She could only see the distant clover of the freeway ramps rising out of the woods in the middle distance. "What?" she asked him.

"There! Right there!" he shouted again.

And then she saw it: a parking lot just before the on ramp. Maybe if Dennis could make a perfect turn, maybe if he could time it just right they could . . .

"Pull in there," Brian said, breathless now, leaning up into the front seat.

The Mazda swung out to the left, into the other lane. Dennis slowed the Lexus and pulled sharply into a gravel parking lot, the Mazda roaring by them and onto the freeway ramp. The Lexus lost traction on the gravel, and the back end of the car swung around. Suddenly the car was in a tight spin. Dust and rock bounced around them, and Mary turned to see Dennis's face, which was a mask of fear. She closed her eyes tight, and she prayed that they wouldn't swing back out onto the road and be hit by an oncoming car.

They didn't. The car came to a stop, its struts popping and gravel dropping from the underside of the chassis in little metallic clicks.

They sat in silence for a moment as the dust rolled up over the car. When it had settled, Dennis opened the door and got out. He looked around for the Mazda, but it was nowhere to be seen.

Mary got out of the car. Her knees were weak, and she had to lean against the Lexus to steady herself. The blowing dust began to choke her, and she coughed violently, spitting on the ground. Soon the urge to vomit was uncontrollable. She fell to her knees and looked at the gravel, felt pebbles digging into her legs, but she could not release it. Instead, she cried. She sobbed into her hands and tried to find a point of release, some window out there where she could throw it all away, all of what was inside her, all the pain and frustration, all the knowledge, just throw it out and be rid of it, lose it on the wind.

"Here." It was Brian. He was behind her with his hand on her shoulder. Then he was helping her up. Then they were standing by the car again, trying to decide where to go next. It was all operatic to her now, a scripted thing, and she was acting not on her own volition, but of some other accord. She was acting for the good of Professor Williams's script.

"We could have died," Brian said.

"Look," Dennis replied.

They followed his finger to the sign that rose high over the freeway.

TRIP'S U-STOR-IT.

Immediately Mary knew what it meant. "Pig's motorcycle," she whispered.

They were standing, of course, on almost the exact spot where Professor Williams had taken that last photograph of the storage facility, the one that showed them where Polly could be found.

39

They walked up and down the aisles, checking the many storage garages for markings or anything that would suggest that one had something of interest inside it. They all knew they had been sent here. There was no question about it. Everything that had happened in the last two days had led them here. But now that they were here, the question became where to look. There were perhaps five hundred garages in the facility—too many to check one by one.

Dennis suggested that they stand at the very spot the photograph was taken and look at the facility from that vantage. They tried to remember the photograph exactly as it was, but it proved to be difficult, considering all that had happened in the last forty-eight hours. They stood across the road, in the yard of a little white clapboard house. They were pretty sure that was where Williams had stood to take the picture. They could see both rows of garages. The photo had been taken to the side, so that the easternmost bank of garages was in the foreground.

"That one there," Dennis said, his fingers making a lens. He pointed toward a garage.

"Which one?"

"The one in the middle. Center of the shot. It has to be that one. He was trying to point us there."

They walked in a straight line, trying to keep their eye on the door of the garage Dennis had spotted, and when they got there Brian tugged on the lever.

Nothing. The garage was locked.

Mary leaned on the garage door, her back against it. She felt so tired, so zapped, that she could have lain down on the gravel and gone to sleep for a hundred years. There was so much weight on her, so much awful tension.

Brian was walking down the bank of garages, which contained about a hundred in all, pulling on every lever. "Brian," Mary whispered. But he was intent. She could hear him grunting with every failed pull from where she stood, the sound of it guttural, animalistic.

Dennis was crouching beside her, tossing gravel. The sun was high and hot now, blistering down on them. She could still taste the metallic residue of the gravel dust on her tongue.

"It has to be here, doesn't it?" Dennis asked her.

"Why else would he show us those photographs? Why else—"

"I found it!" Brian shouted from the other side of the wall.

They ran around the first bank of garages and found him in the middle of the other bank, the ones Williams had left in the background in his photograph. *To confuse us,* Mary thought. *To keep the puzzle going on just a little longer.* He was standing in front of the garage, which was still closed. "I think this is what we're looking for," Brian said matter-of-factly.

They all stepped back and looked at the garage door. Mary's breath caught in her throat, and she nearly choked again on the dust. The door had two giant red letters spray painted on the front:

$$\mathcal{P}$$

Dennis opened the door.

Sitting inside the garage, at a small table, was Leonard Williams.

He was sitting in a rolling chair that could have been the one from Seminary East. His hands were tied behind him. There was a typewriter on the table with a sheet of paper rolled onto the platen. "Professor Williams?" Mary asked. The man's head was hung, and there was a dirty gag stuffed in his mouth. He didn't look up at his students, but it was clear he was alive: he blinked away the sunlight when it fell through the open door on him.

There was nothing in Mary's mind but raw, coursing fear. Brian had her hand now and he was pulling her inside.

They entered the garage. Williams was still looking at the floor. His eyes, however, were open and aware. Someone had assaulted him. He had a shiny knot under his right eye. He looked, Mary thought, more ashamed than anything.

They approached Williams, but he did not acknowledge their presence. His eyes remained down, at the concrete floor. "The typewriter," Dennis whispered. They made their way around the table and looked at the sheet of paper. When she saw what was written there, Mary's knees buckled and Brian had to hold her upright. "I want to go home," she said, although she didn't even realize she was speaking aloud. It was just a string of words, a sort of notation, an expression of her fear. It was an involuntary reaction—nothing so much as her mouth sending out a distress signal for the mind that was locked up now, frozen with a kind of obliterating dread.

For the, read the page. Over and over again, filling up the white sheet entirely until there was no white space.

For the for the for the for the for the

Winchester

40

8 hours left

They untied Williams and got him to the car. He was mumbling, despondent. He had been beaten badly. His eye was swollen almost shut, and a couple of teeth were bloody and loose. Mary used her cell phone to dial 911, but they were so far removed from civilization that the call wouldn't connect.

As they were driving back toward campus, Williams began to speak. His words were like a bomb in the nervous silence of the car.

"I set it all up," he said weakly. His head was still down, his eyes trained on the floor. Mary thought he looked like a child who had been caught stealing candy from a store.

"Set what up?" asked Dennis. They were passing through Cale, where they had spent the previous night. Mary didn't know if it had all been worth it. She wondered, as she had six weeks ago, what Professor Williams's role was in his own game. It was the last day of the quarter. The deadline. In three hours, at 6:00 p.m., when Logic and Reasoning 204 officially ended, would something happen, or would the time pass with no incident? Would it all turn out to be, in the end, just a puzzle? The beaten man next to her told her no.

"The whole thing," said Williams flatly. "The Collinses' house. The detective. The party at the house on Pride Street. The bar owner at the tavern who led you to me. The little boy and the woman, Della, whom I hired to play my wife. My wife's name is Jennifer, by the way. She wanted nothing to do with all this, so I had to bring in someone else to . . . play her role. We don't have any children of our own. The call from the policeman that night to your room, Mary. Marco and the inn, of course. And the storage facility. But of course you weren't supposed to find me in that garage. You were supposed to find . . . other things."

"What other things?" asked Mary.

"Information. Facts. Evidence I found when writing my books."

"But the book is a fake. We saw it. It's just those two words over and over again."

"That's the work of my enemies," he said.

"Your enemies?" Dennis asked.

"These are people who didn't want that book to be seen by the people in Cale or Bell City. Didn't want them to read about Deanna and Polly. So they censored me. My enemies—they have powerful friends. They can do these things. This is why I have to speak in code. This is why I have to create a puzzle."

"Who are they?" Mary wanted to know.

Williams mumbled something. He looked down again at the floor and closed his eyes.

"Talk to us, damnit!" shouted Brian. He was in the back with Williams, and he grabbed the man and shook him. Williams pulled away from Brian and stubbornly turned his gaze out the window.

"Brian," Mary said calmly.

"What had you found out about Deanna Ward?" asked Dennis.

Williams inhaled before he spoke. As always, his gestures were soft, unassuming, almost meaningless in their simplicity. "Five years ago, I started writing another book," he told them. "I had gotten some new information from one of my contacts in Cale. It was solid stuff. As I was writing the book, I learned that I would not be asked back to Winchester. They were going to fire me if I continued on with what I knew. Well, I couldn't lose my job. You can't be disgraced like that in the academic profession. Word gets around. You don't get hired again. So I ceased and desisted, and I put all my information in that storage garage in Bell City."

"Polly is your niece," Mary said.

"Yes. Jennifer and I raised her. We couldn't have any children of our own, so in 1967, when a relative of Jennifer's asked us if we could take this little girl, we jumped at the opportunity."

"Deanna's father," Mary went on. "He was seeing Polly. Sleeping with her."

"Laughable," Williams said, looking up at her. He had a harrowing look on his face, as if he had seen the unspeakable and was just now trying to rationalize it all. "You all have done well in the class, but there are things that you still do not understand."

"Tell us, then," Brian said. "Who put you in that garage?"

"Pig Stephens," Williams said. "They thought I knew too much. About Deanna Ward. They had heard from someone that the class was getting too *specific*. It used to just be a game, you know, an exercise in logic. But a couple of years ago I began to see the possibilities. If I could tell my students where my information was, and if they could find it, then I would be in the clear and the *students* would solve the crime and not me. It was a kind of cloaking device."

"But your enemies figured out what you were doing," said Mary.

"Yes. Somehow he found out about it and sent his henchman. Now they have the information I gathered, and there's no doubt in my mind that it's all floating out in the Thatch River by now."

"Who's 'he'?" asked Mary, but of course she already knew.

"Orman," said Williams. "Ed Orman. If anyone has the answers to this puzzle, it's him. But if you get close to him . . . well, you see what happens." Williams gestured toward his damaged right eye.

"Did you send us that tape?" Brian asked. "The one with Milgram and the . . . those voices?"

"I don't know what you're talking about," Williams whispered. He looked away, out the window to the bare Indiana landscape.

"Why would he be afraid of the information you found?" Mary asked.

Williams breathed in, steeled himself before he answered. "Ed Orman is Polly's father."

The weight of Williams's revelation nearly doubled Mary over. *Of course*, she thought. *Ed Orman lied to us about Williams's disappearance because he was afraid of where we were going. When Brian called him to complain about the class, that was his chance to take Williams out of the picture.*

"So what's the connection to Deanna?" asked Brian.

"She's Polly's half sister," Williams said. "Why do you think they looked so much alike? A woman named Wendy Ward went to Winchester for a semester back in the midseventies. She studied under Ed Orman, and they had a thing. This was before he was a dean. He was a respected professor, one of the finest researchers the university had. He had worked with Stanley Milgram at Yale, of course. That was his claim to fame. He didn't want to sully his reputation, you see, and so he kept the affair secret. A man of his stature, admitting an affair with a student? A townie at that? It would have been professional suicide."

Mary said, "But he couldn't hide the fact that she was pregnant."

"When Wendy got pregnant with Polly, he had it arranged so she would go back to Cale. I don't know how he got her to stay quiet, but I assume he paid her a good deal of money. A year later, Wendy met Star, this biker who was the complete opposite of Ed

Orman, and they had their first child together, Deanna. It was clear they couldn't take care of two young children, so Star called a relative to ask her if she would be interested in 'helping him out,' as he put it."

"Jennifer," Mary said.

"Yes. My wife is a cousin of Star's. I was just finishing my PhD at Tulane and was looking for a job. Jennifer ran the idea by me, and it was intriguing. I interviewed at Winchester and got the job. Ed was against my hiring, of course, but he had no clout at the time. By the time he moved up into his perch at Carnegie, I had written a book and was tenured. Of course, he even tried to take that from me . . ."

The plagiarism incident, thought Mary. *Ed Orman tried to frame him.*

"At the beginning of my career I was a visiting lecturer, making very little money. All Jennifer and I could afford was the trailer out in Bell City. I drove the hour and a half from Bell City to DeLane to teach. Wendy wanted Polly far away from Orman, anyway. At a remove. She was afraid of him for some reason. At that point, you see, I didn't know what I do now about the man. I thought Polly was just the result of an unfortunate fling, something that happened between two consenting adults. I couldn't have been more wrong."

"What did Ed Orman think about your role in Polly's life?" Mary asked.

"He distrusted me. He was paranoid, constantly worried that I would blow his cover and tell someone who Polly really was. But of course I didn't want to sacrifice my relationship with Polly. For all she knew, we were her parents. She was just a little over one when we adopted her, and she never knew anything else but Jennifer and me."

Dennis said, "It must have been awful on you at Winchester."

"Of course," Williams admitted wearily. "I was living a lie. I never talked about Polly. I *couldn't*. Ed had a muzzle on me. It sent me into a dark depression. Finally, we were able to get away from it. I was offered a job in Strasburg, and in nineteen ninety I taught in France. But when that was over, I returned to Bell City and resumed my daily commute to Winchester. To my lie of a life. I wanted to be open about my family, to not live in this secrecy, but of course Wendy and Star would have none of it for fear of Orman."

"Did Star ever come to visit Polly?" Mary wondered.

"All the time. I think he was trying to understand Wendy's old life. Her life before him, the one she'd had with Ed Orman at Winchester. That's what started the whole thing, of course."

"Started what?" Dennis asked. He was driving slowly, trying to take his time so that Williams could tell the whole story.

"Star came out to visit Polly two days after Deanna went missing," Williams went on. "He sat down on the couch with her and asked her if she would be their daughter now that Deanna was gone. Star was distraught, out of his mind. He was calling Polly 'Deanna.' It was excruciating to watch, and it made me hate the son of a bitch who had taken Deanna."

"In your . . . game," Mary said, "you led us to believe Star did it. Why?"

"I needed to get you to the trailer and then to the Wobble Inn. The only way to get you to the trailer was through Bethany Cavendish's story, and the role she played was of the distrustful aunt. She is Wendy Ward's cousin, but her story about Star was trumped up. She knows what I know: that Ed Orman is the culprit here."

Dennis asked, "When did you start researching Deanna Ward's case?"

"I began what Jennifer came to call my 'crusade' to find Deanna's abductor in ninety eighty-seven. Somehow Ed Orman's people found out about it. That's when they dove into my dissertation and found that I had borrowed from John Dawe Brown. *Everybody* borrows from time to time. Yet they planted the information in the paper, and it became a big deal. The word *plagiarism* was there beside my name, and in academic circles that does irreversible damage to your reputation."

"Yet they kept you on," Brian said. "Why?" He had moved as far away from Williams as possible, his body wedged against the back door of the Lexus. The professor's story had not allayed Brian's fears, Mary knew.

"I would have been forced out of Winchester completely if not for Dr. Lewis and some of my allies in the Philosophy Department. They were longtime enemies of Orman's. I confided in one of them, Drew Peasant, and he became my research assistant on *A Disappearance in the Fields*. When they found out Drew was working for me, they got rid of him. At this point, I had tenure and he didn't. I still think about him. I should have never brought him in to this mess, but at that time I didn't know the lengths they would go to, to protect themselves."

"The book is nonsense, though," Brian said. "It's blank. We thought it was . . ." He faltered. *A prop*, Mary thought. *That's what he wanted to say.*

"When the book was published," Williams said, "Orman tried to have it censored. He wrote an anonymous letter to the *Cale Star* blasting me and my credibility. And of course he somehow got copies altered so that they were unreadable. Many people in Cale have never read the book because Ed has made it so that the library and the bookstore on 72 do not stock copies."

"Oh, they stock them," Brian said.

"Let me guess," Williams added. "They're mostly gibberish."

Brian nodded.

"The book went out of print faster than most books even though it sold fairly well," Williams said. "There's no doubt in my mind that Ed was threatening my publisher. But at that point I couldn't do much. I could just wait and see if he confessed to his role in Deanna Ward's disappearance. I had implicated him in the book, even though I didn't have the concrete information to accuse him outright."

"But why would Ed Orman abduct Deanna?" asked Mary. They were entering DeLane and were only about ten minutes from the Winchester campus. Any information they wanted out of Williams they had better get now, because Mary had a feeling that he wasn't going to be as receptive to their questions once he got home, with the presence of Ed Orman and Pig Stephens bearing down on him again.

"Ed was wildly in love with Wendy; he still had this burning passion for her. Wendy was beautiful. Just like Deanna and Polly. I think it started as a game, as something he was doing just because he felt like he could get away with it. This is the kind of man Ed Orman is. He is brutally egotistical. He believes that his brilliance is unmatched, that he can intimidate you until he gets what he wants."

"He feels the same way about you," Dennis said dryly.

"Yes. Well. Who do you believe?" Again, he gestured toward his scratched and bloody face. "It's my theory—and this is what I was working on in the follow-up to *A Disappearance in the Fields* until I was ordered to stop—that Ed had Pig Stephens, this former cop who does all of Ed's handiwork, kidnap Deanna."

"Why would he do that?" asked Mary.

"To ruin Star and Wendy. He wanted to pin Deanna's abduction on Star, the crazy father. Maybe, just maybe, Orman thought, Wendy would return to him if Star were out of the picture, or at least suspected of such an awful crime. Star had a massive criminal record from his time with the Creeps, so it wasn't that much of a leap to suggest that he might have had a hand in his daughter's disappearance."

"But abducting your own daughter?" Mary said incredulously. She thought of Eli and Polly in Williams's tale. She thought of how adamant Williams had been that day when she'd suggested Eli might be the culprit.

"It sounds crazy," Williams said, "but look at it this way: here you have a thug, a man with a violent past who admitted to giving up a girl to possibly be murdered in New Mexico a few months before."

It did make sense to Mary. There was no randomness, Williams had said. Most every crime is perpetrated by someone in the victim's orbit. The police must have thought, *It's only logical that Star Ward is to blame.*

"The police arrested Star," Williams said, "and they took Polly back with them. We tried to tell them that Polly wasn't the girl they wanted, but they wouldn't listen. She looked so much like Deanna, and I think those cops wanted it to be Deanna so bad. Polly was confused. She was just a girl. Nineteen at the time. They were asking her questions and answering them for her. When they looked at her, she turned her face away because she didn't want to be Deanna. She told me later that it was the *way* they were looking at her—as if they were trying to see this other girl, this lost girl. It was all illogical—the police drawing conclusions from evidence that just wasn't there. It came out in the papers that Polly was asked if she was Deanna, and she said yes. That's a lie. That never happened. They made a mistake, and it was never responsibly acknowledged."

"But his plan backfired," Mary said. "The charges against Star wouldn't stick."

"At first, it looked like Ed Orman got exactly what he wanted. The police were wrapped up in their theories about Star for weeks, and Ed had the husband out of the picture. But of course Star was released. They realized they had nothing on him. He and Wendy and their two boys left Cale for California six months later, and Ed fell into a great despondency. When he came out of it, another student was there to console him. This time she was a master's student in behavioral psychology. Now she's in the doctoral program at Winchester."

"Elizabeth," Dennis whispered.

"That's right."

Mary stared at Williams. A tiny vein pulsed on his neck. The gag had been knotted so tightly that they could only slide it down onto his throat, and now it was cinched there, dripping sweat.

"But you haven't answered the question," Mary said. Many holes had been filled in by Williams's story, but *the* hole, the evidence that would clearly implicate Ed Orman, hadn't been discussed at all. "Where is Deanna?"

"Ah," said Williams. "The question of questions. In my book, I wanted to push forward the idea that Pig Stephens—an ex-cop, but still a horrifically violent man, a deviant who had been disgraced by the police department—had accidentally killed Deanna in a struggle and he and Ed Orman had been forced to hide her body. But my publisher wouldn't let me go through with it. Not enough hard evidence, you see. Every time I got close to finding Deanna, she would disappear. This has been going on for nineteen years now, and I really am no closer to finding her than I was back in nineteen eighty-seven."

They were on Montgomery Street now, driving into campus. It was a normal Wednesday at Winchester. The quarter was ending, and parents' vehicles were pulled into the service entrances behind the dorms. It was 4:30 p.m. Soon, they would all be going home for the fall break and these questions would still be unanswered. Mary had just one more thing to ask Williams.

"Where's Polly now?"

"She's getting her degree in criminal justice at Indiana State, down in Terre Haute. It's difficult, this forty-year-old woman sitting in a classroom with teenagers. Kids your age. She's lived a tough life, as you would expect. But she got things turned around, and now she's going to school full-time. She visited me on campus just a couple of weeks ago and she's supposed to be coming back into town today or tomorrow for the break. She knows everything, of course. It was difficult to keep it from her after *A Disappearance in the*

Fields was published, but she knows who her real father is, and she has her own suspicions about Ed Orman. He knows that he's too old to stop us from living our lives now. He was against Jennifer and me moving onto campus a few years ago, but that passed."

"And what about Wendy Ward?" Mary asked. "Does he still obsess over her?"

"I wouldn't know. All I know is that he doesn't interfere with Polly, thank God. He has resigned himself to the knowledge that he has a daughter, even though I know she must bring back terrible memories of what he did to Deanna and the cover-up that has gone on for years. That's one reason he locks himself up in his office: he's ashamed of his history at Winchester. I think it eats at him every day, and I intend to see to it that it continues to for the rest of his time at the university."

"Locked away," Dennis·said, "writing his book on Milgram."

"Did you know he and Milgram were never colleagues?" Williams said. "Not really."

"How so?" Dennis asked.

"I mean—"

But they were on campus now, and he fell silent. They crept down Montgomery and hit the light at Pride Street, the boundary that separated the two hemispheres of Winchester.

"What are you going to do?" asked Mary. She was desperate for some conclusion, some kind of closure to the game. Finding Williams was not enough; it seemed incredibly cruel to leave Deanna still missing, and Ed Orman's deception unchallenged.

"I'm going to do the same thing I've done for all these years," Williams admitted. "I'm going to keep quiet. I'm not going to say anything. I'm going to teach Logic and Reasoning in the Winchester term, just like I always have, and I'm going to hope I have students who are as inquisitive as you three. Right now? Right now I'm going to return to my study to have a bourbon." He paused. "I love my study. We added it on to the house a few years ago. Have you seen it, Mary?"

Mary turned to look at him. There was something in his eyes, a gleaming and almost imperceptible trace of secret information.

They fell silent, each of them gazing outside the car. It was finally fall. The sun that had been out earlier was gone behind a bank of clouds, and the air was crisp and sharp. The wind whistling through Mary's cracked window had the bite of winter.

"Where to?" asked Dennis as the light turned green.

"Home," replied Professor Williams.

So Dennis drove him to the house on Pride Street, and standing outside waiting for him was Polly's adoptive mother, Jennifer Williams. She did not look anything like Della—this woman was plump and short, and her face contained a multitude of hurt lines. The professor got out of Dennis's car and ran up the drive toward her, and they embraced as if they hadn't seen each other in many, many years.

41

4 hours left

"So this is it?" asked Brian. They were in Mary's room in Brown. Dennis had dropped them off with the promise that he would call them before he left campus, and now they were sitting at what Mary called her "dinner table," which was really a card table with a frilly tablecloth draped over it, eating McDonald's cheeseburgers.

"I guess so," admitted Mary. She would be going back to Louisville this evening, and all of this would be left behind. Since her cell phone had apparently been out of range in Bell City, her mother had left five messages since Tuesday afternoon asking if she was coming home for the week. The last message bordered on hysteria, so she texted her mother a brief message: *Been studying hard for exams. Everything's still a go for tonight.*

"It doesn't seem right," Brian said. "Orman shouldn't be allowed to just get away scot-free."

"If Williams's story is true."

Brian flinched. "You think he's lying?"

"I think it's difficult to trust him considering what he made us go through."

"He said it himself, Mary. He was trying to protect himself. He was trying to lead us to the clues that would tell us what we needed to know about Ed Orman and his role in Deanna's disappearance."

She couldn't get the feeling out of her mind, though—the feeling that Williams was somehow deceiving them again. *It's just your paranoia*, she told herself. *You've just freaked yourself out during the two days in Bell City and Cale.*

After they ate, she walked Brian out. A moment passed between them before he walked away, the knowledge that whatever they had begun wasn't over. He took her hand, and for a moment they stood on the quad, looking in each other's eyes. They had shared something, something so significant that neither of them would ever forget it. "Be careful in Kentucky," he told her. "We'll see each other after the break and we could . . ." He didn't finish the thought. He didn't have to. He walked away from her, off toward Norris Hall, leaving her standing alone outside her building.

Back inside, Mary checked her e-mail. She had nineteen new messages. There were forwards from her mother, petitions and jokes and recipes that she found—the detritus of the Internet. There was a note from Dr. Kiseley, her lit professor, asking her where she had been this morning. She would have to e-mail Kiseley before she left and figure out how to get her final paper to her. There were four or five institutional messages from Dean Orman concerning the cancellation of Professor Williams's Logic and Reasoning 204. Nothing else of significance.

She responded to Kiseley and told her that she would e-mail the paper within the week, blaming a family emergency for the delay. Then she threw some clothes into her old suitcase and went out to her mother's old Camry. Her heart was thudding, but it was a plaintive noise. There was a certain sadness inside her: the knowledge that Deanna would not be found, and that she, Mary, was at least a bit responsible for that fact. She had been so close to the truth but had been unable to find the missing girl.

Yet Mary had a feeling that if she looked, if she tried hard enough, logic could still lead her to Deanna.

Ed Orman, she thought. *Elizabeth Orman, his wife. Deanna Ward. Wendy Ward, Deanna's mother. Star Ward, Deanna's father and Wendy's husband. Polly Williams, Ed's secret daughter. Jennifer Williams, Deanna's aunt, Polly's adopted mother, and Leonard Williams's wife. Professor Leonard Williams. Pig Stephens, the potential abductor and murderer of Deanna Ward.*

Even after all this time it was still a puzzle, one of Williams's tangrams. Paper silhouettes. Yet she had been given a wealth of information by Williams, some of it definite and some of it presumed, and she still was no closer to finding Deanna. Maybe, like Williams had said, she just had to resign herself to the fact that some crimes remain unsolved—and hidden. After all, she had to get on with her life, didn't she? Mary sighed and started the car. She saw on the dashboard clock that it was 6:05. Williams's six weeks had finally passed, but Mary felt like she was moving toward another, more pivotal, deadline. Mary's mother would be expecting her at 9:00 for dinner at the Bristol Café, where they always met when Mary came home.

She turned out of the parking lot at Brown and then took a right onto Montgomery. In three hours, she would be in Kentucky and this nightmare would be behind her.

42

Mary drove along Montgomery and came to the stoplight at the corner of Pride Street. Students carrying overstuffed suitcases passed in front of the car. It was just a six-mile drive to I-64, which would lead her back to Kentucky. But Mary was feeling the tug of something. It was a conscious thing, an awareness of something left unopened, like a wound. A lack of closure. An imperfection.

I love my study. Have you seen it, Mary?

She turned right onto Pride. She narrowly avoided a student who was crossing the street, and he cursed at her as she hit the gas and sped down Pride. She had no idea where she was going—she just drove, hoping her intuition would take her wherever she needed to go.

Professor Williams's house was just down on the right. She slowed in the front and noticed that his pickup was not in the driveway. She stopped at the curb and got out.

What are you doing, Mary? she asked herself.

But she was already walking toward the front door. She rang the doorbell and waited. The maple tree that towered above the Williams's house was blazing orange.

When no one came to the door, Mary went around the side of the house and looked in one of the windows. She expected bare walls and dusty floors, just like at the tavern or the Collinses', but it was the same living room she had seen on the night of the party. There was the couch Williams had been sitting on when she'd left that night, and the dinner table was cluttered with dishes that had recently been used. Even the butter was still out.

Mary went around to the back door. She walked up the landing steps and looked through the inlaid glass on the back door. The same thing from this angle: a normal house that looked positively lived in. She saw the kitchen, and beyond it the hallway that led to the Williamses' bedroom.

You're an idiot, Mary. You've let this get to your head. Now let's go home. Let's get as far away from this as we possibly can.

As she was turning to leave, something inside caught her eye. She could see a door at the front of the hallway. Williams's study. The door was open, and inside was a desk. On the desk, something was glinting in the shifting evening light. Mary squinted to see this object, and just as she got her face to the glass someone was behind her, stepping through the fallen leaves in the yard.

"Can I help you?" the person said.

Mary turned and saw the woman.

Polly.

43

"I . . . I've . . ." Mary stammered. "I have Professor Williams in logic class, and he has a paper of mine that I need."

"Didn't the term end today?" Polly asked. She was wearing a peacoat and she had her arms crossed in front of her, protecting herself from the cutting breeze. Polly didn't look forty years old to Mary.

She carried herself like a young woman, but her face was damaged from years of tragic worry. She had the dog on a leash, and she reached up and clipped the leash to the clothesline that ran between the two maples in the Williamses' backyard.

"Yes," Mary explained, "but I'll get an incomplete if the paper isn't finished before the Winchester term starts."

"Oh," said Polly. "Do you know where it is?"

"Yeah. I think he told me that he would leave it on his desk."

"I'll let you inside, then. Dad is off God knows where. He keeps everything important in his study, though, so I'm sure you'll find it somewhere in his clutter."

Polly unlocked the back door and the two women went into the house. As Polly went about cleaning up the dishes that were spread across the table, Mary found her way to the study. She checked to see if Polly was watching her, and then she began to search Williams's desk.

What the hell are you looking for?

She didn't know. She opened drawers and shuffled papers, still keeping her eye on Polly in the other room. Outside the clouds passed across the day's last sunlight, and again an object glinted on the desk.

Mary located it, right there in the center. A paperweight.

The paperweight was sitting atop a manila envelope. As Mary removed the weight and picked up the envelope, Polly said from the other room, "Do you like his class?"

"Oh, sure," Mary called. "He's . . . interesting."

"Other people tell me that his class is weird. He won't tell me what he teaches, but I know he's into puzzles. My father is the kind of guy who won't tell you the answer to anything. He makes you figure it out for yourself. He's always been like that."

"Yeah," said Mary, her tone distracted. Inside the envelope there was a note addressed to her.

Dear Mary,
I knew you couldn't leave it alone. There were some things that
I couldn't tell you in the car. I have a feeling that you are one
who will not rest until you know the whole story. Well, that I
can't give to you. But here is the rest of what I know. This is
what Orman and Pig did not find in the storage garage. I hope
it helps.
Sincerely,
Leonard Williams

Inside the envelope there were two photographs she had already seen: the red Honda Civic and the black Labrador. Nothing else.

"Did you find it?" Polly asked. She was standing at the door. She had taken off her coat and was drying a plate with a dish towel. She had long dark hair, and Mary looked in her eyes. She saw in them a lifetime of secret pain.

"Yep," Mary said, holding up the envelope.

"Good. Dad keeps this room such a mess that you're lucky to find anything in there. Every time I come home to visit I spend most of my time picking up after him."

Polly led Mary out, this time through the front. There was much that Mary wanted to ask the woman, but of course she could not. As she was walking to her car Polly called, "Have a great break."

"I will," Mary said.

Polly closed the door and turned on the porch light. It was, after all, getting dark.

44

Across campus, Dennis Flaherty was in his room at the Tau house waiting for the phone to ring. He was thinking of Elizabeth, as he often did, wondering how it had come this far. On the bed beside him was the black garbage bag. He was having trouble opening it. They were at the end now, and it was difficult to finish it even though he knew he had to if he wanted to go on with his life—and if he wanted to find a way back to Elizabeth.

The phone rang.

"You ready?" asked the voice on the other end.

"Yes," Dennis lied.

The man hung up, and Dennis sat in the crackling silence. He wondered if there was another way to do it. Another way to finish this thing.

But there was no use. He knew that soon he would have to be ready to go.

For the first time in as long as he could remember, he crossed himself.

Then he opened the garbage bag and took out what was inside.

45

Mary pulled into the parking lot of the natatorium on Pride Street and studied the pictures again. The red car she had seen in the photographs Williams had sent, of course. But it had also come up in their time in Bell City. It was the car that Paul said was for sale at the house on St. Louis Street. Was Williams trying to lead her back there, to where he had once lived with Jennifer and Polly?

The Camry idled as night fell. She had to turn on the interior light to see the pictures. It was almost 7:00 p.m. and her mother and father would be getting ready, her father showering, her mother out of the tub with a towel around her wet hair. But Mary wouldn't be meeting them at the restaurant. She still had business to attend to at Winchester, and she intended to finish what she had started. She called her mother's cell. She would be home later, she explained, but don't wait up. Yes, everything was okay. Yes, she had done well on her tests. No, she didn't need anything. She would see them both later, and promise—*Promise me, Mom*—that you won't wait up.

She closed her eyes and thought. How was she going to use these photographs, these "clues" of Williams's, to figure out anything? There was a small roar in her ears, the roar of anticipation, and she knew that feeling would go to waste if she didn't figure out what Williams was trying to tell her now.

I don't think it was part of the game, Brian had said regarding the ride he'd given to Elizabeth Orman. *I think she was serious.*

Mary did a U-turn on Pride Street and went back toward Winchester. On the hill to her right, which the students called Grace Hill, she saw Dean Orman's house. She turned into the drive and climbed the hill toward the cottage. "Cottage" really didn't do it justice. It was essentially a mansion fashioned as a nineteenth-century country carriage house. Rising high into the trees was the house's A-frame. The house, Mary knew, had four stories and was over five thousand square feet.

Mary got out of the car and went to the front door. She had no idea what she was going to tell Elizabeth Orman if the woman answered the door. That her husband was an accomplice in a murder twenty years ago? That she knew the woman had slept with Dennis Flaherty? Mary rang the bell and waited. She heard faint footsteps from inside, and the door cracked open to reveal Dean Orman.

"Can I help you?" he asked.

"I think I have some information you'd like to know about Professor Leonard Williams," Mary said. She was flying blind now, talking off the top of her head. It was an exhilarating feeling, and she went with it.

The man's eyes took on a dark and knowing tint. "Come in," he said.

Mary followed him inside. Orman had his newspaper spread out on the floor next to the couch and ESPN was on the plasma television that loomed in the corner. "Forgive my mess," he said, pushing some of the paper beneath the couch. He gestured for Mary to sit, and she took a seat on an antique lolling chair beside him. Orman was more disheveled than usual. He was wearing a Winchester U sweatshirt with jogging pants. There were holes in his socks, she noticed. His orange hair was matted and tufted on one side, as if he had just risen from a nap.

"Talk," he said.

"I was in his logic class this semester," began Mary. "And some of the things that he told us were—let's just say they were highly unusual."

"What sorts of things?" Orman was interested now. He was leaning forward, toward Mary, with his bifocals clutched between his interlaced fingers.

"Things about Deanna Ward."

The man did not move when Mary said the name. She searched him for something, some tic of recognition, but he was stock still.

"Things about the disappearance of this girl," Mary went on, "and another girl, named Polly, who he claimed you knew."

Orman laughed. It was a deep and guttural chuckle, barely registering as an exterior noise at all.

"Leonard says *things* all the time," Orman said. "He's been talking off and on for twenty years. Here at Winchester we tend to ignore his theories. Most of them are innocent, but some of them are in bad taste, let alone potentially dangerous. I have talked to Leonard about this more times than you can imagine. He tells me, each time, that he will do better. But he doesn't. Empty promises, you see. And we think this is why Leonard left."

"Because you spoke to him about his teaching practices?" Mary asked.

"Because he was tired of playing by our rules," said the dean. "Well, when you are part of a business you have to read the company line sometimes. It's the American way, you know. Leonard couldn't abide by that, so he left in the night and will never teach here again."

"You've fired him?" she asked.

"Of course not. We don't fire professors with tenure. But we can make it so that Leonard has no course load. Or that he is reading research grants for a living in the basement of Carnegie. Anything to get him out of the classroom. There was a time when he was a brilliant lecturer. But not now. He's too worried about the nonessential, the clutter of our daily lives, to teach students well."

"Who is Deanna Ward?" Mary pressed him.

The dean looked at her. Again, there was no stir or awkwardness that told her he knew about Deanna. "A Cale girl who went missing years ago," said Orman lightly. "Leonard wrote a book about the case, and for years since then he has been trying to sell his crackpot theory to anybody who will listen."

"What was his theory?"

And then: an almost imperceptible narrowing of his eyes. Was she taking it too far?

"I don't know," Orman told her, resignation in his voice. "I never read the book. It was, as far as I was concerned, a penny dreadful."

She decided to let it rest for a moment. They talked about the class, and how she would get credit for it. Mary feigned anxiety about getting proper credit for Logic and Reasoning 204. Orman walked her through the steps and gave her a timeline in which the grade could be expected on her transcript.

"I'm just trying to keep my GPA," she said. Now, Mary realized, the tables had turned. Now she was doing the acting, and she found herself strangely enjoying it.

"I'm aware of that, Ms. Butler. Winchester is going to do all we can to make up for your lost time."

She stood, then, and Orman stood with her. "Do you mind if I use the bathroom before I go?" she asked him. "It's a long drive back to Kentucky."

He showed her down a hall off to the right, and she stepped into a spare bathroom that contained only a toilet and a sink. Mary paced the bathroom, trying to get straight in her mind what she was going to ask Orman when she came out. *Think*, she demanded of herself. *You're close to breaking him. Push him about Deanna Ward*. As she was standing in front of the mirror, she heard the back door open and close. Then a feminine voice was just outside the bathroom, in the hallway leading to the kitchen. Elizabeth Orman.

When Mary came out of the bathroom, the Ormans were in the kitchen. The woman had brought in grocery bags, and the dean was putting some vegetables in the refrigerator.

"I'll just be going," Mary said.

Elizabeth turned and saw her. Dean Orman said, "Lizzy, this is Mary Butler. She was just talking to me about Professor Williams's logic class."

Elizabeth nodded slightly and went back to her groceries. Mary searched her face for abrasions but saw nothing. Could she have healed so quickly? Was she simply, as Brian had wondered, putting on a performance that night in the woods?

Dean Orman let Mary out, and she returned to her car. She hadn't gotten the information she needed, but she knew she couldn't push Orman about Deanna Ward without him becoming suspicious.

Outside, the night was complete. She fell with a thud into the driver's seat and sat with the heat blowing onto her cheeks. She was, finally, at a dead end. She put the Camry in reverse and started carefully backing down the hill. But as she was pulling down the drive, she saw something in her periphery. When she looked more closely, she saw that the Ormans' garage door was still open and the security light was on. Mary put the Camry into park and got out of the car. She crept around the side of the house and looked into the garage at Elizabeth Orman's car. The car cracked and hissed, its chassis still settling from Elizabeth's trip to the grocery store.

It was a red Honda Civic.

The car's back door was open, and Mary could see grocery bags stacked in the backseat. There was a bumper sticker that read SCIENTISTS MAKE THE BEST LOVERS. She turned to go back to her car when—

"I just don't understand why she came here," said a woman's voice from inside the door that led from the garage into the house. Mary hunched low, so low that she was almost underneath the back end of the car. The woman wouldn't be able to see her, Mary knew, unless she came outside the garage.

As Elizabeth Orman descended the steps, Mary scrambled completely beneath the car. She watched Elizabeth's feet, felt the click of her heels vibrating against her ear. She must have been talking on her cell phone.

"But why?" Elizabeth continued. "I don't understand it. I think we might be losing her." Again, she stopped to listen. Mary heard the voice on the other end, but she could not make out the words. It was just a scratchy, distant, masculine buzz. Elizabeth exhaled loudly, and then said, "I hope you're right. It's just—it's just that we're so close now. I would hate to lose her and have to start all over again."

At that moment, a can of tomato soup dropped onto the ground. It was just two feet from Mary's nose, rolling under the car in a little arc toward her. Mary recoiled, tried to wriggle back toward the opposite side of the car without making a sound. Elizabeth's hand came into Mary's line of vision. Elizabeth knelt without looking beneath the car and felt around for the soup. When she found the can she rolled it toward her with her fingers, and Mary heard her place it in the sack.

"You're right," she was saying now. "I shouldn't worry. It's always like this. I always worry about things that are out of my control. If she goes home, then we'll find a way to get her back. If she does what she's supposed to do and shows up at the other place, then it ends tonight. Thanks. You've been a big help. I've got to get back in to Ed now. We're fixing dinner tonight before the thing, if it goes through. I know, I know. *When.* When it goes through. Anyway, I'll talk to you later tonight."

With that, Elizabeth snapped the phone shut. She climbed the steps and went inside, shutting the door behind her. Thankfully, she had left the garage door open. Mary slid from under the car and, in a hunched-over run, went around to the front of the house and climbed back inside her Camry. After a moment of composing herself, she started back down Grace Hill.

It wasn't until she was at the bottom that she reminded herself to breathe.

46

Deadline

Mary drove along Highway 72 thinking about what she had seen—and heard. Who had Elizabeth Orman been speaking to? Williams? Were they in this together? It certainly appeared that way. But that was inconceivable. Perhaps—and now her mind was racing, careening in a thousand different directions at once—perhaps Professor Williams had gotten to Elizabeth Orman and convinced her that her husband was an accomplice in Deanna Ward's disappearance. That had to be it. That had to be the reason Williams had given her the photograph of Elizabeth Orman's car—to try and show Mary that Elizabeth Orman was in with them, that she was part of their effort.

She came here before she went to the other place, Elizabeth Orman had said.

The other place.

If she does what she's supposed to do and shows up at the other place, then it ends tonight.

Where? Where was this other place? Was it in Bell City? In Cale? Was it Professor Williams's house?

Mary couldn't stop thinking as she drove down Pride. It was getting dark, and she turned on her headlights as she pulled up to the corner of Montgomery.

Other place.

And then she knew. The link had to be Pig Stephens. He was the only character in the play that she hadn't spoken to. She knew nothing about him other than what Williams had told them in the car. He was dangerous, she knew that, and he was in league with Orman.

Perhaps the dean had found out about Elizabeth and Leonard Williams, and he had sent Pig to punish his wife.

Find Pig Stephens, she thought.

But where? She needed a place now, a location to go to. She needed to follow Williams's script so that it could, as Elizabeth Orman had said, "end tonight."

Where could she find Pig Stephens? Where had Brian House found Elizabeth Orman that night?

The light turned green, and she turned right onto Montgomery. Brian had found her just down the road from here. Afterward, he had driven straight to Mary's dorm. He had been to the public library, and had taken the bypass back to campus. So he must have passed on his way—

That's it, she thought. *Has to be.*

The Thatch River. They were trying to point her toward the boat. Ed Orman's yacht.

According to Dennis, Pig Stephens, the former cop, took care of Ed Orman's weekender. Brian had found Elizabeth Orman out where Montgomery Street overlooks the Thatch, about three miles from campus. Mary was sure, suddenly, that Professor Williams was leading her there.

She took a right on the bypass and made her way toward the Rowe County Marina. The marina appeared out of the foliage at the bottom of a hill just below Montgomery Street. The lights of the slips were on and dotting the cove. A few men walked here and there across the dock, mooring their boats. Mary found a parking space and walked down the slick, mossy steps to the slips. She had never seen Orman's boat, but she guessed that it was probably the biggest one in the marina. There were four docks that intersected out on the water, and there were close to a hundred slips along each dock. It would take her an hour to traverse the whole thing.

She walked out onto one of the docks and found the office. She knocked on the door, and a man's voice told her to come in. The man was brown from the sun, and he was smoking a chewed cigar that was frayed on the end like a gag gift. He was sitting at a cramped desk in the office, stuffing paychecks into envelopes.

"Help you?" he asked.

"I'm looking for Pig Stephens," Mary said.

"Pig comes by around about 10:00 p.m.," replied the man. "Keeps an eye on Ed Orman's yacht."

"Ah," Mary said. *The Ancient Mariner?*" She knew that Orman would name the boat after a line or a title from the classics.

"Naw," said the man. "His is *The Dante.*"

"Thanks," Mary said, and she went back out on the docks and began her search for the boat.

It didn't take her long. The mast of *The Dante* rose high above the marina. The boat was close to the bank, Mary assumed because it would be easier for Pig Stephens to pull down and spotlight the docks to see if anyone was vandalizing it.

She stood in front of the rocking boat. The wind was pitching higher, sending spray off the top of the water and onto her cheeks. It was bitterly cold by now, and almost completely dark. Mary had no idea why she was here or what she was looking for, but something of interest had to be here somewhere. Elizabeth Orman was the link to Pig Stephens, and this is where Pig came every night to take care of his client's investment. Was she supposed to wait until 10:00 and talk to Pig personally?

Mary sat on the dock, her legs pulled up into her chest. *The Dante*'s mast rattled in the heavy wake. She closed her eyes, as Williams had instructed them to do so long ago in Seminary East, and tried to make sense of all she had found. The only photograph she hadn't explained was of the dog, the black Labrador. But there would be no dogs here, of course.

The dock rocked gently, and she pulled herself farther into her coat, until almost no skin was exposed. She thought about Deanna Ward, wondered where she could be, all these years later. Deanna, and Polly, and Professor Williams. So many questions answered, but still so many left. She thought about that day in 1986, when Polly was brought mistakenly back to Wendy Ward. What must Wendy have thought when she saw Polly? Was she being punished for her tryst with Dean Orman? Did she feel, in that moment, as if she had deserved that fate?

"Ma'am?" said a voice above her.

Mary sat up and blinked at the man. It was the man she had seen earlier, in the office.

"You were asleep," he said. "We don't really like people to sleep on the docks. Afraid they'll roll off into the water. It's happened a few times." The orange eye of the cigar pulsed and then swung down to his side.

"Yes, I'm sorry," Mary said. She scrambled to her feet. It took her a moment to orient herself, but then it came to her. *The marina.* Then she thought, *Pig.* "What time is it?" she asked the man.

"It's about nine forty-five," he said. "You been out here for a good while. I bet you're about froze to death."

Now that he mentioned it, Mary was numb. Her feet were stiff and aching. Her hands, which she had squeezed tight into the sleeves of her coat, were sore from where she had clenched her fists so fiercely.

She thanked the man and walked away from him toward the bank. In the parking lot, she sat in her Camry with the heat on, waiting. How would she know Pig Stephens? Maybe he was the owner of the black Labrador. Maybe he kept it in his truck, a sort of companion on his rounds at the marina. She assumed he would pull up and stop, get out of his vehicle, and approach *The Dante.* She waited, blinking the sleep out of her eyes. What would she do when he got here? She had no idea. She might approach him, possibly, as she had done to Dean Orman. She figured by now, after playing the game for so long, that she would be used to acting on instinct. At least she hoped so.

To her right, she heard a truck pull into the lot. The truck swung close to the river and stopped. A man got out. He was carrying a heavy flashlight, and he shined it down on the docks. Mary got out of her Camry and walked toward the man. "Pig?" she called, but her voice caught on the wind and was carried away. She called his name again, and the man turned. He swung the spotlight at her, and momentarily she was blinded.

"Who's that?" he asked. His voice was deep, inflected with a thick Southern accent.

"I just want to ask you some questions," she said, the light still piercing her eyes.

"Kind of questions?" he asked.

"Some questions about Ed Orman."

He lowered the flashlight. "Go on," he said.

"What do you know about him?" she asked.

"I just know he cuts me a check every month. That's good enough for me."

"Do you know that he fathered a child with one of his students?"

The man shifted. Mary still couldn't see his face, but she could see that he was overweight, his stomach bulging out over his belt. "What business is it of mine?" Pig asked.

"It's just that your name has come up in some of Ed Orman's doings."

"Doings?"

"The disappearance of a girl named Deanna Ward, for instance." Mary was pressing on now, trying to reach something. Whatever inhibitions she had at the beginning of the day had now dissolved, and there was something enlivening about standing in front of him and talking as if she were the one in control of the situation.

"I don't know what you're talking about," the man said.

"Ed Orman thinks you do."

They let that hang between them. Down the bank, the Thatch rocked and swayed, and the boats banged in their slips, making a cacophony of sound in the night. Just as she opened her mouth to speak, the flashlight exploded on again and she lost her vision. Mary held her arm up to her eyes, and she was able to see his feet—just his boots, walking toward her. She scrambled away from him, but he was grabbing her, forcing her back toward him. Still blind, she smelled his breath, musty and thick and strangely *earthy*.

Mary pulled away from him and ran. She felt him, felt his heat, close behind her. She saw her Camry, its door still open. There was a ringing coming from inside it: her cell phone. It seemed like a thousand miles away, but the car could have been no more than a hundred feet in front of her. *Oh God, Mary. What have you done?* Somehow, she made it to the driver's seat and shut the door. Pig was a step behind her, and when she tried to slam the door his hand was inside. *"Arrrrll,"* he growled, falling back onto the car beside hers. Behind the wheel, she backed out onto Montgomery Street and gunned the engine toward Winchester. By the time she was out on the highway, she had forgotten the phone.

47

Mary drove the long way toward campus, trying to lose Pig Stephens. There was a wail in her ears, a piercing red scream, and she could barely hold on to the wheel. She knew that if Pig caught up to her, he would surely kill her. She had gotten herself into something she could never imagine. But now—now, she knew, there was no way out.

She drove toward Professor Williams's house. If she could somehow tell him that she was in danger, maybe he would help. Her mind was spinning, torturing her with fear. Repeatedly, she checked her rearview mirror for Pig Stephens's truck.

What have you done, Mary? What have you gotten yourself into?

Mary drove into the Winchester campus, going sixty miles per hour in a thirty-five zone. It was 10:30 p.m. now, and the campus was almost entirely deserted. Only a few remaining students strolled around here and there. She stopped at the light on the corner of Pride and Montgomery, her car rocking violently to a stop. She checked behind her, but there was no sign of Pig. *Please*, she thought. *Please God turn, please turn.*

Finally, the light turned green.

As she began to pull through the light, something flashed in the corner of her vision. She jammed the brakes and lurched forward, the seat belt snapping her back into the seat. When she managed to look up, she saw someone crossing in front of her. It was a man. He was leading a dog on a leash.

A black Lab.

Mary watched him cross the street. He was wearing a Windbreaker he had zipped high on his face and a Boston Red Sox cap pulled low over his eyes, and when he got directly in front of her car he glanced at her. That was all, one short glance. But she knew what it meant.

The man began to walk down Pride, and she turned right and followed him. He broke into a jog, but he did not turn into the trees of the campus proper; he kept on Pride so that she could easily stay behind him. He passed Professor Williams's house, and then Dean Orman's mansion on Grace Hill. At the corner of Pride and Turner, he took a right and headed into the heart of campus. Mary stayed close behind. The man ran all the way to the edge of Up Campus, and then he cut into the woods beside the gymnasium. She pulled to the curb and watched him disappear into a ground floor entrance of a shadow-cloaked building about a hundred yards from where she had stopped.

Seminary.

The spires of the Seminary Building were unlit. The high stained-glass windows were dark and devoid of the religious imagery that burned through them during the day. The building had been the convocation hall when the school had first unified into one college, and just a decade ago it had been turned into a classroom building. On this night it had the look of a fortress, something that the darkness protected and kept hidden.

Mary got out of her car. The wind was still sharp, almost bitterly cold now. She walked under the canopy of oaks, which were shuddering in the wind. She made her way through the darkness to the door on the east side of the building, and she went inside. The steps loomed in front of her. She went up, her footsteps echoing in the dark.

48

B rian House had reached the Indiana state line when his obsession got the best of him.

He drove with the radio off. His plan was to drive to I-71, get into
Columbus, Ohio, and then rest for the night before making the second leg of the trip to Poughkeepsie tomorrow morning. It was already 6:00 p.m. He couldn't turn around or he would lose two hours
and wouldn't get home until tomorrow evening. No, he had to go on.
He only wished there were some way to turn off his thoughts, to silence his roaring mind.

They killed Deanna Ward, he thought.

Shut up.

Dean Orman had Deanna Ward killed.

No.

Williams tried to stop them.

Quit this, Brian. Stop.

Williams couldn't stop him, but—

But?

But Williams will not tell the police. He only invents a puzzle for—

For?

For us. To terrorize us. Like Polly at the kilns that night, but—

But he didn't mention Polly.

He didn't mention Polly, did he?

In the car he hadn't mentioned the girl Brian had met. He'd explained everything, the fake wife and Dean Orman and Pig Stephens,
but he hadn't mentioned Polly.

Was that his daughter? Had Williams's own daughter been in on
the game?

No. Impossible. She would have to be in her forties. The girl at the kilns was much younger.

And so what did that mean?

It meant that there were still hidden truths. It meant that the deception was still ongoing. Williams told them he had explained it all, but he hadn't. There were still pieces to the puzzle that needed to be added.

And if the puzzle is unsolved, then that means—

What?

That means he's still lying.

And if he was lying, then the story about Dean Orman was false. It was just another ruse. A hoax. It meant that Williams was trying to implicate Orman. For what? For some long-standing grudge? Professional jealousy. It meant—

What? Say it.

It meant that Williams had killed Deanna Ward.

It was the only logical solution. The thought plagued Brian, scratched at him like a sort of mad itch. At some point—perhaps as he passed the Bell City exit—the thoughts became geometric. Physical. They dashed and prodded their way inside his skull. They had edges that scraped at him sharply.

Leonard Williams killed Deanna Ward.

I think it's difficult to trust him considering what he made us do, Mary had said to him.

And it made perfect sense. Williams killed Deanna, and his guilt continually drove him to the brink of madness. To assuage his guilt he tried to implicate a man who had always been his better, a man who had overstepped him in the academy, who had a legendary friendship with a famous scientist named Stanley Milgram: Ed Orman.

Slowly, pitifully, the crime had driven Leonard Williams crazy.

He orchestrated a scenario where he set the lies in place. A system of intricate mistruths. A false book that made it look like his interest was merely professional. The adopted daughter, Polly. Williams as a hero. Williams as a savior. Yet—

Yet? His conscience egged him on.

It was much easier to link Williams to Deanna Ward than it was Ed Orman.

After all, it was Williams, not Orman, who had lived close to Cale and Deanna Ward in Bell City. It was Williams, not Orman, who had the unhealthy interest in the case, who devised the Polly story with its horrifying details. It was Williams, not Orman, who loved those gruesome and violent tangrams Dennis had told Brian and Mary about.

He wanted to see Williams punished for what he'd done to him. Williams was a potential murderer, and he had entrapped his students in his twisted game because—

Because why? Because the man was fucking sick. It was clear to Brian now. He had finally seen through the lies Williams had told them as they drove back from Bell City this morning. It was all just a smokescreen.

Suddenly he felt an uncontrollable hatred for Williams.

The viaduct. The Thing buried there.

Can you do it? he asked himself.

Could he?

What choice do you have when your world has been turned upside down by a cruel game? What do you do, Brian wondered, when all the clues and signs point to one solution? What do you do when place, time, motive, and circumstance point to one man?

You turn around. You go back to finish it.

Which is exactly what Brian House did.

49

"Hello?" Mary called after the man in the Red Sox cap.

Silence. Inside Seminary there was a high, fixed silence. Nothing moved.

She climbed the flight of stairs to the second floor and went in. Down the hall, a light was burning in Williams's classroom. She walked down the hall toward that light. *What if Orman is in there?* she thought. *What if I'm being drawn into a trap?*

But she couldn't stop now. The game was ending, and she had to complete it or else she could not forgive herself for coming so close to finding the answers and failing. She had to find out how it ended. Deanna Ward was still missing, and someone in that room knew where she was. Stopping now would sacrifice everything she had learned in these six weeks.

Mary walked through the door.

50

Brian arrived on campus a little after nightfall. The dorms were dark and still. No cars crept down Montgomery, and even the streetlights seemed to be darker, throwing off a misty and incomplete gray rather than the blinding orange they normally did.

They say you become obsessive after tragedies befall you. He wondered if that was it—if his ability to quell his own impulses had been shattered after Marcus's suicide. That would explain a lot— the nagging obedience he felt to Williams's game, the paranoia after meeting the girl at the kilns. His craving tonight for some kind of closure.

Brian dialed Mary's cell phone but got no answer. He drove to Brown, parked on the curb, and left his truck running. This dorm, like all the others, was empty. He had to try, though. He had to warn Mary about Williams before she contacted him.

He took the elevator up to her floor, and when he stepped into the hall he saw the hunched figure of a girl. She was sitting on the floor, her back to Mary's door.

"Polly?" he asked.

The girl looked up at him. Her eyes were weary and red. She'd been crying.

"Who?" she asked.

It was Summer McCoy, Mary's friend.

"I was waiting on Mary," the girl said.

"I've been trying to call her," Brian replied.

"Who are you?"

"My name is Brian. I'm a . . . a friend of Mary's."

"She's mentioned you," Summer said. "She thinks you're cute."

At another time, Brian might have pursued that comment, might have asked the girl what exactly Mary had said. But not now. All he said was, "Where is she?"

"I don't know," she replied. "I've been waiting here for an hour. I don't know what else to do. I just need to tell her . . ." The girl trailed off. She put her head down again. Her clothes looked too big for her, somehow; her wrists were thin, her cheeks sunken. She looked emaciated, broken down.

"Tell her what?" Brian asked. So slowly, he was walking toward her. The movement was almost unconscious, as if he were separated from his body now. He wanted to be as close as he could possibly get to her. He needed to hear what this girl said to him, needed to understand why she was here, in front of Mary's door, tonight of all nights.

"I wanted to tell her that what they've been doing is wrong," she said.

"Williams," Brian gasped. He was tuning up again, just like earlier in the truck. The girl blurred, and he shut his eyes to keep the world from spinning. He leaned against the wall opposite her, forced himself to breathe.

"The professor," she said, "and the others. I don't know their names. I never met them in person. Dr. Williams showed up at my dorm one night and asked me if I would do something for him. Take a picture with a boy. It was nothing. Just a snapshot on a couch— the couch was green, I'll remember that for as long as live—with his arm around me. They told me that they were going to send it to Mary for that class she was taking, the logic class. It was nothing. And I did it. I didn't know what the picture meant. They paid me, you see. It was nothing but I—I needed the money. But then I heard about Dr. Williams disappearing from campus and I called the number they'd given me."

"The number?"

"It was on the back of Dr. Williams's business card," she said. "Just in case I had problems. Just in case Mary started asking me stuff. Questions. A man answered. It wasn't Dr. Williams. This guy was younger, like a student. I asked him if Dr. Williams was okay, and he told me not to worry about it. He said that it was nothing, just a rumor. So I drove to his house."

"You drove to Williams's house?"

"Yes. On Pride Street. And there in the driveway was Dean Orman's car. I knew it was his because I'd seen it around campus. He parks it in the lot at Carnegie, where I do my work study."

"What was Orman doing at Williams's house, Summer?"

The girl continued. Her stare was broken, her voice wavering. She didn't want to go on, Brian knew, but couldn't stop now. "I was going to just knock on the door. Just tell them I wasn't comfortable with whatever they were doing. I didn't like to deceive Mary. She's like my best friend at Winchester. Why would I want to do anything to her, you know?"

"You saw them in there, didn't you?"

She nodded. "I heard a bunch of voices coming from inside. Like a big party was going on. So I walked around to the side of the house and I saw . . . I saw . . ."

"What did you see, Summer? Tell me."

"I saw them tying Williams up. They were taping his hands with, you know, masking tape. Or duct tape. Something. They were putting his hands behind his back and leading him around the room. But—"

"But what, damnit?" Brian asked. He was getting impatient with her. The hall was spinning, and it was all he could do to steady him-self against the wall.

"They were all laughing. Like it was all a joke. Dean Orman was there. A few other people I didn't recognize. And then—oh God—and then Williams turned and *saw me.* Through the window. He saw me. Or at least I thought he did. Later I couldn't be sure. Thought I might have just imagined it. But I swear he looked—"

"Dangerous," Brian finished for her.

"Exactly," Summer said. "Dangerous. He looked like he had caught me in something. And so I ran. I drove off campus and stayed at a friend's apartment in St. Owsley. I flunked both my classes. I haven't told my parents anything. I just couldn't . . ."

"Have you heard from them?" he asked.

"No. They called my cell, but I didn't pick up. I eventually just turned it off. I haven't spoken with Mary for a week or two. She probably thinks I'm dead."

Mary's got her own problems right now, Brian thought but didn't say.

"But last night it just got to me," Summer went on. "I thought about what I'd done. For fifty bucks, you know. Fifty bucks! For a fucking picture on a green couch. I couldn't keep silent anymore. I thought Mary was in danger. The way Dr. Williams looked at me through that window, I thought maybe Mary was in trouble. I wondered if maybe I was responsible somehow . . ."

Brian waited, but she didn't go on. She put her head down again and started to sob. It was a weeping at first, and soon it was a deep, ragged sob.

But he was no longer focused on the girl. He thought about what she'd said last: *I thought Mary was in danger.*

Williams was trying to hurt Mary.

Brian didn't bother with the slow elevator at Brown Hall. He bolted down the stairs and burst out into the cold night. He knew exactly where he needed to go, knew that the only way to end this was to get to Williams before he could do any more damage.

I thought Mary was in danger.

Brian went to his favorite place on the Winchester campus: the viaduct. He threw his leg over the barrier and climbed across. He started down the bank toward Miller's Creek, slipping here and there in the mud. There were no students around, thank God—no one to see him crawling on his hands and knees into the muck, just as he had in an early dawn three years ago, just days after he'd returned to Winchester. A security light on the viaduct gave him some light, enough to see his own hands becoming smeared with black as he dug.

Soon, he felt it. It was still wrapped in the towel he'd put it in.

He pulled it up out of the dirt, the ground below him making a sucking sound, and removed the towel. The Thing appeared in the sickly light off the viaduct. It was a gun—the 9 mm Smith & Wesson Marcus had used to shoot himself. Brian had kept it because there didn't seem as if there was anything else to do. For weeks he'd carried it around in his truck, the Thing pulsing with some invisible energy from the glove compartment. When he came to Winchester, he'd wrapped it in a towel and packed it away. When he got here there was nowhere to keep it, nowhere to really hide it. And so he'd brought it down to the banks of Miller's Creek and buried it, the closest thing he could think of to actually destroying it.

Afterward, his arms and knees covered with the black muck of the creek side, the Thing hidden in his coat pocket, he walked toward Up Campus. Toward Leonard Williams's house.

51

The first thing Mary noticed when she entered Seminary East: the room was full of people. They were people she had seen before, all of them familiar to her. The second thing she noticed was that Elizabeth Orman was standing at the podium, where Professor Williams had stood during their classes. The woman was smiling a strange, almost beatific smile.

52

Brian walked slowly. He'd cut his knee on a rock, and the dirt in the torn skin began to burn when he reached Pride Street. There were no cars. The campus was completely silent; the only sound was the traffic moving up and down Montgomery three blocks ahead of him.

Williams's house came into view up ahead, and Brian began to jog. He heard the dog barking, saw the man's pickup truck in the drive. He put his hand in his pocket, felt the weight of the gun, held it still as his coat jostled. Brian had shot a gun only once, with his father years ago. He had no intention of shooting one tonight; he wanted only to have protection in case . . .

In case what?

In case Mary was there, in the man's house.

And they were laughing, Summer McCoy had told him.

Laughing? Why had they been laughing?

He was right in front of Williams's house. It was dark; no lights were on inside at all.

Weird, thought Brian. *Maybe they're in the basement.*

He approached the house, and as he did something caught his eye in the distance. It was the Seminary Building looming over the evergreen trees just across Loquax Avenue. The lights were on up there in Seminary East.

Why the hell would the lights be on? Brian wondered.

He went around to the side of Williams's house to get a better look. Yes, they were definitely on. He saw them on the east side of the building as well. And was that—

He squinted to see.

There were people up there. A whole crowd of them. They were sitting in the student desks, and someone was at the podium addressing them. But he couldn't see who it was. The side of the building obscured his vision.

At that point Brian knew.

He knew where he needed to go.

53

"I'm glad you made it," Elizabeth Orman said to Mary. "We were worried there for a bit." She gestured at the crowded room. There were perhaps twenty people there. Some stood against the wall, but most sat at the desks. They, too, were smiling at Mary. "And I assume you know these people," Elizabeth said. "I guess no introductions are necessary."

"No," Mary managed, her voice hollow and ruined.

No introductions at all. In fact, back in the back corner, Mary recognized the boy they'd taken to the park, the boy called Paul. When he saw her looking at him, he waved.

"What is this?" Mary asked.

"This is the Polly Experiment." Mary looked at Elizabeth Orman. The woman was in a black dress, different from the one she'd been wearing earlier. Her hair was perfect, her jewelry flashed in the fluorescent light. She had been preparing for this, Mary knew. This was her big night.

"What are you talking about?" Mary was bracing herself against the wall, the crowded room reeling around her.

"It's my dissertation," Elizabeth said. "I'm a PhD student in behavioral psychology, and you and Brian House have been my subjects."

"You were performing a test on us?" Mary asked.

"Not *on* you, no," Elizabeth said. "Not at all. I was using you to test certain results. Certain hypotheses. For instance: Did you know that a human being cares for a person that they've never even met? Did you know that a human being will go out of her or his way to save this hypothetical person given the right circumstances? If a human being feels that another is in danger, then that human being will 'care for' this other person in a profound, utterly human manner."

"But not always." It was a man's voice. He was somewhere in the middle of the room, and when he stood up Mary gasped.

Troy Hardings.

He was dressed in a suit. It was silk, Mary saw: the light glinted off it when he moved. The facial hair was gone, the smirk had been replaced by a rigid smile. He looked completely professional, like a businessman—or perhaps someone acting like a businessman, Mary reminded herself.

"This is Dr. Troy Hardings," Elizabeth Orman said. "He was my faculty adviser for this project."

"To register the impact of this study, we have to remember Kitty Genovese," Hardings said. "We have to remember the so-called by-stander effect. What the Polly Experiment proves is that human beings are more apt to help a *potential* victim, an *assumed* victim, than they are if they, say, saw a woman being stabbed below their window at night."

"Deanna," Mary said weakly.

"Yes," Elizabeth Orman replied. "Deanna Ward was completely fabricated. A lot of things in the Polly Experiment were fabricated. Or 'exaggerated,' as Troy liked to say. The night Brian saw me beside the road, for example. That was a ruse to pull in Brian. We thought he might be straying, so we found the perfect method of bringing him back. And the day you found Troy in the office. That was all done on the fly—we had no idea that you were coming up. We had literally nailed Leonard's name to the door five minutes earlier."

"And these people?" Mary asked. She closed her eyes. She couldn't look at them, couldn't turn to face the crowd. It was not embarrassment that she felt, not shame or guilt. It was fear: fear that there was another twist in the game coming, another misdirection. Mary didn't know if she could handle it. Not now.

"We hired them to play roles," Elizabeth explained. "They all did a beautiful job. And of course you know who we hired to play the part of your professor."

Leonard Williams stood up from his chair and nodded. "In real life he's in a theater troupe here in DeLane. His stage name is Mike Williams. And he was often disguised, so there was no way you could have uncovered him." Mary thought about the first time she'd seen him, of the acne pits on his face. Makeup, she knew now.

There was a pause, a moment where nobody spoke. Then Williams approached Mary. He was smiling, trying to disarm her with his charm. In an instant he was beside her, putting his hand on her shoulder. "Mary," he said softly.

And then something happened.

54

Brian crept slowly onto the floor where Seminary East was. The door was open, and yellow light spilled out and bathed half the hallway. He heard a woman's voice coming from inside, but because he was sliding along the wall he couldn't see anyone in the room.

"In real life he's in a theater troupe here in DeLane," the woman said.

And then another voice. This second voice was very low and weak, barely discernible. "Mary," it said. And he did discern it: it was Leonard Williams.

Brian moved faster down the hall, his hand on the gun in his pocket. He had turned it now so that his finger was on the trigger.

When he stepped inside his knees almost buckled. He almost pitched forward into the crowd, but somehow he maintained his balance and stood, staring at them.

They were all there. All the actors. Marco, the Collinses, the boy from the park named Paul. Bethany Cavendish from the high school. The waitresses they'd met in Bell City. Even Dean Orman, sitting toward the front and wearing his fedora. All of them were here, waiting for him.

And there, leaning against the back wall, was the girl from the kilns. She'd pulled her hair back. She looked very young, thirty or so, and she was staring at him in a way that was so sickening, so fucking sickening.

"Polly," he said.

Ashamed, the girl looked down at the floor.

"Brian," someone said to his left.

When he turned he saw not Elizabeth Orman, who had spoken to him, but Leonard Williams.

Williams's hand was on Mary's arm. He was—was he pulling on her? Pulling her toward him?

"Brian," Elizabeth said again from the front of the class.

But he paid no attention. Williams was staring at Brian so oddly, so coldly that Brian knew he was trying to impart some information. The professor's gaze said something, it spoke of something awful.

What? Brian mouthed.

But Williams still stared at him, his eyes hooded, his hand still tight on Mary's shoulder. She looked shocked and terrified, as if she were in tremendous pain. Did Williams's mouth move? Did he say some word, reveal something?

What the fuck do you want? Brian mouthed. *Let her go!*

"Brian, we want you to know that this began during your freshman years," Elizabeth Orman said. But Brian already had the Thing out of his pocket and he was aiming it at Leonard Williams.

55

When Williams released his grip on Mary's arm and fell backward onto the desk, coming to rest right in front of Edna Collins, everyone laughed. They thought it was part of the game, another trick. Another wrinkle thrown in the narrative.

But Mary knew better. She saw Brian's hand, saw through the wispy smoke that he was holding a gun. A gun that had just been fired.

The atmosphere changed around her. It became charged; the whole room dimmed as if a fuse had blown somewhere. The dog tore away from the man he had been kneeling beside, the man in the baseball cap, and ran out of the room.

At that point everyone moved.

Dean Orman was the first to Williams. "Get an ambulance!" he shouted.

A couple of the other men collapsed on Williams. It was all moving fast, so fast. They were tearing off his shirt. They were slapping him, trying to keep him awake.

And to her right Brian was moving. He was not trying to escape, but rather he was coming into the room, toward the frantic throng of actors and actresses.

He was walking toward Elizabeth Orman with the gun.

"Brian," Mary said softly.

56

M ary said his name, and he stopped.

That movement—the stopping, the turning around to face her—was what allowed the man in the Red Sox cap to reach him.

"Stop," the man said. He was dressed strangely, Brian saw. His jacket had been zipped high and the cap had been pulled down low so that his face was obscured. The dog he'd had beside him, the black Lab, had run out of the room. The man held the snapped leash limply in his right hand.

"I couldn't," Brian said to this man, this stranger. "I just couldn't let him continue hurting us."

"I know, I know," the man said. "But put the gun down and we'll figure it all out." His voice was soothing, familiar.

Suddenly, Brian knew who he was.

Brian reached up and unzipped the man's jacket and revealed Dennis Flaherty.

57

D ennis took the gun away from Brian and put it on the table. Mary was so close to Dennis that he could hear her voice. "Why?" she said.

"Let's talk about this later, Mary," he said. He was holding Brian by the shoulders. Both boys looked vulnerable, weak, as if they had stepped into a nightmare that they couldn't wake up from.

Dennis took a few steps toward where Williams lay, but he couldn't get through to the man. Mary went around to the other side and found her way to him. They had him on the floor, and she could see by his pallor that he was dead. He was gray and still. She knelt and touched his hand, and he was unresponsive to her touch. "Professor," she whispered. Nothing. The man who had played Marco was performing CPR, and all the actors and actresses were watching passively now. The air had been taken out of the room. They had finally reached the end.

58

Some time later, after Marco had stopped trying to save Williams, after some of the actors and actresses had left the room to retch in the hallway, Mary looked at Dennis. She didn't have to say anything: he knew what she needed him to say.

He took a deep breath. "I was intrigued. When I figured it out, I thought it was so brilliant. A real-life behavior experiment, you know. So I joined them. They sent me to Cale and Bell City. I was their emissary. I made all the phone calls so they could track us. I called the Collinses beforehand; I called the diner from the store where we stopped to get directions. I went in to speak to Bethany Cavendish this morning and we sent out Paul. They needed someone to help them, and so I did. And there was also . . ." Dennis trailed off.

"Her," Mary said.

"Excuse me?"

"You wanted to be near Elizabeth." It was Brian. His head was leaned back against the wall, and Dennis still held him by the shoulders. Mary knew that if Brian wanted to break free he could, but he was resigned to this now. He had conceded defeat.

"That's absurd," Dennis said, his voice nearly a whisper. "I was going to say that there was also my father. How I wanted to be like him, more 'serious-minded,' as he liked to say. More academic. More worthwhile." But Mary could see that was also a lie. The truth was that Dennis's part in the study had, in fact, everything to do with Elizabeth Orman and little to do with his interest in the science or with his father.

"How pathetic," she said to him. Dennis didn't respond, and in that silence she saw that in some twisted way he agreed with her.

"No," Dennis said. "It had nothing to do with her. Not after I got involved with it. Not after I started talking to Leonard and Troy Hardings. It became a—a purely academic thing. I began to see what my father saw. The proof opening up, the answer revealing itself. The study was so perfect, so mathematical."

"Except you forgot one thing," Mary said.

"What's that?" Dennis asked.

"The human element. It's what you always forget, Dennis. That your actions mean something to other people. That what you do has consequences."

She looked down and caught Brian's gaze, and he simply shook his head. His face revealed the gravity of his mistake. Tears streamed down his face, and Mary noticed that his hand, the hand that had held the gun, was trembling slightly.

Then Mary was being led away from them, into the crowd of people. Soon she was in the back of the room with Edna Collins beside her, and through the mass of people she saw the events of Seminary East unfold: Elizabeth Orman sat on the rolling chair and buried her head in her hands; Troy Hardings came to Elizabeth and stroked her hair, and Mary saw what he was saying to her by reading his lips: "It will be okay"; the ambulance arrived, the stretcher was rolled in, and they took Leonard Williams away; the word "dead" began to ripple through the room. Then, much later, when only ten or twelve of them remained, a detective came in to talk to her. He was wearing a flannel jacket and had a mustache. He could have been an actor for all Mary knew, but she was too exhausted to care.

"What's going on here?" he asked, and Mary told him what she knew.

TWO MONTHS LATER

59

Mary Butler had begun to pick up the pieces of her life.

She was back in Kentucky and planning to enroll at another university next fall. She had answered question upon question about her role in Elizabeth Orman's study. It was decided, finally, that she didn't know what Brian House had been planning. It was also decided, by a faceless ethics committee put together by Winchester University, that the mistakes that had occurred in Elizabeth Orman's Polly Experiment were completely happenstance. There was no breach of ethics, the committee found, and Elizabeth was allowed to continue her studies at Winchester.

None of this mattered now to Mary except for Brian's fate. She had moved on. It had taken her a while, of course. She had spent three or four dark weeks in her parents' home, sleeping between those bouts of questions. She thought of Brian often. He was awaiting trial in DeLane, and the district attorney was planning to charge him with first-degree manslaughter. Mary had been subpoenaed, and would testify at the pretrial in two weeks. It would take no preparation. She had memorized the story by now; she knew it so well that she could recite it with her eyes closed.

She took walks with her mother. She cooked dinner for her parents. She tried to regain some normalcy. But it wasn't easy. She had, once again, trusted too much and had been hurt because of that trust.

Dennis had been dismissed from school. He had been Elizabeth's and Troy Hardings' patsy after all. The school had uncovered his relationship with Elizabeth, and they had ruled that he had an "unhealthy obsession with the doctoral candidate and her work." Mary knew that this was not the case; Dennis had told her the truth in Seminary East that night. He took the fall for Elizabeth, and Mary saw something in that: he still loved Elizabeth. Perhaps she had seduced him into the study, perhaps she had stuck the knife in his back and twisted it, but he could not give her up. Poor Dennis. He called Mary one night and simply sat on the other end of the line, weeping.

Williams, of course, was dead by the time he reached the DeLane Baptist Hospital. One shot to the gut opened him up, destroyed his insides. They found cancer there, Mary heard, and it had been terminal. Eating him away in there, destroying him. She didn't know if that was true or not. She wanted it to be.

Only one question remained: Who had sent the videotape of the Milgram experiments?

Mary had a feeling that she knew, and one day in the middle of winter she e-mailed him to test her theory.

To: eorman@winchester.edu
From: quinnsrednotebook@gmail.com
Subject: Milgram

Thank you for trying to warn us, Dean Orman.

It took him only ten minutes to respond.

To: quinnsrednotebook@gmail.com
From: eorman@winchester.edu
Subject: Re: Milgram

I am so sorry. I told Elizabeth that it was going too far, that things were breaking down. I sent the videotape as an object lesson. They, as you know, got ahold of it. Thus the audio at the end, the voices of Hardings and a boy named Net. All that chicanery. You know now: never trust those who seem to have extramural motives. Elizabeth and I have finally drifted apart. I suppose you heard that, though. After Leonard died we just couldn't look at each other any longer. She wants to pursue her studies; I want to settle down, retire, live my life. My good friend Pig Stephens is recovering from the broken hand you gave him. He sends his best wishes. We go out fishing from time to time on the Thatch. We ponder life and how it winds and unwinds. It's all masculine and pathetic and, yes, disingenuous. But it is what it is. I miss her some nights. But she had a drive unlike mine; it was the same drive Stanley had. I probably married her because of that, because I became— what?—subservient to her ambition. I noticed it from my dealings with Stanley, and I'm drawn to that kind of rigor. I admit it: I'm a sucker for a strong mind.

Don't be ashamed, Mary. You are not alone. I was thirty years old when it happened to me, so I had some years on you. I too have spent my life trying to figure out how it was that I was … deceived. I know how it feels, you see. I know how *you* feel.

I'll see you in DeLane soon for the legal mess.

All the best,
Edward Orman

New Haven, Connecticut

August 7, 1961

M ilgram.

They were ready inside the laboratory at Linsly-Chittenden Hall at Yale University. There was a strong scent in there—like burning flesh. Milgram could smell it through the closed door. Why had they done that? He wondered if it was on purpose, to create some sort of deeper effect on his subjects. It certainly wasn't his idea. He thought, *Will I ever be the same after this is through?*

"Stanley?" asked James McDonough, the man who would be acting as Milgram's learner. "Are you all right, Stanley?" He assured the man that he was.

Milgram was looking at the shock machine, at this creation that would make him famous. *Slight shock. Moderate shock. Strong shock. Very strong shock. Intense shock. Extreme intensity shock. Danger—severe shock.* Milgram touched it, ran his palm across the cool surface. The machine seemed to pulse with some hidden life. It had become like some kind of a weapon. He had dreamed about the goddamned box for weeks. He had gone back to mescaline so that his mind might dodge the machine in his defenseless sleep.

"Stanley," said McDonough. The man was not nervous. It seemed that nobody was nervous except Milgram himself. "We're ready now."

Milgram went into a back room, where he could watch the proceedings through a two-way mirror. He saw his experimenter, the man who would play the "scientist," appear in the open room. The experimenter was wearing a gray coat. *Not white*, Milgram had demanded. Definitely not white. White presented the idea of medicine. Of sterility. People automatically distrusted white for that reason. So Milgram's experimenter would wear gray, and upon seeing him in the coat for the first time Milgram thought he looked like a slab of granite. This was exactly what Milgram had intended.

He then saw his subject enter the room, a middle-aged man with red hair wearing a light smoker's jacket and a wet hat, for it was raining outside. The man took a seat, and the experiment began.

"I'd like to explain to both of you now about our Memory Project," the gray-coated experimenter said to the man and also to McDonough, who was already in his act, nervously twitching in the chair next to the subject. The plan was to place McDonough in a separate room and have the subject shock him. There wouldn't really be shocks, of course. No electricity, either. The box was a grand hoax. The point was that the subject should be *obedient* to the experimenter. The subject should respect the experimenter's authority, only because the experimenter wore a coat and spoke with a deep voice and held a clipboard.

"Psychologists," the gray-coated man went on, "have developed several theories to explain how people learn various types of material."

Milgram stopped listening. He had fallen away somewhere, to that other plane.

"Okay, now we are going to set the learner up so he can get some punishment," the experimenter said. "Learner, let me explain what's going to happen, what you're supposed to do. The teacher will read a list of word pairs to you."

Milgram shut his eyes.

"So he later reads to you," the experimenter was saying, " 'strong: back, arm, branch, push.' You would press this one—"

McDonough hesitated. "Well," he said, as he had been instructed, "I think I should say this. When I was in West Haven VA Hospital a few years ago, they detected a slight heart condition. Nothing serious. But as long as I'm getting these shocks—how strong are they? How dangerous are they?"

The experimenter ignored McDonough's question. He went to the subject. "All right," he said. "Now listen carefully to the instructions. First of all, this machine generates electric shocks." He slid his hand over the box, his palm making a hiss as it moved across the black surface.

Milgram thought of Eichmann. He thought of Mengele's pressure chambers. He had heard from his father that Mengele had frozen Jews alive until their bodies could be cracked apart limb by limb. One Jew, his father said, was pointing. Perpetually pointing, a statue on the frozen ground at Auschwitz. They called him *zarah:* the compass.

"Before we begin," the experimenter said, "I'd like to ask you, the subject, your name."

The subject's voice came through the static and into Milgram's tiny room. "Orman," the man said. "Edward Conrad Orman."

Acknowledgments

Writing a book is hardly a solitary effort, and I am fortunate to have worked with some gracious, fiercely intelligent folks during this process. Thanks are in order to my wonderful agent, Laney Katz Becker. Laney's guidance and support—and her novelist's eye—made this book so much better than it was when it first showed up, bloated and misshapen, on her desk. To Anna Stein, whose tenacity pleased and scared me at the same time. To my editor, Sally Kim, who was so kind and attentive and who really made the editing process a sort of perverse delight. To Dr. Thomas Blass, whose book *The Man Who Shocked the World: The Life and Legacy of Stanley Milgram* was an invaluable resource. To James Leary, who helped me kick this book's butt when it needed kickin'. To my family in Whitley City, of course. And finally to my lovely wife, who is just days away from giving birth to Jenna Marie at the time of this writing. *My passion burns for you . . .*